Praise for *The Corruption of Zachary R.*

In staccato chapters dealt out like a deck of
cards—snappy, latent, repeating—Richardson
tracks Zachary R.'s descent into psychosis. . . .
[He] tenders characters that, due to the story's
brevity and swiftness, are quickly sympathetic
and pack a compressed punch. . . . An artful,
beguiling voyage to a place no one wants to go.

-Kirkus Reviews

There is a certain yin and yang to Richardson's
work that moves us to quickly invest ourselves in
his characters. The novel sails along in short
bursts of revelations. . . . [Richardson] writes with
a poet's heart and a suspense novelist's eye.

-ForeWord Reviews

Praise for *Trust Fund Baby*

Filled with memorable characters and thoughtful moments, this well-paced story provides lessons as well as entertainment. . . . An impressive story of corruption, religion and friendship, and the lengths people go to for love.

-Kirkus Reviews

Richardson is a master storyteller, with a great command of the language. The economy of word and raw humanity in his work are astounding.

-Brenda Petrakos

American Strays

Douglas Richardson

Weak Creature Press
Los Angeles

Contents

For Jen

Book One

The Corruption of
Zachary R.

PART I

1. Committed

The bun held the burger. The wrapper held the bun. The brown bag held the whole apparatus, concealing what was happening to the burger: worms, microbes, malodor.

Zachary R. was committed on a thin autumn Saturday, Nebraska football on a New England lawn, a dad mowing at halftime, vibrations on his right-angle chin.

His teenage daughter, keeper of the ash, put on the Revolution Dress and went to the blood drive on an empty stomach. She returned home like scurvy over anemia, crashing the Nova through the living room window. He kissed her and sent her to her room with a grapefruit and a Hershey's, and he set about surrounding the house with orange cones to distract the eyes of the neighbors.

The burger had festered for days in the abandoned shed on the riverbank and Zachary R. wanted to care for it, so he set off on foot saying,

"Service to mankind, Service to mankind." For eight miles, however, he went tenement to tenement eating numbers right off the doors, stealing the identities of tenants to the delight of landlords and Goth Girls, who clutched their Damien lockets and swooned at the sight of the rusty nails in his lips and the brown blood hugging his neck.

A month later, in the asylum, he claimed to the Cracked Snail, "I have Neosporin." Only the snail heard him.

A year later, someone important heard him say, "I like rivers and women." These words got him permission to mow the asylum lawn, vibrations on his right-angle chin saying, "Service to mankind, Service to mankind."

2. Seven Women Walking in Lab Coats

Zachary R. sat in the exact middle of the asylum lawn on a chair that made a pattern on his legs.

He was daydreaming about pine trees and leisure until he looked through the iron bars of the gate and saw seven women walking in lab coats, cameras raised to cover their spying faces. These women were posing as health care journalists. Their badges indicated that they were doing a photo exposé for *Psychiatry Today*, but their black painted eyes and lips and fingernails indicated otherwise.

Zachary R. looked down at the Cracked Snail and asked, "How do I bed one?"

The snail replied, "Approach the redhead.

"Tell her she's somewhat gorgeous, that chess is nearly impossible.

"Tell her you need to look far away to erase her naked image from your mind."

Zachary R. heard the sound of a plane. He looked at the sky.

3. Chess

Bishop takes knight. Pawn takes bishop. Pawn takes queen.

Zachary R. lay in bed in the asylum, tense as a gargoyle, unbearably awake because of chess with his father.

The lessons soldered his cerebrum. His cerebrum short-circuited: Leave the knights on the back row. Be aggressive with the rooks. Move the queen out as quickly as possible.

So many hypotheticals. So much losing.

And the board itself, each square a minor concussion.

Insomnia troubled him until dawn, when at last he slept for an hour, then awoke erect as a saint with no one to touch.

Sometimes it calmed him to picture Earth from space:

The blue and white eye.

The slow reentry.

Mother with child in subway.

4. Keeper of the Ash

Solitary, poor, nasty, brutish, and short.

Zachary R.'s teenage daughter, a Hobbes scholar with a nose ring, understood how in one moment a bag lady could look down at the veins in her thighs and in the next moment be the victim in a fatal hit-and-run.

Sarah R. was her name and she was filled with pity, which is four-fifths of piety, which is an obsession with the sanctity of death, which meant her father had obligated her to guard the urn with her mother's ashes.

Sarah R. arrived in New Orleans in early February, on the Wednesday before Mardi Gras. She checked into a bargain motel, unpacked, threw on the Revolution Dress, drank all the liquor in the minibar, shaved her head, and went to the corner for a hot dog. She watched mustard and onions splatter on the sidewalk, disrupting a trail of ants. She felt omnipotent like Hobbes' Leviathan, until she stumbled into the street and was nearly struck by a speeding bus. The hot dog vendor picked her up and escorted her back to her room. He kissed her on the cheek and slipped his business card in her cleavage.

5. The Dungeon

Sarah R. woke Thursday afternoon in Necropolis, in New Orleans, the estuary, city of brackish voodoo, turtle soup, and hurricanes.

It was true. The hot dog vendor had slipped his business card in her cleavage the night before, only it wasn't a business card for his hot dog cart. Rather, it read of his capacity as bartender and part owner of the Dungeon, a bar in the French Quarter.

The Dungeon was situated at the end of a long, narrow alley. Its hours were from midnight to an undisclosed hour just after sunrise.

Sarah R. slipped into the Revolution Dress and arrived at the Dungeon after midnight on Friday morning, sans urn, on an empty stomach.

She was there for more self-destruction.

Blue Hawaiians and blow jobs were the drinks of the night.

There were mannequin menageries and foul rubber masques. T-shirts were being sold.

She danced with a grateful deadhead who said as if in a dream, "You are adroit."

She looked up that word after she woke Friday afternoon.

6. The Same Sensation as a Feather Boa

All Saturday afternoon and into Saturday evening, Sarah R. wandered the streets of the French Quarter in a vain attempt to find the deadhead from the night before. In addition to the word *adroit*, she recalled him saying something about returning to Kentucky and the word *Godspeed*.

She stopped at Café Du Monde for chicory coffee. The hot dog vendor wheeled his cart along the sidewalk, but he did not stop to chat with her. Instead, he winked an avuncular wink and moved through the cold February night.

Sarah R. returned to her room and lay in bed, but she did not sleep.

Sunday morning she put on the Revolution Dress, ate eggs Benedict that made her eyes throb, and took the urn in a cab to Lake Pontchartrain, where she paid a fee and boarded a tour boat.

About a mile offshore, Sarah R. maneuvered her way to the bow and, in a moment of sheer adolescent impetuousness, emptied the contents of the urn into the brackish water.

The captain of the vessel, who had watched Sarah from the start (it wasn't every day he saw young women board his tour boat with urns under their arms), was bound by law to inform her that the disposal of human ashes had to be formally cleared by the Neptune Society. Sarah R. replied, "When some of the ashes blew back into my face, it was the same sensation as a feather boa."

The captain was sufficiently bewitched by this response to invite her for turtle soup and mint juleps after the boat had docked.

She declined the invitation. Relieved, he removed the handkerchief from his shirt pocket, wiped the residue from her face, and made an awkward remark about how the Neptune Society would be outraged if they ever found out.

Sarah R. returned to the city, swinging the empty urn low as a pendulum.

7. The Revolution Dress

Stardust in her backpack, flask in her pocket, opium in her veins. But nothing intoxicated Sarah R. more than the Revolution Dress.

It made her burn with weakness.

It made her reckless and charitable.

It was blood drives and blackjack, kittens and heroin.

It was apples and arsenic and trick-or-treating with foster parents.

When the hot dog vendor was asked to describe Sarah R., he said, "Her charm was like a shade of burgundy I hadn't noticed before."

Of course he wasn't describing Sarah R., but the Revolution Dress.

The Revolution Dress was five times eight, eight times thirteen, thirteen times twenty-one, twenty-one times thirty-four, and so on, but then it was all divided by zero.

8. Antipsychotic Oblivion

Droperidol. Haloperidol. Lorazepam. Diazepam.

Believing his discharge from the asylum was imminent, Zachary R. complied with his regimen. The antipsychotics had the following side effects:

Sheep and clouds.

Sky and grass.

Sand and water.

Fire and ash.

He imagined that Sarah handed him the urn. He opened it and stared at the ashes, searching for humanity. He closed the urn and looked out the asylum window. Again he imagined Sarah.

"Can you forgive me?" he asked.

9. Antipsychotic Hallucination

The medication moved through his body like panic moves through a crowd, every nerve scraped and startled, every memory ambiguous and addled.

He entered a forest where boxcars stretched endlessly through tunnels in hills with shacks and cigarettes.

The Cold Angel ran her veil over his scalp. Fog passed above and diagonally. "They're there for you to ride," she said. "Why won't you play in them?"

The Cold Angel joined at his side, rubbed his back like winter, and asked, "Whatever happened to the child in you?"

He wept, but not over his lost childhood. He wept because of what the boxcars had done.

"Lie down under a picnic table and sleep," she said, "and the train will go away."

10. Memories of the Carnival

The best day of Zachary R.'s life was the day his daughter was born. The second-best day of Zachary R.'s life was the day his daughter was conceived, which was at the carnival. Therefore, Zachary R. liked the carnival. He made a bullet-point list of his memories of the carnival on that day:

- Hay bales
- Ropes

- Logs
- Parachutes
- Flashing colors
- Historical photos
- Brown
- Earth
- Smoke
- Among strangers
- Rolls of tickets
- Stolen
- Torn
- Dropped into a slot in a metal box

11. Flyswatter by the Toilet

In the days and nights leading up to his committal, Zachary R. kept a flyswatter by the toilet for use as an emetic. Each time before he got sick, he swung the flyswatter while reciting these words:

Forehand

Backhand

Microphone

Guitar

Spider on shoulder

Cockroach on soap bar

Slipping

Slipping

Slipping

12. The Last Night at the House

Toilet was sterilized. Flyswatter was packed. Fridge was warm and empty. Asylum was in the past.

Zachary R. had just closed the door of his house for the last time when it occurred to him that the walls needed sponging with mild dish soap.

He turned the doorknob, but the door was locked and the key was in a business reply envelope on its way to *Playboy* magazine.

He considered the definition of insanity: "to do the same thing over and over and expect different results." He went to the bar anyway.

Zachary R. spoke to no one there, except for the bartender the seven times he ordered drinks. The bar was crowded with the din of human voices, but sometimes single voices could be heard saying things like:

"Cigar boxes and romance novels are the brass knuckles of sex."

Or, "I am nostalgic for the dark-road signature of the skunk."

Or, "Are you lonely as the cello? No, I am lonely as an aisle of concrete in the moonlight."

When he realized it was he who had uttered these things, Zachary R. knew he should leave.

He exited out the back, stinking of bourbon but feeling better about his chances of entering his ex-home.

He picked up several substantial stones on the way, expecting he would need to bust a window to get inside. To his moderate surprise, however, the door was unlocked when he arrived. He went room to room looking for signs of an intruder, but found none. Perplexed, and more than a little drunk, he entered the kitchen and opened the cupboard that held the cleaning supplies. He took a sponge and some dish soap and began sponging.

He sponged the dining room and the study, the hallways and the bedrooms, all without incident. But when he arrived in the living room, his attention was diverted by several ants and a termite on the windowsill.

He watched the ants surround the termite and the ensuing carnage: Six ants amputated six termite legs, two ants amputated two termite wings, and a ninth ant arrived to carry off the termite body.

Zachary R. paused and then proclaimed, "International harvesters."

Then he thought, "What is this merciless carnival I am allowing in my home?"

He emptied the entire bottle of soap onto the victorious ants and sponged the whole ensemble.

He reached into his pockets and grabbed the substantial stones. He knocked out the boards where the living room window had been, and he ripped and tore the carpet on the living room floor. He busted out the remaining windows and pounded divots into the walls.

He busted and pounded until the vicious energy was gone. Then, exhausted, he went outside and sat on a stack of pine logs that he had cut with a sharp axe. He thought about the dead and wondered where he was in the years before his birth. He smiled the eyeless smile of eradicated dreams.

PART II

13. Bernrd Red

Countless boys came into existence the same year as Zachary R., but none had as much influence on his fate as one of the many boys who were called Bernard. Because the father of this Bernard, for various reasons, refused to lend the boy his last name, this Bernard adopted the street name of his mother, the roughhouse prostitute. His mother's street name was Chloe Red.

And one day, for various reasons, Bernard Red decided to remove the "a" from his name to promote the sensation of being hit in the head with a rock.

There are many rumors surrounding Bernrd Red, all of which have been substantiated. One such rumor was that Bernrd Red was a pious child until he got hit in the face by a girl.

14. The Roughhouse Prostitute

Bernrd Red was a pious child until he got hit in the face by a girl; and by girl, it was the girl he referred to as "Mother," which is to say, his mother had him when she was fifteen years old.

Bernrd Red's father was one H. Charles Branhoover, a well-to-do and good-for-nothing banker in the city all three lived in: Pittsburgh, Pennsylvania.

All three lived in Pittsburgh, but not under one roof. Branhoover didn't want the scandal that would surely have arisen from a fifty-one-year-old man living with his fifteen-year-old lover and their baby. So he set lover and child up in a one-bedroom apartment, and he hired a crew of good-natured but aggressive nannies, who delivered money and groceries and ensured that the boy, whom mother and father named Bernard, received an education fit for a Branhoover, even if the child couldn't take the Branhoover name.

The nannies taught Bernard to read and write, and up to Algebra-level mathematics, all while immersed in Mozart and the music of the sixties and seventies. And all this was accomplished by the time Bernard turned eight, when he was enrolled in the Pittsburgh public school system.

Chloe Red loved her boy, but she knew life wasn't all Mozart, Crosby, Stills, Nash & Young, and mathematical precociousness. There was also the knowledge she possessed, street knowledge. Chloe Red resented the bossy nannies and the money and her secret life, so she resolved that her contribution to her son's upbringing would be to instill a little of the hard reality of the streets, which is to say she taught him how to fight and how not to be a sissy.

Bernard, of course, preferred his time with the nannies and the music and his studies over his time with his mother. Of course, his mother didn't like this fact.

The fighting lessons became less like lessons and more like punishments. The blows Chloe administered to Bernard became less and less playful and instructive, and rose from taps to the stomach to blows to the arms and the face. When the blows to the face began, Bernard Red began to change.

15. Bernrd Red, Crosby, Stills, Nash & Young

When he was very young, Bernard Red loved music. His mother's clientele even said of him, "That boy of yours has a real affinity for music." These remarks were made mainly in the family room, where the record player was located. Not only did he love the Mozart foisted on him by aggressive nannies, but also he loved "Puff the Magic Dragon" and "One Little Two Little Three Little Indians." Actually, regarding the latter, he mainly liked it because the record label was tan and red, which he imagined to be the colors of the Indians. Tan and red coated his mind like pink bismuth coated his parents' stomachs.

Bernard Red's favorite band was Crosby, Stills, Nash & Young, even though he told everyone he liked Led Zeppelin best.

He played CSNY at every opportunity until he entered the public school in the third grade and it was discovered that he excelled at math, surpassing even Betsy Sullivan, who was also the class bully.

Betsy Sullivan didn't like it when Bernard Red outdid her on every math exam, so one morning she confronted him at recess. He tried to appease her by inviting her over to listen to Led Zeppelin. Betsy responded by hitting him square in the forehead. Bernard hit her back, but by that time the teachers had descended upon the commotion, witnessing only Bernard's retaliation.

Three days later, after serving his suspension for hitting a girl, Bernard Red sat in the principal's office filling out reinstatement forms when he blurted out, "Betsy Sullivan is a fussy wet salami."

From that day on, Betsy Sullivan regained her favored status among the faculty.

From that day on, Bernard Red dedicated himself to collecting substantial stones for breaking school windows and bruising student skulls.

From that day on, Bernard Red began omitting the "a" from his name on all of his homework, which one of his more eccentric teachers said gave her the same sensation as being hit in the head with a rock.

16. Preppie Hoodlum

By the time they entered high school, Bernrd Red and Betsy Sullivan had put aside their differences. In fact, the two of them had been an item since middle school, when, as a happy couple, they terrorized their fellow students and each other to their mutual delight and to the chagrin of their teachers.

Bernrd Red would call Betsy Sullivan a fussy wet salami just so they could fight and make up with barbaric sex in the afternoon before Betsy's parents got home (and sometimes at Bernrd's home, but not as often because Chloe Red was usually there with her johns earning extra money on the sly because Mr. Branhoover was cheap). At night they would sneak out and meet up to gather substantial stones for busting out the windows of the school, which made them whirl and pop and believe they were in love.

By now, Bernrd Red believed in the strength of violence and the weakness of music. He renounced Mozart and Led Zeppelin and he obliterated Crosby, Stills, Nash & Young from his mind.

Betsy said he should try to get into punk rock but Bernrd Red refused, saying punk was for poseurs and pussies seeking attention. So Betsy Sullivan dressed like a punk rocker to antagonize Bernrd Red, and Bernrd Red dressed like a preppie hoodlum to antagonize Betsy Sullivan, and they whirled and popped and busted out the school windows until graduation, when Bernrd Red ended their relationship without explanation.

17. Self-Styled Cooler

Bernrd Red was silently distraught over the end of his relationship with Betsy Sullivan, despite having been the one to call it off. He understood that breaking up with Betsy was a cowardly thing to do, but he did it anyway to maintain his image as a preppie hoodlum.

Although Betsy cried and broke things around the house, her broken heart only took about a week to mend, and then she settled down, went to nursing school, became a nurse and an adult, and never gave her ex another thought.

Bernrd Red, on the other hand, bummed around the streets of Pittsburgh promoting the sensation of being hit in the head with a rock. If there was a street brawl or a bruised skull or a broken window, Bernrd Red was likely to blame.

His father tried his best to rein in his wayward son. But when Bernrd Red threw a rock through the window of Mr. Branhoover's bank with a note attached that read, "Dear Mr. Branhoover: Hi

Dad. Sorry I forgot your birthday whenever it was this past year. Here is your belated birthday present. Don't get mad. Rocks make good paperweights for a busy bank executive's desk. Your son, Bernrd Red-Branhoover," Mr. Branhoover wasted no time getting his son out of town for good.

When Bernrd Red learned that "out of town for good" meant he was being sent away to the School of Hotel Management at the University of Nevada, Las Vegas, he cooperated in every way possible to expedite his expulsion from Pittsburgh.

In Las Vegas, Bernrd Red became an "A" student and a self-styled cooler at the Golden Horseshoe downtown, where he won on the come line and quieted the craps tables with no expectation of reward other than the desire to watch other gamblers lose. He caught the appreciative eyes of the pit bosses and the casino owner, who made Bernrd Red his protégé, which Bernrd took full advantage of.

Bernrd Red and the casino owner rigged the roulette wheel and canoodled with showgirls. Bernrd Red's slogan at the rigged roulette wheel was "Always bet on black," but the rigged roulette wheel was rigged to land on red. Bernrd Red enjoyed watching the various expressions of dismay on the faces of the gamblers when, despite his advice to bet on black, and the gamblers following his advice, he moved his chips to red at the last second, just before the dealer waved his hand over the table signaling no more bets, and the ball landing on red. He enjoyed watching hotel security escort enraged gamblers out of the casino as they screamed idle threats at him.

It didn't take long for the gaming authorities to sniff out the scam at the Golden Horseshoe, which made Bernrd Red an offer he couldn't refuse. They gave him his degree in Hotel Management, set him up as a concierge in a bed-and-breakfast on a road called Bath in a seaside village out West, and told him never to come back.

On Bernrd Red's last day in Las Vegas, the casino owner gave him a pinky ring with a giant ruby as an expression of his gratitude. He thumped Bernrd Red on the back, winked an avuncular wink, and said, "Always bet on Red."

18. You, Your Best Friend, and Your Vilest Enemy

During his time in the asylum, Zachary R. was visited by Bernrd Red, which is to say that the grudge he held against Bernrd Red manifested itself in the form of imaginary visits. The first such visit went like this:

Zachary R. sat up in bed in the asylum listening to the Electric Light Dirge for Cello and Organ, when Bernrd Red entered the room.

Bernrd Red despised music. Zachary R. hit pause and asked, "Would you like to sit with me and listen to this lovely dirge?"

Bernrd Red replied, "If you don't turn off the music, I am going to betray you, your best friend, and your vilest enemy."

"Looks like you get to fuck yourself three times, then," said Zachary R.

The two men fought feebly. Asylum staff separated them. Zachary R. was placed in isolation. His mowing privileges were suspended.

19. Bigger Moths Need Bigger Flames

When their first son, Bernrd Red, was sent west to become a self-styled cooler at the Golden Horseshoe in Las Vegas (and later a malevolent concierge at a bed-and-breakfast on a road called Bath in a seaside village), his parents, H. Charles Branhoover and Chloe Red, decided it was okay at last, that it wouldn't ruin Branhoover's reputation in the banking industry, for them to formally announce their mutual admiration by getting married.

Of course, as is often the case, the only two people in all of Pittsburgh who believed their version of the story of their relationship were H. Charles and Chloe Red themselves.

And so they got married and Pittsburgh went along with the whole apparatus of their farce. And then Mrs. Chloe Branhoover announced she was pregnant with the couple's "first" child, who, if a girl, would be called Hilda Janice Branhoover and, if a boy, Haley James Branhoover.

H. James Branhoover, the Branhoovers' second son, was born on a thin autumn Sunday. He was raised like a prince and he behaved like one, too. He ran away to Hollywood because bigger moths need bigger flames, and he leapt to his death from the roof of a youth hostel.

PART III

20. The Wrinkles Around Your Eyes

One night, during the days and nights leading up to his committal, Zachary R. dreamt about a Red Cross nurse in a nun's habit. In the dream, she motioned for him to follow. Fog passed above and diagonally. He looked at her and asked, "What do you want me to do?" Because she also wore a veil, he could not interpret her reply. He awoke thinking about the Cold Angel.

He arrived at work that morning lit by the black sun of empathy, thinking "Service to mankind, Service to mankind." He took the elevator to the top floor, to his station in the file room, where he clocked in and settled down. Then he took the elevator down one floor to the litigation department, where he made a photocopy. The lines of his hands appeared along the blackened edges, reminding him of the wrinkles around the nurse's eyes. He looked at the floor and tightened his lips in sad reflection.

But the sound of others working their machines scintillated his brain:

Keyboards clicking. Phones ringing. The mechanics of a bustling office. Graves being dug in the continents of the world.

So the nurse asked, "Is that a map of the New Hampshire mountains you're copying?"

And he replied, "How did you access my brain?"

"It was you who accessed my brain," she said. "So, when did you decide to quit your job and save the world?"

And he said, "I decided here at this copier, while thinking about the wrinkles around your eyes."

21. The Cold Angel

When the Cold Angel was alive on Earth, she was a Red Cross nurse who traveled widely in service to mankind.

She cried a lot and suffered from insomnia, which deepened the wrinkles around her eyes and lowered her core temperature a full degree below normal, to 97.6 degrees Fahrenheit.

She died of malaria in the jungle of Southeast Asia, the parasitic protozoa of the disease occupying and destroying her red blood corpuscles. The bitter irony of such a fate for a Red Cross nurse did not escape her, nor did her hatred of mosquitoes, which she took with her into the afterlife and which gave her the power to summon and control the movement of fog, which reminded her of smoke, which repelled the disease-carrying insects.

The Cold Angel's feelings toward Zachary R. were ambivalent. On the one hand, she felt motherly pity for him on account of his naïve and compassionate nature, which she displayed herself and which was a prerequisite for a life in service to mankind. On the other hand, these were the same qualities about him that she despised. There is a certain ignorant arrogance, a narcissism, in those who believe they have the power to change things for the better. The Cold Angel was convinced that it was these qualities which made her cry, lowered her temperature, and caused her to suffer a horrific death in the jungle.

She could see that Zachary R. was likely to suffer her fate, so she came to comfort him and to send him on his mission, which she hoped would show him his folly and reform him before it was too late.

22. Red Cross Nurse in a Nun's Habit

When the Cold Angel was alive on Earth, her first mission to Southeast Asia in service to mankind was to a primitive village in the Philippines. The inhabitants there were suspicious of Western medicine but not of Western religion, so in order to gain their trust, the Red Cross nurses wore nuns' habits with crucifixes rather than the all-white uniforms with bright red Red Cross crosses.

The Cold Angel met with such tremendous success in the village, inoculating the children and teaching good hygiene, that she took to wearing the nun's habit on all of her missions, including Thailand, Vietnam, Cambodia, and Laos, even gaining recognition for her tireless service from the Vatican.

It was not long before the Cold Angel converted to Catholicism, took her vows, and became a bona fide nun.

When asked—after her death—to describe the Cold Angel, the sisters in her convent firmly and unanimously asserted their belief that she was headed for sainthood. They considered the drop of her core temperature to be a sign, perhaps even a precursor to the miracle of the stigmata, which they all hoped for dearly, checking her hands and feet each morning for wounds, which they never found, except for the mosquito bites that she suffered frequently and which eventually led to her death.

As the Red Cross nurse in a nun's habit lay dying, she prayed to God for one more mission in service to mankind. Her prayer was not answered, but it wasn't ignored altogether. God, that bald family man, rewarded her in the afterlife by making her a shivering angel, called the Cold Angel, complete with veil, hands like winter, and the power to summon and control the movement of fog, all in service to mankind, which meant in service to Zachary R.

23. The Goth Girls

The Goth Girls gathered once a century in the cathedrals, prisons, and streets of the world to select a troubled man to torment and to protect.

Having wearied of tormenting and protecting a well-known German composer in the eighteenth century, in the nineteenth century they opted for John Brown of Harpers Ferry. Not only did they admire his violent piety, which is five-fourths of pity, but also they were attracted to his paranoid hair and to how he complemented the pillory.

In the twentieth century, they selected Harry Houdini, for not only did they admire his malevolence toward the claustrophobic, but also they swooned to the song of his name.

In the twenty-first century, they wanted a joker, a man who ate numbers off apartment doors, a man who spoke to a cracked snail in the searing mental sun, a man who refused sex because he thought it would diminish his chances of becoming a Messiah or Rock Star. But mainly they wanted a man who made them giggle.

That man was Zachary R.

Their selection was made on a thin autumn Friday, the day before his committal, the day when Zachary R. coughed blood into the toilet and it formed the shape of a rose.

PART IV

24. Like Negligent Acupuncture

On the corner of the street of the twilit bungalow was a pole dedicated to a button dedicated to the regulation of traffic.

A seven-year-old Zachary R. pressed that button and pressed it again just to be sure. The woman in front of him, his mother, turned in her tissue-fiber nightgown and said, "I already pressed the button and you knew that, but you pressed it again anyway."

She reached for a knitting needle, which protruded from a rip in her bag.

"You looked like you were waiting for a train," he said, "to hop on a boxcar. That's why you forgot to press the button."

She clinched the needle and winced like negligent acupuncture when it punctured a bag of birdseed, spilling the contents onto the sidewalk to the delight of pigeons and Goth Girls, who were searching for a joker to torment and to protect.

"Just kidding," he said. "Sometimes I have to press the button no matter what. I apologize."

Her chin dropped and her eyes widened with approval. An entry was made in the Book of Do's and Don'ts.

25. The Book of Do's and Don'ts

Zachary R.'s mother's frayed nerves were caused by her encounters with the Book of Do's and Don'ts, to which she was made privy in her dreams.

The book was three-by-five feet and was kept in Argos, Greece, in the exact center of an all-marble edifice with an opening in the roof that allowed a pillar of light to shine down upon the open pages.

Each night when Zachary R.'s mother went to bed, she did so fearfully yet unaware that she would face a full accounting of the day's do's and don'ts.

The Book of Do's and Don'ts was not a book of rules. Rather, it was a running commentary on the main events with moral implications which occurred on that day. For example, the entry made on the day when her son pressed the button and she winced like negligent acupuncture was as follows:

Do's	Don'ts
1. Wearing your tissue-fiber nightgown in public. Who cares what the neighbors think?	1. Getting irritated with your son when he pressed the button, even though he knew you had already pressed it. He's just a mischievous boy, after all.
2. Explaining to your son why you were irritated with him. You	2. Wearing your tissue-fiber nightgown in public. You should

should always have a reason for being upset with him. You should never be upset with him "just because." Well done.	care about the negative consequences this could have on your son.
3. Clinching the knitting needle and wincing like negligent acupuncture when it punctured your bag of birdseed, spilling the contents onto the sidewalk. Not only did this feed hungry pigeons, but also it made your son laugh at you and then feel bad about it, which made him apologize for pressing the button.	3. Clinching the knitting needle. Don't threaten to stab your son over such a minor offense. Actually, don't ever threaten to stab him.

4. Accepting your son's apology, showing him your approval with your widened eyes. You really can be a good mother sometimes.	

When Zachary R.'s mother awoke in the morning, her nerves were shot, but she couldn't determine why.

26. The Twilit Bungalow

In the days and nights leading up to his committal, Zachary R. spent the hours in reverie at work and then, after he quit, along the rivers and tributaries and seashore of Massachusetts, and finally in the mountains of New Hampshire.

He wore a heavy coat and bit into a bad burger in a shed along the riverbank.

He made photocopies in a skyscraper. He crouched under a table that pine cones bounced off of. He walked the aisle of a hardware store and reached into a barrel of nails that rattled and brushed his spine like silk, urging him to nap.

Job was lost. Wife was cremated. Pram did not squeak.

He believed in the morning. He believed in Messiahs and Rock Stars. He believed he could still be one or the other, or both at the same time. He believed he was on a mission to save the world.

But there was also the childhood memory of the twilit bungalow with sunflowers painted thick on the mailbox and grease stains on the driveway and tires propped against a chain-link fence and a parrot out of its cage that shit on the kitchen stove and his chess-obsessed father and his mother and her frayed nerves and tissue-fiber nightgown lying in bed for three years straight and her young son who gazed out the living room window fogged in breath that said, "I want to take some kind of endless train."

27. The Book of Do's and Don'ts

An entry was made in the Book of Do's and Don'ts concerning the twilit bungalow, to wit:

Do's	Don'ts
1. Providing a twilit bungalow with sunflowers painted thick on the mailbox. The home that you and your chess-obsessed husband have provided for your son has created a sense of security for him, albeit tenuous. He	1. Providing a twilit bungalow with sunflowers painted thick on the mailbox. Why do you and your chess-obsessed husband insist on keeping your home in a state of perpetual dimness? This quirk of yours is

also secretly loves the sunflowers on the mailbox, because they remind him of a van Gogh painting he saw in a book.	liable to drive your son nuts. Also, the sunflowers on the mailbox are poorly rendered in comparison to the van Gogh painting your son saw in a book.
2. Having grease stains on the driveway and tires propped against a chain-link fence. It is essential for a family to have a car in this day and age. Good job.	2. Having grease stains on the driveway and tires propped against a chain-link fence. You neglect your car like you neglect your son. You are an awful mother.
	3. Allowing the parrot to be out of its cage to shit on the kitchen stove. No explanation should be necessary for

	this one.
	4. Lying in bed for three years straight. If you got out of bed, you would see your son gazing out the living room window, sick with worry that he is the cause of your condition. It will be a miracle if he doesn't wind up in a mental asylum someday.

When Zachary R.'s mother awoke in the morning, her head hurt and her mouth was dry, but she couldn't determine why.

28. Mother with Child in Subway

An eight-year-old Zachary R. stood on the shoulder of a foggy road waving his arms. A traveler saw him and pulled over. He grabbed the traveler's arm and led her to the place where his mother lay motionless. He reached for his mother's body and said, "I am afraid to die." The traveler felt for a pulse and found one. She told him not to worry, that his mother was alive. She considered asking him why he said, "I am afraid to die" rather than, "Please don't die," but she decided it would be better to remain silent. When he stopped shaking, she asked him what had happened. Zachary R. told the traveler that his mother was showing him how to climb a pine tree when a pine cone came loose and fell, bouncing loudly off a picnic table, startling her, and causing her to fall. The traveler believed this explanation, but it was a lie. The truth was that he had been linking together boxcar after boxcar on an imaginary train that he said went forever through tunnels in hills with shacks and cigarettes. He said it was an endless train that never stopped. This made so little sense to his mother that she suffered a nervous breakdown and collapsed unconscious on the hard dirt.

Either way, the only truth that mattered was the truth of his injured mother, who had taken the boy to the New Hampshire mountains to get him away from chess, from his father. The traveler realized that she wouldn't be able to lift the boy's mother, so she retrieved a sleeping bag from the trunk of her car, lay it next to the woman, rolled her onto it, and then dragged her to the car, where the two of them managed to slide her onto the backseat. The traveler instructed Zachary R. to sit in the back with his mother, who was now conscious. Zachary R. said he was sorry about the endless train, but his mother just moaned and glared. The traveler, sensing the tension, rummaged through the suitcase on the passenger seat and pulled out her family album. She handed the album to

Zachary R. He looked intently at each photo, but the one he liked best was a photo of a boy and his mother alone in a subway train. He pulled the photo out of its pocket and looked at the back. The inscription read, "Mother with Child in Subway."

29. The Book of Do's and Don'ts

An entry was made in the Book of Do's and Don'ts concerning the incident in the New Hampshire mountains, to wit:

Do's	Don'ts
1. Taking your son to the New Hampshire mountains to get him away from chess, from his father. It was decent of you to notice	1. Suffering a nervous breakdown and collapsing on the hard dirt when your boy described the endless train. This just in:

the stress that chess and your husband were causing your boy, but perhaps you took him to the mountains because of the stress that chess and your husband were causing you. In any event, there should be at least one entry in the Do's column, so here it is.	Young boys have wild imaginations, which should be encouraged, not discouraged. A nervous breakdown? You cannot be serious.
	2. Moaning and glaring when your son said sorry about the endless train. Your son's apology was sincere, and you knew this. Why didn't you accept his apology? And really, did he need to apologize for

	having an imagination?
	3. Forcing your son to find a surrogate mother in the photograph in the traveler's family album. This is the equivalent of telling him his only viable option for survival in this world is to be saved by zero.
	4. Have you noticed that, once again, there are more don'ts than do's? This by itself qualifies as a don't.

When Zachary R.'s mother awoke in the morning, her chest was tight and she could barely breathe, but she couldn't determine why.

30. You Can Be Married and Still Die of Loneliness

Compassion is the method, convergence is the goal.

This was Zachary R.'s unspoken mantra during his childhood. Unspoken because he was a quiet boy who acted on principle, even if he couldn't articulate what the principle was.

His parents could see that he wanted them to be together and happy. And they were together, if together meant living in the same house.

The rumor was that Mr. and Mrs. R. had come together three times. Once on their first date—there was no Internet back then and neither of them was given to writing letters. Twice on their wedding day—Mr. R. looked at the imminent Mrs. R. and recited the words. Mrs. R. did the same. Mr. R. kissed Mrs. R.'s wincing face, though his mind was on knights, rooks, and bishops. Thrice when Mr. and Mrs. R. converged to create Zachary R. When Zachary R. was released from his mother's womb, he was placed in the maternity ward and then driven home by his parents, who, though they lived in the same house, went their separate ways.

The three of them lived in the twilit bungalow, but Mr. R. spent all of his time in the game room, which was dedicated to one game, chess. Mrs. R. dedicated her time to receding into the neurosis of her recurring nightmare—the Book of Do's and Don'ts—of which she was entirely unaware.

Zachary R. would come between them, sweetly, delicately, and say things like, "What time is dinner tonight?"

Or, "Mom and Dad, come look at the endless train I am building myself."

Mr. R.'s exclusive response was to grunt and shut the game room door, which was painted in sixty-four black and white squares, like minor concussions.

Mrs. R.'s customary response was to poke her head out her bedroom door and say, "It is so obvious what you are up to" and then vanish into bed in her tissue-fiber nightgown.

Zachary R.'s only company in the twilit bungalow was the parrot out of its cage that shit on the kitchen stove and his own imagination, which conjured up boxcars and the endless train that went through tunnels in hills with shacks and cigarettes.

Sometimes his mother would come out of her room to check on the boy, but mainly she wanted to see him to test out her pitiful cries for attention, such as, "You can be married and still die of loneliness."

Zachary R.'s response to such things was to knock on his father's door and ask if he wanted to play chess, which he always did.

31. The Book of Don'ts

An entry was made in the Book of Do's and Don'ts concerning Mrs. R.'s remarks to her son, to wit:

Don'ts
1. Notice anything different about this entry? No doubt, you can see that there is only one column this time. Awful. Just awful.
2. Saying, "It is so obvious what you are up to" in response to your son's compassionate attempt to unite the family. Indeed, it *is* obvious what he is up to, which should make it all the more easy for you to find a way to come together. But instead, you would rather shut the door on him and go lie on your pressure sores.
3. Saying, "You can be married and still die of loneliness" in a pathetic plea for

sympathy. I've got news for you. You're
not the one in need of sympathy. Your
son is, and you know it. Maybe he would
be better off without you.

When morning arrived, Zachary R.'s mother
did not awake. Her body wasn't discovered until
three days later, when Zachary R. knocked on his
father's door and the two of them went into her
bedroom in silence, sensing that something was
wrong. When Mr. R. explained to Zachary R.
that his mother was gone, the boy began to sob at
the foot of the bed, saying over and over, "It's my
fault. It's all my fault."

Mr. R. took the young Zachary R. in his arms
and stroked his hair, assuring him that it wasn't
his fault at all. Then he carried Zachary R. into
the game room, where the two of them fell asleep
seated on fold-out chairs on opposite ends of a
chessboard.

The next morning Mr. R. made funeral arrangements for his wife.

32. My Job Is to Father You

At the funeral of Mrs. R., Mr. R. searched his mind for a way to comfort his son, who was still convinced that he caused her death. Zachary R. sobbed on and on about the boxcars and the endless train being why his mother was dead. Finally, Mr. R. said, "Listen, son. I've been thinking about why your mother died. She died because she loved you so much that it paralyzed her, made it impossible for her to do anything. So it's nobody's fault. Do you see? And I know if she could be here now, she would say she loved you and that it wasn't your fault."

Zachary R. looked directly at his father and said, "You won't be paralyzed, right, Dad? Because of chess. Right?"

"That's right, Zachary. Chess makes me strong. But I love you too, just like your mother did."

"But if you love me as much as she did, then why aren't you paralyzed?"

"I do love you as much as your mother did, Zachary, but my job isn't to mother you, my job is to father you."

"And fathers don't get paralyzed because they know how to play chess?" asked Zachary.

"You're damn right," said Zachary R.'s father.

PART V

33. Mustard All Over Your Face

Pawn takes pawn. Bishop takes pawn. Knight takes bishop.

A fourteen-year-old Zachary R. surveyed the midgame chessboard. His mind was supposed to be on his first junior chess tournament, which was forthcoming, but he was thinking about prisons and cathedrals instead.

His father had just made his move and was now in the kitchen frying hamburgers while keeping an eye on his son's hand as it jerked over the pieces. His father went from stove to fridge to cutting board, creeping like a critic hoping to be offended.

Zachary R. made his move. Knight takes bishop.

His father's eyes widened with approval. He placed the burgers on the buns, making small circles of mustard in the exact center of each.

"Excellent move, Zachary," he said. "I believe you'll have checkmate in less than ten moves. Have a burger."

Zachary R. leaned back in his chair and took a medium bite. A dab of mustard squirted out the corner of his mouth, leaving a small yellow stain on his pubescent face, his right-angle chin at sixty degrees and growing.

His father's expression changed from approval to disgust. "You've got mustard all over your face," he said.

Zachary R. knocked the burgers and the chess pieces off the table and ran down the street toward the hill of shacks and cigarettes, where he waited impossibly for an endless train.

34. Hit in the Head by a Pebble

Zachary R. lay in bed in the asylum thinking about how he threw away certain victory because of his fault-finding, embellishing father.

Bernrd Red shined a flashlight into the room and said, "Don't embellish on his embellishments. At least this isn't a story about a boy and his dog."

Zachary R. couldn't disagree with this statement. For once, Bernrd Red was promoting the sensation of being hit in the head by a pebble, rather than a rock.

The two men talked almost cordially for several minutes, and even though Zachary R. still was unable to convince Bernrd Red of the merits of music, he did get him to remove the ring from his pinky.

And then something very uncharacteristic, even inspiring, happened. Bernrd Red gave Zachary R. a bear hug. But it wasn't clear to Zachary R. whether the hug was malevolent or affectionate. The hug was malevolent, as Bernrd Red slipped the ring back on his pinky behind Zachary R.'s back.

Zachary R. wheezed to regain depleted oxygen.

He rolled his neck.

The bees and bones inside him buzzed and popped with such force that he fell asleep drooling.

35. Scholar's Mate

White's opening moves: King's pawn to e4, queen to h5, king's bishop to c4, queen to f7.

Checkmate in four moves, a scholar's mate, for Zachary R. in the opening match of his first junior chess tournament.

His father grunted and shook his fist in the air.

Zachary R.'s opponent, a meek child, began to cry.

Zachary R. quickly moved his chair aside, walked around the table, and put his hand on the child's shoulder.

"Don't worry," said Zachary R. "My dad checkmated me like that the first time I played him. I promise, after if happens to you the first time, it will never happen again. You'll see it coming a mile away."

Zachary R. smiled. The meek child smiled back.

This was Zachary R.'s first experience lit by the black sun of empathy.

Suddenly Zachary R. felt the jarring thud of his father's hand as it wrapped around his small bicep and pulled him out of the tournament room.

"Well done, son," said Zachary R.'s father. "Don't let it go to your head. And don't talk to your opponent after the match. It's poor form."

"Yes, sir," said Zachary R.

"Don't call me sir, Zachary. This isn't the army."

"Okay, Dad."

So much information. Too much of it confusing. The messages: You played well, but don't feel too good about it; it's poor form to talk to your opponent after the match, even if it obviously made him feel better; this isn't the army, so I'm ordering you not to behave as if it were.

36. The Black Sun of Empathy

The black sun of empathy is black because it operates on the inside. It is sun because it produces light and heat.

The black sun of empathy operates on the principles of "do unto others as you would have others do unto you"; "the needs of the many outweigh the needs of the few"; "from each according to his ability, to each according to his need"; "boy, you're gonna carry that weight a long time"; and, "the purpose of life is to die saving someone else's life."

Many famous and heroic men and women followed the principles of the black sun of empathy. None of them lived long, to wit: Gandhi, Martin Luther King, Jr., Joan of Arc, Jack and Bobby Kennedy, Benazir Bhutto, John Lennon, Jesus.

Zachary R. experienced the black sun of empathy and, like Joan of Arc, he also spent time under the searing mental sun.

37. Fool's Mate

The opening moves: White f3, black e5. White g4, black Qh4.

Checkmate in two moves, a fool's mate, for Zachary R.'s opponent in the semifinals of Zachary R.'s first junior chess tournament.

Zachary R.'s father grunted, shook his fist at his son and walked out of the room. Zachary R.'s opponent, an arrogant child, tormented Zachary R. as Zachary stood up to reach across the table to shake the child's hand.

"How did you manage to make it all the way to the semifinals?" asked the child. "Guess your side of the draw was for retards."

"Can't you see that I let you win?" replied Zachary R.

"Yeah right, fool's mate," said the child.

Zachary R. yanked the arrogant child across the table by his handshaking hand and dragged him to the tournament floor, frantically punching his ears and forehead.

Tournament officials quickly descended on Zachary R. and pulled him off of the arrogant child, who had pissed his trousers because of the shocking ferocity of Zachary R.'s attack.

This was Zachary R.'s first experience under the searing mental sun.

38. The Searing Mental Sun

The searing mental sun was painted thick and blinding on the inside of Zachary R.'s skull, like the sunflowers on the mailbox of the twilit bungalow, like the van Gogh painting he saw in a book. And the thick and blinding paint dripped from inside his skull and colored his mind searing yellow, the intensity of which made it impossible for him to keep his balance, caused him to tilt and moan and draw spirals that became portraits of the Cracked Snail.

The searing mental sun and the black sun of empathy mixed together to misguide Zachary R., who did both good and bad like everyone else.

39. No Pontius Pilate

Zachary R. was so naïve and disconnected, so cut off from himself and others, so compassionate, so self-obsessed and sexy with his right-angle chin, that even when he had ulterior motives, he was the last to know.

This meant he could genuinely believe he was acting calm and kind, but friends, family, and bystanders could plainly see he was calmly and kindly sharpening an axe with a tilted stare.

In other words, Zachary R. was no Pontius Pilate.

There was no Roman rationalization in his eyes.

No imperial impropriety in his heart.

No washbasin for his bloody hands.

In other words, Zachary R. was bad at politics.

Indeed, there was an infuriating innocence to him that friends, family, and bystanders found more offensive than an axe to the head. "It is so obvious what you are up to," they would say.

It was as if they had been banished to his Bethlehem in their Las Vegas state of mind.

40. Messiah or Rock Star

Zachary R.'s childhood ended with the death of his mother. He forced himself to forget about the boxcars and the endless train that went through tunnels in hills with shacks and cigarettes. He lied to his father and agreed that his mother's death wasn't his fault, even though he still believed it was. He dutifully continued to play in all the chess tournaments his dad signed him up for, doing well enough to get noticed by his middle school and then his high school.

Zachary R. was one of the region's best junior chess players, but chess wasn't the only reason Zachary R. got noticed in middle school and in high school. Another reason Zachary R. got noticed was that his confidence grew, which caused the girls to giggle, which motivated him to buy a guitar with the money he earned helping at his mother's church, where the pastor had instilled in her an acute sense of right and wrong, of the do's and don'ts of life, as he liked to call them.

Zachary R. never told the pastor about the boxcars and the endless train and the incident in the forest in the New Hampshire mountains that drove his mother into her tissue-fiber nightgown and into bed forever. He never explained that he went to church in search of forgiveness for that incident, which in his mind led to her demise. And so the pastor mistakenly believed that Zachary R. was just an uncommonly devout young man, like Jesus himself. And the pastor became like Paul to Zachary and mentored the boy on the do's and don'ts of life, as he liked to call them.

The pastor told Zachary R. that he had what it took to be like Jesus, his devotion to service and his highly developed sense of empathy toward his chess opponents being two of his finest qualities. But along with the do's came the don'ts. The pastor explained to Zachary R. that if he continued in his service to the church that he could change the world, but if he wanted to change the world, he would have to avoid the temptations of the world, and by temptations, the pastor meant sexual relations with the ever-growing number of young women who, the pastor noticed, were paying attention to his young disciple.

The pastor called Zachary R. to his office and said, "You're not interested in all that, are you?"

"I'm sorry," said Zachary R. "I'm afraid I don't understand what you mean."

"I mean those girls you're talking to," said the pastor. "There must be at least seven of them."

"I'm not doing anything wrong," said Zachary R.

The pastor stretched out both of his arms and put both of his hands on Zachary R.'s shoulders. "Not yet, Zachary," he said. "But if you want to be like Jesus, you have to refuse to have sex with those girls. Having sex outside of marriage is a don't, Zachary."

Zachary R. lay in bed that night, tense as a gargoyle and unbearably awake because of what the pastor had told him. But after hours of deliberation, he decided he would stop flirting with the girls in order to increase his chances of becoming a Messiah or Rock Star, which, if he succeeded, would absolve him of the sin of his mother's death.

Insomnia troubled Zachary R. until dawn, when at last he slept for an hour, then awoke erect as a saint with no one to touch.

41. Rock 'n' Roll High School

Under the tutelage of his father and the pastor, Zachary R. became one of the most disciplined and successful kids at his high school, becoming a confident student and chess player, and refusing sex with the seven or so young women who would have been willing or even agreeable to having sex with him.

One girl in particular, a kind and unassuming redhead with typical redhead features—fair skin, pale blue eyes, and a sensitive, colorful, energetic personality—took a keen interest in Zachary R. and had her girlfriend show him a family photo in which she thought she looked pretty. The girlfriend showed Zachary R. the photo in math class and innocently asked him what he thought about the girl on the end in the green dress.

Zachary R. said, "I recognize her. She's in my English class. I think she's gorge—I mean, I think she's somewhat gorgeous, that chess is nearly impossible." Zachary R. felt the twofold pain of lying and denying his true feelings. He felt sharp melancholic daggers in his stomach and heart.

The girlfriend frowned and put the photo back into her backpack. Her opinion of Zachary R. diminished significantly with that remark, which was unlucky for him, since she was popular and a gossip.

News got around that Zachary R. was stuck up and a chicken, yet many students still admired him from a distance due to his imperviousness to their overt antipathy toward him, his clean lifestyle, his unswerving faith, his good grades, his success at chess, and his guitar prowess. They saw him as aloof and above their petty criticisms, which only increased their pettiness and his aloofness.

The pastor, on the other hand, was pleased with Zachary R. and explained to him that Jesus, too, was misunderstood and even hated in his time. Zachary R. was glad to know his chances for Messiah or Rock Star, for his mother's forgiveness, were intact.

The girls who once liked him, and especially the redhead, who was heartbroken but still had a high opinion of him, were baffled as Zachary R. withdrew and his appearance and personality became less and less attractive. These same girls, and even the redhead, began to pay attention to the other boys, which frustrated Zachary R. and made him suffer under the searing mental sun.

Despite his talent at guitar, he lost any desire to start a band. He began to talk to himself in class, which got him sent to the school psychiatrist. He lost all patience for chess and started to lose, which irritated his father, who stopped speaking to him entirely.

His grades suffered, but not enough to prevent him from graduating. And graduate he did, but he refused to attend the graduation ceremony. Instead, he informed the school psychiatrist that he wanted his diploma mailed.

He thought about running away to Hollywood to start a band out there, but this was just a thought.

The summer after high school, Zachary R.'s father gave him three months to find a job, saying that come September, job or no job, he was kicking him out of the house.

Zachary R. moved out in July when he landed a file clerk position at the Law Offices of Miller & Associates, where they happily employed the organizational skills he had gleaned from chess and the discipline he had learned from the pastor of his mother's church.

Zachary R. lived the first years of his twenties like a monk, until he saw his future wife asleep in the hall with the blue carpet.

42. Stuffed and Perched in a Cage

While it is not exactly clear what happened to Zachary R.'s father, it is widely believed that he happily lived out the rest of his days at his local chess club and in the game room of the twilit bungalow, where he had his wife's parrot stuffed and, at last, perched in a cage.

43. The Book of Do's

Soon after Zachary R. found a job and took an apartment, he quit chess, guitar, and church. But, the three did not quit him. And he spent his days in three places, too—at home, going to and from work, and at work itself. As far as going to and from work was concerned, Zachary R. rode the bus, and later, after he had saved enough money, he purchased and drove the Nova.

And in all three places he spent more and more time in the searing mental sun. He no longer played chess, but he saw chess pieces in everything. He no longer played guitar, but his love of music grew. He especially liked the requiems of Mozart, Fauré, and Richafort, and the Electric Light Dirge for Cello and Organ by an obscure American composer.

He no longer attended church, but he did not give up on the dream of becoming a Messiah or Rock Star. On one night in particular, he dreamt of a cathedral in Bethlehem that had a telescope where the rose window should have been and he climbed a ladder and looked through the telescope, which saw all the way to a marble edifice in Argos, Greece, and he looked down an opening in the roof that allowed in a pillar of light that illuminated the open pages of a three-by-five-foot book called the Book of Do's and Don'ts. Though he could not see her, he could hear his dead mother begging the Book to leave her alone, and he saw the one entry in the Book that was intended for him, to wit:

Do's
1. Go in search of rivers and women. The rest is meaningless.

Zachary R. awoke in the morning feeling good for the first time in his life, but he couldn't determine why.

PART VI

44. You Smell Like Rain

Zachary R. first noticed Annabel R. asleep on the blue carpet in the common hall of his first apartment. He stared at her for a long time and the longer he stared, the more his mind emptied.

His troubles floated in the vacuum of her dormant image. He nudged her awake and said, "You smell like rain."

Her eyes twitched, opened a little, then closed again.

Zachary R. went back to his room and forgot what she looked like, but he wondered about the inside of her apartment and what might happen if he spent time with her there.

45. The Blue Carpet in the Hall

The first time Zachary R. saw Annabel R. asleep on the blue carpet in the hall was not the first time she had slept there. Annabel R. had just been kicked out of her father's house, and moved into her own apartment, where she acted out the story of "The Little Match Girl." The blue carpet in the hall reminded her of the cold Danish alleyway where the little girl struck the matches and saw visions before she died.

Now Annabel R. lay on the blue carpet and pretended to freeze to death, pretended to see visions, pretended that if she came home without money, her father would beat her, which essentially wasn't pretend, except for the fact that money had nothing to do with it.

The first time Annabel R. had a real vision on the blue carpet was the first time Zachary R. noticed her there, his mind emptying, his troubles floating in the vacuum of her dormant image.

She dreamt that it was the vernal equinox and a young man with eyes that blossomed like sunflowers invited her to the carnival.

When she awoke, there he was just staring at her until finally he said, "You smell like rain."

Annabel R. thought, "I am going to know this man and it is going to be important."

She thought about what she liked about him that wasn't sentimental . . . That she dreamt him before she met him. No. Sentimental. That his eyes blossomed like sunflowers. Better, but still sentimental. That he noticed she smelled like rain. Made her heart leap, but still sentimental. That when she woke and saw him staring at her, he didn't speak for an uncomfortable length of time. That was it. Zachary R. was mostly silent. That was what she liked most about him.

Annabel R. wrote "Mostly Silent" on a matchbook and slipped it under his door.

46. Mostly Silent

Annabel R. knew she was going to know Zachary R. and it was going to be important. She slid a matchbook under his door with the words "Mostly Silent" written on it, which was, by Zachary R.'s underdeveloped sense of romance, the most bewitching of surprises.

But the vernal equinox was fast approaching and Zachary R. hadn't so much as uttered a hello, let alone knocked on her door and formally introduced himself.

But this didn't mean Zachary R. wasn't interested. On the contrary, he was so smitten with the mysterious sleeping match girl in the hall with the blue carpet that he was devising a strategy not just for a first date, but also for a way to get her into his life for the long term.

On March 18, he thought, "Should I bring her flowers? No. Too common." On March 19, "Dinner and a movie? No. She is too original to be impressed by such gestures."

And then, on March 20, the day before the vernal equinox, Zachary R. saw a band of gypsy kids posting small poster ads for the carnival, which was to stake a patch of earth at the foot of the hill of shacks and cigarettes and open on March 21.

Zachary R. liked the carnival. He lay awake all night hoping that when morning came, he would see Annabel R. in the hall with the blue carpet.

47. The Carnival

Wheels and ropes. Beetles and straw. Logs and parachutes. Sage and thaw.

The next morning Zachary R. saw Annabel R. in the hallway with the blue carpet, but this time she was awake, leaning against the wall, following the path of the sunlight as it moved along the opposite wall.

He stared at her until she said, "Today is the vernal equinox. What are you doing?" He opened his backpack and showed her a small poster ad for the carnival, which had staked a patch of earth at the foot of the hill of shacks and cigarettes.

She went back inside her apartment for a moment and reappeared in a burgundy dress. Her hair was parted down the middle.

Zachary R. wore an indigo T-shirt and sideburns, which complemented his right-angle chin. His eyes blossomed like sunflowers.

They set off on foot toward the patch of earth that the carnival had roped and logged, beetled and strawed. They joined a procession of coolers, crows, and firecrackers, and in less than an hour they arrived.

Colors flashed. The grand wheel spun. Hot dogs rolled on metal rods. Paper cups and wrappers blew over shoes and ants.

At the carnival Zachary R. felt vital to the mechanics of the world. He looked deeply into Annabel's eyes, but she did not kiss him.

Instead, she led him to the photo booth by the fortune-teller. She sat him down and drew the curtain. No photos were taken.

They rode the parachutes. They fired guns. They burned sage in the name of loneliness, but it was so warm that the sky seemed to descend and nothing was distant.

Zachary and Annabel moved through the carnival in such gentle oblivion that gypsy kids had no trouble stealing rolls of tickets from their pockets.

48. The Photo Booth and the Brass Knuckles of Sex

Zachary R. did not object to sex in the photo booth, especially since Annabel's dress concealed the mechanics of the act. What was surprising was that they occupied the booth for twenty minutes and no one drew back the curtain, not even the gypsy kids. Most likely all of the carnival patrons were conditioned to recognize the piston-like sound of the working parts and elected out of empathy to direct their attention toward the fortune-teller.

Either way, Annabel became pregnant with Sarah R. And, of almost equal importance, conception occurred in the photo booth rather than later that night in Annabel's apartment, because the sex that occurred in Annabel's apartment was hell compared to the sex at the carnival, which wasn't quite heaven, but was close.

Back in Annabel's apartment, Annabel ordered Zachary R. to sit on her bed while she retrieved a cigar box from the floor of the closet. She sat down beside him and opened the box, which contained brass knuckles and a romance novel called *Savage Splendor*. She ordered him to strike her with the brass knuckles while she read from the book. The sunflowers in his eyes wilted, but he obeyed. He struck her harder than she anticipated, which frenzied her and made her whirl and pop. Love came and went.

Zachary R. turned gray and began to weep. Annabel R. put her hand on his shoulder and fell asleep.

49. Solstices and Equinoxes

Morning sickness. Minor concussion. Birth of Sarah. Postpartum depression.

In the early days after the carnival, Annabel fell ill. At first, she thought it was the familiar aftereffects of the ritual beating she had received during sex: brass knuckles, *Savage Splendor*, and the ensuing concussion and nausea.

Then she remembered that her pregnancy test was positive and that the pregnancy was likely causing her morning sickness.

It was clear to both of them what needed to be done.

A wedding date was set for June 21, the summer solstice. This made sense from a romantic point of view (the carnival and the conception of Sarah R. occurred precisely on the vernal equinox) and a logical point of view (Annabel R. would not be showing at the end of the first trimester).

112

The honeymoon didn't immediately follow the wedding. Instead, because of the solstices and equinoxes, they decided to honeymoon the week of the autumnal equinox.

Sarah R. was born on December 21, the winter solstice, exactly nine months to the day after conception.

By now, the novelty of the solstices and equinoxes had worn thin. In fact, as Annabel R. held the newborn in her arms, she thought the baby was cursed. She fell into a deep postpartum depression for the rest of her days, which were numbered: seven hundred and thirty, to be exact.

50. Guests Dressed Up Like Dragons

Flash of bulb. Jet of plane. Swift of cloud. Drop of rain.

The wedding occurred on a wet summer Sunday of turbulent chairs and guests dressed up like dragons.

Zachary R. dressed up like a groom and made an appearance. Annabel R. was there too. He looked at her and recited the words. She did the same. He kissed her wincing face. Lights and noise were made when a jet flew over the ceremony. Zachary R. looked at the sky, his eyes blinking in the pinprick rain.

51. Frozen Little Girl

When she was little, Annabel liked to read, and she imagined herself downtrodden or orphaned, or both. She liked Hans Christian Andersen's "The Little Match Girl," especially the visions the little match girl had when she struck each match and also that the little match girl went to heaven to be with her grandmother and God when she died. On the other hand, Annabel had no tolerance for the sentimental and she held maudlin in contempt, so she made sure to keep the little match girl a secret by keeping a cigar box under the bed with a matchbook, a rag doll, and a locket with a photo of a pale boy called Damien, which she didn't care for, but she couldn't find a suitable photo of a frozen little girl.

Annabel R. guarded the cigar box and her sentimentality vigilantly.

Her father also kept a cigar box with secret contents. Photos of his wife, Annabel's mother, who had run away with a magician; photos of naked women and girls; and a pair of brass knuckles.

He demonstrated his love for his daughter using the contents of the cigar box. His daughter grew accustomed to her father's violent love, which fulfilled her downtrodden fantasy. She missed the ritual after high school ended and her father kicked her out.

In fact, on the day her father said goodbye, she pilfered the brass knuckles from his cigar box, placing them in her own cigar box along with a romance novel called *Savage Splendor*.

Annabel R. never set foot in her father's house again, but she continued her father's ritual with all of the boys and men in her life.

She went to the carnival with Zachary R. and conceived a child there. And back in her apartment that same night, she received her beating, which made her whirl and pop.

She cheated on Zachary R. with at least two men. And she received her beating from each of them.

PART VII

52. Lean Monday

Sarah R. spent all of Monday in her motel room in an apoplectic daze because she had scattered her mother's ashes across the lake. She sat on the floor at the foot of the bed, hugging the empty urn, trying to comprehend the finality of her actions.

She sobbed over the mother she never knew, who died when Sarah R. was two. She sobbed over her father, who was sick in a mental asylum and whom she had deceived.

She forgot to eat. She forgot to drink. She thought, "If tomorrow is Fat Tuesday, then today is Lean Monday."

Sarah R. fell asleep at dusk, still seated at the foot of the bed, still hugging the empty urn.

She woke at eleven thinking about the deadhead. She shaved her head, showered, threw on the Revolution Dress, and set off on foot to the Dungeon, where Mardi Gras began precisely at midnight.

53. Fat Tuesday; Ash Wednesday

Sarah R. spent the first six hours of Mardi Gras at the Dungeon, where the Dungeon Master poured her two-for-one drinks and listened attentively to her story about the deadhead from Kentucky.

The Dungeon Master, because he liked Sarah, didn't divulge the truth, which was that he knew the mysterious Kentuckian's identity. He was from out of town, it was true. But he was from just across the bridge in Mississippi and was a regular at the Dungeon until recently, because he was afraid of the possibility of running into a certain underage woman with a bald head who wore a burgundy dress that compelled him to utter words such as *adroit*, which he didn't know the meaning of but said anyway, as if the dress had coaxed the word out of him by some kind of voodoo.

Out of avuncular concern for Sarah, the Dungeon Master cut off her drinking privilege at six a.m. He kissed her on the cheek and sent her on her way toward Bourbon Street, which was already crowded with partiers who threw beads her way in recognition of her bald head and the Revolution Dress.

Suddenly, Sarah R. felt hungry. Because she didn't immediately see a hot dog cart, she opted for the nearest restaurant, a brightly lit twenty-four-hour diner.

The diner was so bright, in fact, that she had no trouble identifying the Kentuckian and his girlfriend sitting in one of the booths.

At that moment, the booze and the Revolution Dress took over.

"It's over, isn't it!?" she screamed at the deadhead.

The deadhead from Mississippi looked at his girlfriend with an expression that said, "I have no idea who this bald madgirl is."

What he did or didn't do was irrelevant to Sarah R. The crush was over.

She ran out of the diner and threw her beads into the street. The police on their horses paid no attention. She screamed obscenities at the languid trees. She cursed this city, this Necropolis, the Dungeon, the lake and its brackish voodoo, and the bright diner that had betrayed her.

She returned to her room, disrobed down to her bra and panties, and set fire to the Revolution Dress, which had also betrayed her.

When Sarah R. came to, it was to the face of a nurse with ash residue brushed across her forehead. The thought that she had died and gone to Hell for her bad deeds on Mardi Gras was quickly replaced by the thought that the day after Fat Tuesday is Ash Wednesday and that the nurse had just returned from church.

"Where am I?" asked Sarah R. cautiously.

The nurse didn't mince words. "You're in a hospital," she said. "You nearly burned down a motel last night."

Sarah R. winced. "What does the ash on your forehead mean?"

"Today is Ash Wednesday," said the nurse. "The first day of Lent. The ashes are an expression of sorrow for sins and a reminder that we are dust and will return to dust unless we repent and hear the good news."

"That's scary," said Sarah R. "I guess Fat Tuesday was my Ash Wednesday."

"Clever," said the nurse. "Not funny at all, but clever. You're lucky nobody got hurt in that motel you almost burned down."

But Sarah R. was no longer listening. She was thinking about all of the ashes in her young life. Her mother, the Revolution Dress, the motel, and even her father, who was returning to dust, slowly, with each passing day.

When the nurse left the room, the authorities entered and the interrogation began.

* * * * *

An entire week went by and Sarah R. was still in the hospital, but by now the authorities felt she had sufficiently regained her bearings and could return to society. She was reminded over and over that she had nearly burned down the bargain motel and that, luckily, nobody was seriously hurt.

During her stay in the hospital, Sarah R. told the authorities about her parents and where she lived, as the driver's license in her purse was a fake.

She told them about the descent of her father and the foreclosure on their house in New England.

She told them about the death of her mother and of scattering her mother's ashes across Lake Pontchartrain.

Because this was the state of Louisiana, and because there were many more Mardi Gras nutcases to be questioned, the only action the authorities took was to issue a citation for unauthorized disposal of human ashes into state waters. A hospital doctor prescribed a drug regimen of painkillers and antidepressants, and discharged her via wheelchair back onto the streets of New Orleans.

Sarah R. turned gray. She took her pills and staggered down the street to the nearest park, where she collapsed. The hot dog vendor knelt down beside her and emptied a bottled water from his cart onto her face to revive her.

She woke reluctantly, but the kind expression on the hot dog vendor's face made it easier for her to face consciousness and the truth about her predicament.

"The doctors and the detectives in the hospital questioned me about my dad," said Sarah R.

"They care about you," said the hot dog vendor.

"And they callously reminded me of my mother's death by ticketing me for scattering her ashes across the lake," she said.

"That's unfortunate," said the hot dog vendor, brushing away the grass that had left an imprint on her cheek.

"While I can't vouch for the sensitivity of doctors and detectives," he continued, "I hope I can convince you that hot dog vendors doubling as Dungeon Masters have better manners."

54. The Hot Dog Vendor

The man who was a hot dog vendor had, depending on one's point of view, multiple jobs, multiple personalities, or, as is the case with many a New Orleans native, multiple masques. Or, depending on one's point of view, the man possessed multiple all of the above.

Each job, or personality, or masque took an interest in Sarah R., but each had his own motives.

It was true. The hot dog vendor had kissed Sarah R. on the cheek after she was nearly struck by a speeding bus. He was a kind and simple man whose affectionate disposition crossed modern social boundaries. Yet, because of his noble countenance, no one ever protested. In fact, his bold but gentle gesture of affection toward Sarah R. came across as a refreshing and welcome anachronism.

This was why Sarah R. also did not protest when he slipped his business card in her cleavage. But the job, or personality, or masque who crossed that boundary was the Dungeon Master.

It was true. The Dungeon Master's motives, if not outright impure, were at best suspect. If he wasn't unethical, he was at least cynically self-interested. The Dungeon Master needed customers, especially young female customers, for his bar, and Sarah R. was eager to oblige the man's efforts to survive in this Hobbesian world.

It occurred to Sarah R. that the man probably had additional jobs, or personalities, or masques that he didn't reveal to her. But of this she was unconcerned. She understood it was best not to pry.

PART VIII

55. The Cracked Snail

Pellet of poison. Boot of orderly. Zachary's mower. Snail's soliloquy.

The Cracked Snail had committed itself to the asylum lawn long before Zachary R.'s arrival, when it learned it was the only snail who could communicate with humans.

The snail made this discovery one mad day as it was meandering among the blades thinking "Service to mankind," when from high above the boot of an orderly crashed down on its shell, cracking it and revealing its innards, which glistened in the searing mental sun. The snail screamed in pain and cursed at the orderly, who, to their mutual shock, heard the snail and went running for solitary confinement.

And so the Cracked Snail determined it would talk to the asylum patients, but would do so selectively so as not to worsen their already fragile psyches.

Years later, when Zachary R. was committed, the Cracked Snail took a keen interest in him due to his right-angle chin and his eyes, which blossomed like sunflowers. But the snail did not speak to him out of concern for his fragile psyche, which was confirmed beyond all doubt a month into his stay, when he first claimed to the snail that he had Neosporin. After all, no human in his right mind would offer Neosporin to a snail, crack or no crack.

But after a year in the asylum, Zachary R. said to someone important, "I like rivers and women." These words got him permission to mow the asylum lawn, much to the Cracked Snail's amusement and chagrin. The Cracked Snail's already keen interest in Zachary R. was heightened due to the intensity with which Zachary R. mowed the asylum lawn. The poison pellets did wonders to relieve the pain of the crack, but nevertheless the Cracked Snail had no desire to have its wound worsened by the blade of a lawn mower. And so the Cracked Snail kept extra vigilant watch over Zachary R. when Zachary mowed the asylum lawn.

On one such occasion, Zachary R. was mowing the asylum lawn, admiring the precision of grass, when he noticed a glint in the blades. He cut the engine and then stared for hours at the Cracked Snail, until finally Zachary R. again claimed, "I have Neosporin."

"Thanks," replied the Cracked Snail, "but you shouldn't use Neosporin on a wound of this magnitude. And, more importantly, as to your intense level of concentration in mowing the lawn, if you could spare some of that intensity for painting my portrait, I would like that very much."

Betraying neither shock nor horror at the fact of being spoken to by a snail, Zachary R. replied, "I don't know anything about painting."

"Don't be so modest," said the Cracked Snail.

56. The Lavender Bush and the Night Sky

Zachary R. wandered the perimeter of the asylum lawn in the searing mental sun. He stopped when he saw the Cracked Snail. He stared briefly and then proclaimed, "I'm lost."

The Cracked Snail replied, "Go to the corner and look into the lavender bush." Zachary R. went to the corner and looked into the lavender bush. He saw five bees. He continued to look into the lavender bush. He saw twenty bees. He continued to look into the lavender bush. He saw a hundred bees.

That night he sat up in bed, unbearably awake because of chess with his father. He thought about the bees in the lavender bush. He rose out of bed and went to the asylum window. He looked into the night sky. He saw a thousand stars. He continued to look into the night sky. He saw ten thousand stars. He continued to look into the night sky. He saw knights, rooks, and bishops.

57. Proselytize with Those Eyes

Zachary R. sat in the exact middle of the asylum lawn, thoroughly engrossed by the Cracked Snail as it slithered among the green blades in the searing mental sun.

Up the entire length of a blade it went, innards glistening, until the blade bent down for a soft landing, and then continuing along the dirt, stopping to nibble on a poison pellet, and back up another green blade until the blade bent down for another soft landing. All afternoon this continued, inducing a monk-like trance in Zachary R., whose eyes blossomed like sunflowers. Finally, the Cracked Snail stopped and, in a poison pellet-induced stupor, proclaimed, "You could proselytize with those eyes."

58. The Asylum Lawn

As depressed as an orderly, Zachary R. lay in the exact middle of the asylum lawn and imagined rows of pine trees in a pool of heat waves, the searing mental sun, the black sun of empathy, Annabel R., Sarah R., the Goth Girls, the Cracked Snail, shacks, cigarettes, chess, his father, his mother, the endless train, the Cold Angel, the flyswatter, the carnival, Bernrd Red, the lavender bush, and the night sky all beating down.

PART IX

59. News from the Working Parts, Part 1

A fortnight out of the asylum, the foreclosure finalized, the boxcar journey complete, Zachary R. released himself to the soft prison of Hollywood in search of his daughter.

He cleared a spot for observation just off the Walk of Fame, on a stretch of pavement between medium buildings.

He gathered magazines, popped pills, worked a dainty jackhammer.

He wrote a suicide note on the back of a clipboard and sealed it in a business reply envelope.

He rolled up a *Newsweek* and a *Hustler*, and peered through them like binoculars. Unable to concentrate on the boulevard, he lifted his head to examine the sky, which was the same as examining the past. He saw knights, rooks, and bishops.

To his left was a beer bottle and a hat rack with a sailor's hat on it. He dropped the magazines and ignored the hat, but he uncapped and recapped the bottle several times, mimicking the working parts of Hollywood billboards.

He sampled his fingers: semen on the index, beer on the middle, stardom on the ring, asthma on the pinky, murder on the thumb. He turned and punched the building behind him. Pain traveled from his hand to his mind and back to his hand.

He looked at the boulevard. There was no sign of his daughter. He watched the megaphone arm of a police car cock and then heard the words, "Driver of the blue truck, get out of the way." He heard the blue truck ram the car in front of it and the ensuing siren.

He watched girls mine for teeth jewels and boys fake gayness for the sake of slavery, but really they all missed trick-or-treating with foster parents.

Zachary R. took notice of the boys because the boys had caught a glimpse of his right-angle chin and the dainty jackhammer, which no longer worked due to the pain in his hand. Nevertheless, the boys pushed up their sleeves, pursed their lips, and moved toward him. Zachary R. leapt to his feet and bull-rushed them, believing their flirtation would wither in his malodor. He was correct. The boys ushered him along, shirts raised to cover their noses.

He continued walking until he came upon a corpse at the base of the hills by the youth hostel. Searchlights crossed overhead. He heard Haydn. A soft breeze moved his arm hairs. His hand began to swell. He reached for the lifeless body and said, "I am afraid to die."

60. Wind in Empty Boxes

Woodward and Bernstein. Bonnie and Clyde. Heckle and Jeckle. Jekyll and Hyde.

Morning came and Zachary R. was back on his stretch of pavement between medium buildings. Eyes were all around him: vendors and vice, bankers and bondsmen, and two newsmen questioning a male and a female detective about a corpse found by the youth hostel near the Hollywood Bowl.

Zachary R. did his best to look tilted and full of space. He sampled the fingers on his injured hand, which was now swollen to the point of immobility.

He was unbearably awake and black with hunger.

He zipped his pants and put on the sailor's hat. He thought about the night before, about Haydn and the corpse, and about his time in the asylum when he fought Bernrd Red over the Electric Light Dirge for Cello and Organ.

He boarded the bus to Santa Monica and sat directly behind the driver, who smelled like wind in empty boxes.

In Santa Monica, Zachary R. walked in the wet sand. Gulls and pigeons made him duck and weave to the delight of Goth Girls, who had frenzied the birds to conjure storms from the ocean. He bull-rushed them and said in a mock English accent, "You have a spectacular arsenal of spells." The girls raised their Damien lockets to cover their giggling faces and vanished in the ocean air.

He turned and walked to the pier with the endless carnival. He ordered a beer and a banana and watched the grand wheel until the sun went down. Then he went to the edge of the pier and watched the waves.

He dove in just as it began to rain, expecting the current to carry him to shore. But just the opposite happened. He drifted out to sea, past the continental shelf and into a vast fishing net that scooped him aboard a Yin Yang liner bound for

143

all ports south around Cape Horn and then north to Rio and the Caribbean, with a final destination of New Orleans, where a ramp was extended and he disembarked.

Zachary R. woke along the shore of Venice Beach, coughing up ocean. He wished for a possibility other than life or death.

61. Dumbfounded as a Refugee

Zachary R. stood on the sand of Venice Beach, dumbfounded as a refugee. He took three steps east and fell face-first onto a mound of seaweed, causing a splash of flies that attached en masse to his body.

He rolled like he was on fire, rolled until the flies had flown or were smashed, rolled until the bananas and the beer from the night before reemerged in his mouth mixed with bile. He spit out the entire apparatus, which diminished his vertigo. He stood again, free of entanglements.

He scraped his salty wet clothes with a stick, and set off on foot toward the hill of shacks and cigarettes. He walked for eight miles, recalling the joy of nails in his lips and the comfort of flowing blood.

By evening he had returned to his stretch of pavement between medium buildings.

He felt in his pockets for burger money but found only sand and tar.

He turned gray and curled up where pavement and building met, where the warmth of the day had been retained.

Three Goth Girls surrounded him to block the chill, but this did little to prevent the ensuing fever and the further blackening of his injured hand. Puzzled, the girls painted their nails white and prayed.

62. The Street Boys and the Dainty Jackhammer

After all he had been through in the soft prison of Hollywood—his injured hand, the corpse, the bus ride to the ocean and diving off the pier and being washed ashore and coughing up ocean, the flies on the beach and rolling in the sand like he was on fire, the long walk back to Hollywood, back to his stretch of pavement between medium buildings with no burger money and fever and the further blackening of his injured hand—Zachary R. had forgotten about the boys who fake gayness for the sake of slavery, the street boys, but the boys did not forget Zachary R.

The boys had taken notice of Zachary R.'s right-angle chin, and they hadn't forgotten the glimpse of the dainty jackhammer and how he made them wither in his malodor.

So the boys kept an eye on the alley and waited for Zachary R.'s return. When he returned from his bus ride to the ocean, the boys pushed up their sleeves, pursed their lips, and moved toward him.

There were three street boys in all and Zachary R. was in no condition to bull-rush them this time. The defense of his malodor, the dark-road signature of the skunk, had been diminished by the sea.

The first boy spoke: "If it isn't the bum with the pretty chin and the dainty jackhammer."

Then the second boy: "And he smells pretty, too, like the ocean and not like a skunk. Much better." He took a deep whiff.

And then the third boy: "He does smell better. Must be trying to impress us this time. Let's see that chin smile. Let's have a look at that dainty jackhammer."

All three boys laughed loudly. The third boy shoved him to the ground.

Zachary R. turned gray. He covered his ears with his hands and moved his knees to his chest.

The third boy yanked Zachary R. by the arm with such force that he went from lying down to sitting up straight.

Zachary R. grimaced in pain.

"No smile from that pretty chin?" the first boy taunted. "No glimpse of that dainty jackhammer?"

Zachary R. grimaced again, giggled terribly, and said, "I'm neither gay nor gay, so I guess the three of you little cocksuckers will just have to fuck yourselves tonight."

The only memory Zachary R. retained from this night was the sound of what seemed like every trashcan in the alley crashing down on him and the laughter of the street boys, which sounded like crows and made him see sunspots.

63. Puke, Porn, and a Pit Bull

Street boys, crows, and sunspots. Zachary R., all slender and milky, thought dark thoughts as he dragged himself along his stretch of pavement. He cursed God over his committal, which separated him from daughter and home.

"Just let me die here in peace," he pled.

His plea was not granted. A murder of crows shrieked above, while all around him hovered puke, porn, and a pit bull.

But God did not ignore him altogether: That bald family man good-vibed him with a thunderclap that startled the pit bull and sent it into a cardboard box.

That night it rained cold and hard. Water ran down the sides of buildings and down the hills. Water joined puke and disappeared into a storm drain. Water saturated porn and bled colors into pavement.

The morning sun revealed a new city, like the beginning of ancient ruins. Zachary R. hummed

Haydn. He thought fondly of the Electric Light Dirge for Cello and Organ. The swelling in his hand seemed to recede.

64. The Wheels of a Trashcan

The wheels of a trashcan rolled slowly over Zachary R.'s stretch of pavement between medium buildings, crunching and popping gravel, and causing his neck to tingle with delight.

Memories of carnival straw and smoke.

Thoughts of Annabel.

"Why do the police whisper all the time?" he thought.

"Why are they always looking at me?"

Thoughts of Sarah.

"Where could she be?" he said out loud.

Zachary R. reached inside the trashcan and pulled out a large brown bag.

Inside the bag were a hamburger and a bathrobe. He bit into the burger, but it tasted of worms, microbes, and malodor. He tried on the bathrobe, but it smelled like Ben Gay.

65. Like a Ghost Ship

A bus stopped near Zachary R.'s stretch of pavement between medium buildings in the early morning hours. The inside of the bus was dark, like a ghost ship. The electric letters that moved along the top read, "NOT IN SERVICE."

The driver swung open the door and stepped outside for a cigarette.

The boulevard was quiet.

Zachary R. approached the driver. His injured hand began to throb.

"Where does this bus go?" he asked.

"Around the perimeter," said the driver.

"Can I go with you?"

"No."

"Why did you stop here, then?"

"To smoke a cigarette."

"Have you seen my daughter?"

"Yes. And your wife, too. They're looking for you."

66. The Goth Girls and the Ghost Ship

Seven Goth Girls filed out the side door of the bus and descended with great conviction upon Zachary R., who was still harassing the bus driver on his cigarette break.

"Why do you think he said he was going around the perimeter?" they asked in unison. "He was afraid of what you might do to him if he told you the truth.

"The truth is that your mother and wife are dead, and your daughter is in New Orleans.

"The truth is that your daughter tricked you into coming to L.A. because she is afraid and ashamed of you.

"The truth is that you are going around the perimeter of the truth by living in this alley and acting crazy.

"The truth is that you are not responsible for your mother's death, but you are responsible for Annabel's death, though only partially. Her death was largely her own fault and that of her other lover, Bernrd Red."

"That's enough truth for now," said Zachary R.

He felt ill and at peace simultaneously.

The redheaded Goth approached him and held his injured hand.

67. The Arrest

It looked like Easter clouds on the morning of Zachary R.'s arrest for the murder of H. James Branhoover of Pittsburgh, Pennsylvania.

Though his name had a princely air, Mr. Branhoover was, in fact, a runaway living in a youth hostel on Highland Avenue, just south of the Hollywood Bowl.

Mr. Branhoover had either fallen to his death from the roof of the youth hostel, or he had been pushed. No suicide note had been found, there were fingerprints on his clothes, and one eyewitness, a gay male prostitute, said he saw a homeless man reaching for the body and muttering, "I am afraid to die."

Zachary R. sat alone in a holding cell, watching sunlight shine through the lone barred window and move across the floor as the hours passed by.

Finally, two detectives, one male and one female, entered and escorted Zachary R. to an interrogation room.

It didn't take expert detective work to determine that Zachary R. had nothing to do with the death of H. James Branhoover, or to determine that Zachary R. was in need of medical attention for his injured hand and for his broken mind and desolate spirit.

It would have taken expert detective work, however, or even clairvoyance, to uncover the unlikely connection between Zachary R. and H. James Branhoover. Fortunately for Zachary R., the detectives did not possess such powers.

Zachary R. told the detectives about his daughter, his mother, the Cold Angel, boxcars, subways and endless trains, his father and chess, his wife and Bernrd Red, his pleasant conversations with the Cracked Snail, the peace of mowing the asylum lawn, and the tormenting and nurturing Goth Girls.

The detectives were good listeners, but their logical minds were incapable of comprehending Zachary R.'s story. At least they got him to a hospital to get his injured hand looked at.

As for H. James Branhoover, a suicide note was eventually found. He had sealed and mailed it in a business reply envelope for *Playboy* magazine.

The ladies at the subscription processing center in Boulder, Colorado, were moved by the poignant words and the urgent message contained in Mr. Branhoover's note. In fact, one of the ladies photocopied the note and shared it with her son, who had run away twice before.

The note dispelled romantic notions of the lives of runaways and demonstrated just how ugly Hollywood really is. The lady's son never ran away again. Instead, he waited until he turned eighteen and then he moved to Las Cruces, New Mexico, where he got a job, found a wife, went back to school, and eventually became a professor in the Humanities Department of New Mexico State University.

68. Worms, Microbes, Malodor

Zachary R.'s hand was put in a cast at the hospital, but the doctor there was less concerned about the broken hand than he was about the infection that had begun to spread.

The doctor, realizing that Zachary R. was homeless, was determined not to let him take the bed of an insured patient, but he wasn't totally devoid of pity. He had asked enough questions during intake to determine that Zachary R. had been previously placed in an asylum in Massachusetts, and he attempted to devise a way for Zachary R. to be committed to a comparable facility in California.

The doctor knew that Zachary R. was in need of intravenous antibiotics for the infection in his injured hand, which had begun to move up his arm en route to his brain. He also knew, however, that he needed to process Zachary R. as quickly as possible in order to bring in the next— insured—patient.

A redheaded nurse with black lipstick and white painted fingernails brought Zachary R. a bottle of antibiotics and told him to return in a week for follow-up and for possible admission to the state hospital—the asylum—for his broken mind and desolate spirit.

Zachary R. explained that he found the asylum in Massachusetts to his liking as he was escorted out of the hospital in a wheelchair and deposited back into the soft prison of Hollywood.

He set the bottle of pills in a flowerbed and forgot about them as he made his way back to his stretch of pavement between medium buildings, his mind on knights, rooks, and bishops.

That night he felt a deep chill course through his body as the infection moved closer to his brain.

PART X

69. A Penny for Your Two Cents

Zachary R. knew his marriage was a mistake, but he naively hoped the wedding ritual would instill in Annabel R. a modicum of love— or at least respect or sentimentality.

But this was not the case. Annabel R. was a day-tripper despite all the promise of the Mostly Silent matchbook slipped under Zachary R.'s door and their day at the carnival. Bernrd Red, the bed-and-breakfast concierge, understood this immediately when he saw Annabel R. at check-in on the first day of her honeymoon with Zachary R. Whenever possible, Bernrd Red would promote the sensation of being hit in the head with a rock by stealing the services of unscrupulous brides.

When Bernrd Red laid eyes on Annabel R. at the concierge desk, he could see that she would be an easy conquest. He fiddled with his pinky ring under the desk.

When Annabel R. laid eyes on Bernrd Red, the concierge, she could see that he would be a willing participant in her cigar box ritual. She began to sweat.

Annabel R. asked Zachary R. to inquire about the nineteenth-century bicycles at the rental shop across the street.

Zachary R. went gallantly, chivalrously, to do so. "The wedding has softened her," he thought.

When Zachary R. was out of earshot, Bernrd Red sneered at Annabel R. and said, "A penny for your two cents."

Without hesitation, Annabel R. told him her thoughts and invited Bernrd Red to meet her in the honeymoon suite just as soon as she could send her new husband on another errand.

She flashed the contents of the cigar box at Bernrd Red. A pair of brass knuckles. A romance novel called *Savage Splendor*.

Bernrd Red chuckled and handed her one of two keys to the honeymoon suite. He kept the other key for himself.

As Annabel R. was preparing the honeymoon suite for her paramour, there was a knock on the door.

She opened it fearfully, not knowing whose face would appear. It was Zachary R.'s face. He was holding brochures and maps of local hiking trails.

"The giant bicycles aren't for tourists," he said. "Only the staff are allowed to ride them."

"Of course," said Annabel R.

"I got some maps of hiking trails," said Zachary R.

"That's sweet of you," she said. "Would you mind going hiking without me today? I became ill while you were out. Pregnancy is getting to me."

Zachary R. obliged her, but he forgot to ask about a key to the room.

Some time later, Bernrd Red called the room and Annabel R. answered, confirming that she was alone and that her husband was off hiking for the afternoon.

The ritual beating began from the moment Bernrd Red walked through the door. Bernrd Red required no instruction from Annabel R. as to what to do, which frenzied her and made her whirl and pop.

Love came and went, and came and went again.

Zachary R., meanwhile, had gone no more than a mile down the road when it occurred to him that he didn't have a key to the honeymoon suite.

He felt the most considerate thing to do would be to return to the room at once, before his pregnant wife fell asleep. He made only one stop on his way back, to get pink bismuth for her stomach.

Zachary R. was several paces from the door when he heard the familiar sound of brass knuckles on flesh, as well as the whirling and popping.

He dropped to his knees and grabbed his haunches. Then, in a moment of terrible clarity and calm, he walked back down the hallway, out the door of the bed-and-breakfast, and into the mountains, where he hiked the longest trail on the map.

But before he turned the other cheek and walked away into the mountains, he turned around and looked in the window of the honeymoon suite, where he saw on the nightstand the glint of a ruby ring and a concierge badge with the name Bernrd Red written on it. Worse than these, he saw the grinning chin and the angry eyes of Bernrd Red. They would haunt him forever.

70. Wind Chimes and Lavender

Zachary R. woke to the face of his cheating wife, their heads on pillows in the honeymoon suite of a bed-and-breakfast on a road called Bath in a seaside village out West.

He turned away and opened a window. On the windowsill, silk roses and a ceramic dove.

He looked outside. In the courtyard couples whispered among wind chimes and lavender. On the sidewalk nineteenth-century bicycles went by, giant wheels in front, miniature wheels in back.

He grabbed his haunches and moved his knees to his chest.

His wife woke, said "Quit it," got dressed, rubbed a drop of rain on her neck, and went surfing alone. In the South, buildings and lungs collapsed.

Zachary R. turned gray. He pulled on his jeans and staggered shirtless up the road to a park, where he collapsed and curled up in the grass. A young Goth Girl with red hair and black lips knelt beside him, placed her hand on his shoulder, removed her coat, and covered him.

In the East, silver clouds enveloped the New Hampshire mountains.

In the New Hampshire mountains, a traveler pulled to the side of the road.

71. A Penny for Your Thoughts

On the third and final day of their honeymoon, Annabel R. woke to an empty bed. Remorse coursed through her bruised, concussed, scraped, and startled body. Why had her husband not returned? Could he know about Bernrd Red, the concierge? How could he? He didn't have a key to the room. He isn't waiting outside the door, is he?

Annabel R. slowly rolled out of bed, put on baggy warm-ups to hide the bruises on her pregnant body, and gently opened the door of the honeymoon suite. Zachary R. was not there.

Annabel R. felt relieved, but only for a moment, as relief was replaced by fear for what might have happened to him.

She went back inside for her sandals. Then she set off on foot up Bath Road until she found her husband lying in a park covered by a heavy black coat that was not his own.

Annabel R. knelt beside him, placed her hand on his shoulder, removed the heavy black coat, and stroked his hair until he woke.

He stared at her until the memory of who she was returned. "You smell like rain," he said.

"Yes, I know," said Annabel R. "It's the scent of the perfume I wear."

Suddenly Zachary R. began to recall the events from the two previous days. He saw the face of Bernrd Red. The sunflowers in his eyes wilted.

Annabel R. stroked his face with her fingers and said, "A penny for your thoughts."

"I want to go home," said Zachary R. "What time is the flight?"

72. Pregnant Pause

The post-honeymoon flight home was quiet and tense for Zachary R. and Annabel R. and for the baby in Annabel R.'s womb. The baby kicked and squirmed in unison with the turbulence at thirty-five-thousand feet.

Zachary R. obsessed on the moment of betrayal. His angry thoughts came through loudly to Annabel R., even though his actions spoke of a happy newlywed with a child on the way.

He rubbed his wife's expanding belly, and he held her hand and spoke gently and lovingly and dutifully. He convinced himself that it was all genuine, but his wife and everyone else onboard

171

the flight could feel the rumbling volcano in seat 26A.

So Zachary R. and Annabel R. each had a secret. He withheld having witnessed his wife with Bernrd Red, and she withheld having had the affair with Bernrd Red and at least one other man.

And while there was very little that was genuine in their marriage, there was the overriding fact of their forthcoming daughter, who kept them together.

During the final trimester of Annabel's pregnancy, Zachary R. and Annabel R. continued to live in their separate apartments in the building with the hall with the blue carpet.

And then Sarah R. was born, and the family of three moved into the house where Sarah R. would one day drive the Nova through the living room window.

73. Dutiful Zachary

Dutiful Zachary pushed down his grief and relief that his wife was dead, pushed them down next to his mother in her tissue-fiber nightgown and his chess-obsessed father, pushed them down next to Bernrd Red, who greeted Annabel R. with a rueful smile and read passages from *Savage Splendor*, as if the ritual belonged to them and not to her and Zachary. Bernrd Red, to whom Zachary R. had never uttered a word except in his capacity as concierge of the bed-and-breakfast, but whom—if not for the fact that it would have jeopardized his chances for Messiah or Rock Star—he gladly would have murdered in any number of grisly ways.

Dutiful Zachary indulged the violent fantasy of his righteous murder of Bernrd Red. The fantasy always a sharp axe and a tilted stare with varying methods of delivery, and always the same witness, Annabel R.

And then he pushed down this fantasy to greet a snickering Bernrd Red and a snarling Annabel R., who mocked Zachary R. with the words, "I'm already dead, but you never could have gone through with it anyway. You were a harmless nobody with your wilting sunflower eyes. Everybody could see what you were up to. You're no saint. You're a deluded coward who didn't even have the guts to put a stop to his own cheating wife on their own honeymoon."

Dutiful Zachary pushed down his dead wife. "Sharp axes are for pine trees and leisure," he muttered. "Hold onto your job and raise your daughter," he said to himself.

And these thoughts were pure and these thoughts were righteous, but Zachary R. neglected his grief, and his grief became shame and his shame became anger and his grief, shame, and anger festered like worms, microbes, and malodor.

* * * * *

Sarah R. thought her father was a bit uptight because of his obsession with mowing the lawn, but otherwise she felt safe and content and taken care of during her first fourteen years.

Had she known what he was battling inside, she would have identified his struggle as a Hobbesian choice, a dilemma.

Zachary R. could have confronted Bernrd Red and the pregnant Annabel R. in the honeymoon suite, but that would have had only one possible outcome: a violent struggle that would certainly have resulted in serious injury or death to one, two, or all three involved . . . all four if the in utero Sarah R. was included.

His alternative, which, of course, was what he chose to do, was to turn the other cheek and allow the events in the honeymoon suite that day to run their course. He would push down the pain for the sake of peace that day and peace for the future of the marriage and the baby.

Zachary R. hoped that his wife would outgrow her taste for brass knuckles and romance novels and that there was a possibility for some kind of normalcy in the future.

But Annabel R. gave birth to Sarah R. and a week later she was arranging trysts not only with Bernrd Red—who visited Boston as frequently as he could, expensing flights for "concierge conventions" or anything related or not to the hospitality industry, so long as it brought him to the bedroom of Annabel R.—but also with the gardener who gardened the neighbor's house across the street every Tuesday at eleven o'clock, when Zachary R. was hard at work at Miller & Associates and Sarah R. was in her crib.

But with the ever-increasing frequency and duration of the trysts came increased trips to the emergency room to care for her injuries.

Because there was no attributing her injuries to anything but brass knuckles, the doctors and nurses at the hospital began to suspect Zachary R. of spousal abuse. Eventually, though, Annabel R., to keep her affairs a secret, was forced to admit them to the doctors and nurses.

She was forced to admit that the beatings came at her own request and that her husband was not to blame, that he used to indulge her fetish but now refused. She was forced to make this confession or risked losing her baby, her two paramours, and her cuckold husband, who remained dutiful and true for her sake and the baby's sake and also for the sake of keeping alive his chances for Messiah or Rock Star.

The doctors and nurses warned Annabel R. of the dangers of blunt trauma to the head and other areas of her body, as well as of the seriousness of multiple concussions. They officially attributed her fetish to postpartum depression and, like Zachary R., hoped it was all a passing phase.

* * * * *

Annabel R. must have known her days were numbered, because her behavior began to change. She began to dote on her baby, reading passages from "The Little Match Girl" to Sarah R. in her crib. She began to call off visits from her paramours. After two such postponements, and because he began to hear nothing but the voices of Crosby, Stills, Nash & Young singing "Carry On," Bernrd Red checked himself into the asylum. Upon discharge, he never set foot in Boston again. As for the gardener, he kept right on gardening at the neighbor's house across the street.

Annabel R. even began to take Sarah R. around the block in a squeaky pram that Zachary R. deliberately failed to oil because the sound of the squeaky wheel signified the rehabilitation of his wife and the possibility of happiness.

Zachary R. was beginning to feel vindicated in his decision to remain passive throughout the ordeal, until the morning when Annabel R. failed to wake up.

The autopsy revealed that Annabel R. had died of a brain hemorrhage brought on by chronic blunt trauma to the head.

Dutiful Zachary pushed down his grief and relief that she was gone. He had Annabel R.

cremated and her ashes placed in an urn. He hired a nanny to care for his two-year-old daughter. He continued to go to work every morning at the Law Offices of Miller & Associates.

Dutiful Zachary oiled the squeaky wheel on the pram, which the nanny pushed along the sidewalk in silence.

74. Your Story Is My Story

Zachary R. lay in bed in the asylum, feeling lonely as an aisle of concrete in the moonlight, feeling well. Bernrd Red burst through the door, bull-rushed the bed, and yelled, "My story is your story!"

Zachary R. grabbed a paperweight off the nightstand and threw it at Bernrd Red.

It missed by a wide margin. Both men were relieved.

Zachary R. apologized.

"No," said Bernrd Red. "I understand. What I meant to say is your story is my story."

Zachary R. felt the sensation of being hit in the head with a rock. He lunged for Bernrd Red, but Bernrd Red grabbed him and wrestled him to the floor. When Bernrd Red had Zachary R. pinned, he sneered, and said, "You're more like me than you think. You despise me for beating and sleeping with your wife, for betraying you. You had an infuriating innocence that made me want to hurt you. You betrayed a man you didn't know when you took Annabel to the carnival and knocked her up. I'll bet you didn't know that, did you? She told me all about it and we laughed at your ignorant self-righteousness."

"Whatever," mumbled Zachary R.

75. Bernrd Red Finds the Accommodations in the Alley Disagreeable

Zachary R. sat on his stretch of pavement between medium buildings nursing his injured hand and humming Haydn when from off the Walk of Fame came Bernrd Red.

Bernrd Red despised music. He looked down the alley and locked eyes with Zachary R. He covered his ears and glared as he headed down the alley to menace him.

"Long time no see," said Bernrd Red. "What brings you to a Hollywood alley?"

As he continued his approach, Zachary R.'s malodor thickened and Bernrd Red was forced to move his hands from his ears to his shirt, which he raised to cover his nose.

Zachary R. was preparing in his mind to explain about searching for his daughter when he noticed Bernrd Red's displeasure.

"What's the matter?" asked Zachary R. "Do you find my new accommodations less agreeable than the asylum?"

"You reek!" exclaimed Bernrd Red through his shirt, turning and walking purposefully back toward the Walk of Fame.

"And stay away!" shouted Zachary R., giggling terribly.

And Bernrd Red did stay away; in fact, he never visited Zachary R. again.

PART XI

76. Skyscraper File Clerk

In the twenty years between high school and his committal, Zachary R. worked as a file clerk in the file storage room of the Law Offices of Miller & Associates.

Miller & Associates was a large firm that had been around since Teddy Roosevelt was president. As a result of its size and age, and because of the firm's conservative document retention policy, the file storage room occupied the entire top floor of the fourth-largest skyscraper in Boston.

Zachary R. was one of three file clerks, but due to the private nature of file clerks, there was little or no interaction among them. The floor was quiet except for the sound of shuffling papers. There were no human sounds or even machine sounds, as the photocopier was in the litigation department on the floor below.

Miller & Associates' files were arranged using a twelve-digit sequence of numbers and no color coding.

Numbers, papers, and photocopies. This was how Zachary R. earned a wage.

There was no need for thought since only patterns of numbers occupied his mind. There was a lot of room, therefore, for daydreams and fantasies at the photocopier downstairs. The sound of the photocopier and of others working their machines scintillated his brain: Keyboards clicking. Phones ringing. The mechanics of a bustling office. Graves being dug in the continents of the world.

When he went downstairs to make photocopies, it was as if he had entered the vibrant City of Letters after years in exile in the stagnant City of Numbers, unable to speak or understand the world of words. The numbers had stolen his identity.

77. International Harvester of Souls

One day, during the days and nights leading up to his committal, Zachary R. arrived at Miller & Associates lit by the black sun of empathy. His mind was on numbers, as usual, until he went downstairs to make copies.

Keyboards clicking. Phones ringing. Graves being dug in the continents of the world.

The Red Cross nurse appeared. She removed her nun's habit. She was the Cold Angel.

The Cold Angel ran her veil over his scalp and said, "Isn't it time you quit this job? Isn't it time to save the world? Isn't it time to atone for the deaths of your mother and your wife?"

Zachary R. stared at the wrinkles around her eyes and proclaimed, "International harvester of souls."

He left the papers in the photocopier, took the elevator down to the ground floor, and vowed never to set foot in Miller & Associates again.

78. Shacks and Cigarettes

Zachary R. walked out the front door of Miller & Associates and set off on foot toward the New Hampshire mountains, saying, "Service to Mankind, Service to Mankind."

With his mind no longer occupied by numbers, Zachary R. lost his bearings. He disconnected. He genuinely believed he was on a mission, but friends, family, and bystanders could plainly see that he was disintegrating.

He went into a hardware store for supplies for his mission, which was shacks and cigarettes for all, roofs over their heads and smoke in their lungs, train after train with boxcars full of smoke and lumber, saving the world like a Messiah or Rock Star.

But if there were to be smoke and lumber, there also needed to be nails to bring it all together.

Zachary R. walked down the aisle of the hardware store and reached into a barrel of nails that rattled and brushed his spine like silk, urging him to nap.

He lay down on an aisle of concrete in the outdoor nursery and slept until the store opened the next morning.

Security shook him awake and ushered him out the door.

Job was lost. Wife was cremated. Pram did not squeak.

But Zachary R. still believed in the morning.

He determined that he would need a heavy coat for his trip into the New Hampshire mountains. He found one in an abandoned shed along the riverbank. He reached into the pockets and found a burger and a pack of cigarettes. "This was somebody's home," he thought.

He bit into the burger: worms, microbes, malodor. He threw it down in disgust.

He lit a cigarette. Carnival smoke. Brown earth smoke. Gypsy kids. He flicked the cigarette onto the hard dirt floor of the shed and watched it smolder.

It was late afternoon when Zachary R. felt he should get home to tell his daughter about quitting his job and about departing on his mission.

He fell asleep in the shed while wearing the heavy coat. He dreamt about his mother in her tissue-fiber nightgown and about the parrot out of its cage shitting on the kitchen stove.

Zachary R. didn't make it home that night. Instead, he left the shed and walked south along the river and its tributaries, thinking "I like rivers and women" instead of "Service to mankind," which was what he meant to think.

Now he was confused. He felt ill. The burger had made him sick. He stumbled along the riverbank and vomited violently. The burger was bad. He became feverish. He hummed Haydn. He thought about where he might have been in the years before his birth. He vomited some more. He decided he had better get home to Sarah.

79. Evil Men

Zachary R. and Sarah R. lived in a twilit bungalow on the outskirts of Boston, in a town with a cemetery dating to a time before the Revolutionary War.

The town was quiet and the neighbors were easily woken, which presented a problem for Zachary R. when he discovered that he had lost his keys somewhere between work, the shed, and vomiting up the bad burger.

He circled the perimeter of the house quietly and tested windows to try to break into without disturbing his daughter. They were all shut tight. Then he arrived at the front door and turned the knob, which, to his chagrin and delight, had been left unlocked.

Sarah R. was sitting on the sofa waiting for him.

"Sarah, why are you still up? It must be way past your bedtime," said Zachary R.

"It's only eight o'clock," said Sarah R., unnerved at the sight of her father.

"Why are you wearing that ratty overcoat?" she asked. "It smells. Are you all right? You're pale and you smell like puke. Dad, what's happening? You're scaring me."

"My mom wore a ratty tissue-fiber nightgown and we had a parrot out of its cage that shit on the kitchen stove and all my dad cared about was chess," said Zachary R.

"We lived in a twilit bungalow like this one, but your mom and I agreed this one would be clean. No parrot. No grease stains on the driveway, no sunflowers painted thick on the mailbox, no chess," he said, all lit up by the searing mental sun.

Zachary R. took the urn with Annabel R.'s ashes down from the mantel and explained: "Your mom allowed evil men like her father, and another man I won't even mention, to corrupt her.

"I thought that if I could love her long enough, she would allow her better side to prevail. But in the end, her cheating and her concussions did her in.

"Did you know your mom liked Hans Christian Andersen, Sarah?"

"Dad, what are you talking about!? You never told me Mom cheated on you. You're scaring me. Why are your work clothes so dirty? Why do you smell like puke? There *are* grease stains on the driveway. The Nova has been leaking for years. There's no such thing as a tissue-fiber nightgown. There *are* no parrots. Have you lost your mind?!"

Zachary R. was nonplussed. He wiped his brow. "How old are you, Sarah? Thirteen?"

"No, fourteen. C'mon."

"It's time for you to learn how to drive. It's time for you to start giving. Time to start donating blood. If you don't start behaving, you're going to wind up like your mother."

"Dad, did you quit your job?" asked Sarah R.

"Yes, I did," said Zachary R., now completely deflated.

"Then how are you going to pay the bills?" she asked, meekly, starting to cry. "If we get evicted, then you're the evil one."

The sunflowers in his eyes wilted, but he wasn't going back to Miller & Associates. It was too late. It was too late for work. It was too late for raising a daughter. It was too late for living in a home with a roof over his head. It was too late for Zachary R.

Zachary R. handed Sarah R. the urn. She opened it and stared at the ashes, searching for humanity. She closed the urn and set it back on the mantel. Then she turned and looked hopelessly at her father.

"Can you forgive me?" Zachary R. asked.

80. Aisle of Concrete in the Moonlight

Zachary R. woke earlier than he expected to the next morning because he wasn't done getting sick. He stumbled past Sarah's bedroom and into the bathroom, where he dry heaved three painful dry heaves. There was no bad burger left in his stomach to heave up. He drank water out of the bathroom faucet, and then he reached for the flyswatter by the toilet and recited these words:

"Forehand, backhand, microphone, guitar, spider on shoulder, cockroach on soap bar slipping, slipping, slipping."

A fourth dry heave ensued, but it was a little less painful because of the water. Sarah R. cracked open the bathroom door and saw her father lying on the cold tile still in the heavy coat, knees pulled tight to his chest, and clutching the flyswatter.

"Are you going to be okay, Dad? Should I call 911?" she asked.

"I'm almost better," said Zachary R. "Please don't call 911, I'll be okay in a minute. Go back to bed."

Sarah R. shut the bathroom door. Zachary R. could hear her footsteps heading back to her bedroom. He felt ill again, but not from the bad burger; rather, he felt ill from shame and doubt and fear. He needed to expedite the mission.

Zachary R. rose from the bathroom tile, buttoned his heavy coat, and set off on foot toward the abandoned shed along the riverbank to retrieve the nails and cigarettes that would build a smoking, smoldering habitat for humanity.

When he arrived at the shed, he recalled that he had no nails, lumber, or otherwise for the construction of his worldwide shacks. All he found on the hard dirt floor of the shed was an open pack of cigarettes, one half-smoked cigarette butt, and the remainder of the bad burger, which had decayed almost beyond recognition.

He would need to return to the hardware store to procure supplies.

Zachary R. walked along the riverbank, thinking about rivers and women instead of service to mankind.

He considered the definition of insanity: "to do the same thing over and over and expect different results." He went to the bar anyway.

Zachary R. stumbled among the barstools and pool tables, blurting out, "Cigar boxes and romance novels are the brass knuckles of sex" to anyone who would listen, which was no one, except for the bartender, who kindly offered to pour Zachary R. a complimentary Wild Turkey if Zachary would kindly sit down and leave the paying customers alone.

Zachary R. managed to finagle five drinks for the price of none. He exited out the back, stinking of bourbon, and with a heightened urgency to get on with his mission. He set off on foot to the hardware store to pick up supplies, but by the time he arrived, night had fallen and the store was closed.

He picked up a substantial stone, expecting he would need to bust a window to get inside. To his great relief, however, the door had been left unlocked.

He entered the hardware store and began gathering supplies in a shopping cart: screws and lumber, saws and hammers, levels and pencils.

But then he reached into the barrel of nails that rattled and brushed his spine like silk and urged him to nap.

Zachary R. left the cart behind and made his way to the outdoor nursery, where he lay down on an aisle of concrete.

The Cold Angel knelt down beside him, rubbed his back like winter, and asked, "Are you lonely as the cello?"

"No," said Zachary R. "I am lonely as an aisle of concrete in the moonlight."

81. A Peculiar Shade of Burgundy, Part 2

Sarah R. understood that her father was descending into madness and that she had better figure out a few things about surviving as a fourteen-year-old adult.

She would have to mooch. She would have to learn to drive the Nova. She would have to act at school like nothing was wrong. She would have to do what her father asked and give blood. Maybe she could find a part-time job at the Red Cross. Maybe she could learn to gamble or prostitute herself. Maybe she could become a hitman at school, injecting arsenic into teachers' apples.

What she was most concerned about, though, was guarding the urn with her mother's ashes. With her father no longer able to support her, she gained an appreciation, even an obsession, with the sanctity of death, which she now understood to be the ultimate fact of life.

* * * * *

On the other hand, with her father away on his mission, Sarah R. felt encouraged to do some exploration of her own. She decided to ditch school one morning and take an inventory of the house. She surveyed the main rooms and the garage, which held no major surprises, save for a stack of orange cones, which she hadn't noticed before.

Then she went through the closets and found nothing of interest until she arrived at the closet in the master bedroom, which she knew had an opening in the ceiling that led into the attic.

The first thing she noticed about the attic was that it was warmer than the rest of the house.

The next thing she noticed was a trunk that contained her parents' things.

- Carnival items: a small poster ad with illustrations of trapeze artists and elephants; stuffed animals; a roll of unused tickets.

- A copy of Hans Christian Andersen's *Fairy Tales* with a bookmark at the story called "The Little Match Girl."

- A photo of Zachary R.'s parents, whom Annabel R. never met, his father sitting at the dining room table surveying a chessboard; his mother, looking tired and daft in her tissue-fiber nightgown; a parrot perched on the back of a chair.

- A cigar box with a pair of brass knuckles, a romance novel called *Savage Splendor*, and a CD called Electric Light Dirge for Cello and Organ.

At the bottom of the trunk was a dress in a peculiar shade of burgundy with the word *Revolution* written on the tag inside, where the washing instructions would normally be.

Sarah R. tried on the Revolution Dress, which must have been her mother's, because the word *Revolution* was written in her mother's hand. The dress made Sarah R. burn with weakness. She felt reckless and charitable. She suddenly knew how she would survive without her father, as, essentially, an orphan.

It would be blood drives and blackjack, kittens and heroin, apples and arsenic, and trick-or-treating with foster parents.

82. A Peculiar Shade of Burgundy, Part 1

Insurrection was in the thrift store air when a peculiar shade of burgundy caught the corner of Annabel R.'s eye. She paid the three dollars to the fop behind the counter and she wore the dress out the door and onto the street, where she promptly became aware that her secondhand dress possessed first-rate power.

The dress compelled her feet to walk in a new way and her insides to burn with a strange and powerful weakness. Her burning insides and her new walking feet led her into a scent shop, where she purchased oil that made her skin smell like rain.

Annabel R. took her new dress and her new scent and her new walk into a rough bar, where the boys wore barrels and spoke in verse, and she intoxicated these boys with a charm they had never seen.

The ugliest barrel boy spoke the prettiest verse and when he saw Annabel R. walk into the bar, he spoke and she heard him say that rain and revolution just walked through the door.

Annabel R. swooned, then regained her composure. She ordered red wine, took a pen off the counter, and wrote *Revolution* on the tag inside the dress where the washing instructions would normally be.

83. Wet Green Blades High as His Hips

Once again, security woke Zachary R. from his slumber on the aisle of concrete in the outdoor nursery. What seemed strange to him, though, was that he wasn't arrested either time, even though this time there was a shopping cart full of building materials left in the exact middle of the store. Zachary R. was perplexed by the look of abject pity on the security guard's face as he escorted Zachary R. out of the store for the second time.

The security guard released Zachary R.'s arm once they were outside, and then his look took on another characteristic. It was now abject pity coupled with halfhearted hardness.

"Sir, I'm truly sorry you have nowhere else to sleep. I'm truly sorry you're homeless. My brother has a mental illness, so I know how difficult it is for you people. But I'm afraid if I catch you in here again, I'm going to have you arrested. Please, if you can, get some help."

Zachary R. was indignant. "Nowhere to sleep? Homeless? Mental illness? Who did that security guard think he was talking to?" he thought.

He pushed these questions deep inside, where they took up residence with his mother and father, his wife, and Bernrd Red—all of whom were gone, never to be seen again, but not gone away, not dealt with.

Zachary R. set off on foot, intending to go north into the New Hampshire mountains to atone for the deaths of his mother and his wife.

"I like rivers and women," he said and headed south by mistake.

He headed south by mistake along the river and south along a tributary of the river and south along smaller and smaller tributaries of the river until he heard the sound of a plane, which made him look at the sky, which was now dark.

He looked into the night sky and saw a thousand stars. He continued to look into the night sky. He saw ten thousand stars and the moon. He continued to look into the night sky. He saw knights, rooks, and bishops.

Zachary R. walked south along a tributary looking into the night sky when he felt something fluffy squirm beneath his feet and then, in conjunction with the squirming, he smelled a powerful, yet satisfying, odor.

He looked down just in time to see the white stripe of a skunk vanish into the wet green blades along the tributary.

Zachary R. followed the white stripe into the wet green blades high as his hips the secondhand light of the moon upon the skunk's stripe which lured him to a ledge that descended to the sea and he followed the stripe over the ledge and into the crashing tide that tossed him around and thrashed him about and spat him back onto the shore.

Zachary R. woke the next morning covered with vicious greenhead flies. If it weren't for his heavy coat, his entire body would have been covered with welts and swelling and pain, but as luck would have it, he only suffered bites on his cheeks, neck, and the fleshy part between the bridge of his nose and his eyes.

He stood up and scraped his salty wet clothes with a stick. Then he climbed up the ledge, which was more like a sandbar only a few yards high, and he walked back through the wet green blades high as his hips, and when he returned to the tributary, he started south again but he couldn't remember why.

And then he began to chant, "Service to Mankind, Service to Mankind," which made him recall that his mission was to the north.

Zachary R. turned around and set off on foot toward the New Hampshire mountains where the traveler had pulled to the side of the road to help him so many years before.

84. Hobbes Scholar with a Nose Ring

Sarah R. wore the Revolution Dress as often as she could. Kids at school began to take notice, and not in a negative way. She seemed to possess some kind of mysterious power over them and over herself. The power was the newfound self-sufficiency thrust upon her by circumstance, along with the unique style and peculiar shade of burgundy of the dress and the secret word written on the tag inside: "Revolution."

She began to take risks. She pierced her nose and wore a nose ring. She put rings through her eyebrows and in rows along the tops of her ears.

She began driving the Nova, as her father had instructed. This increased her popularity immensely. She drove her friends everywhere, sometimes charging them for gas money and a little extra for her time. Rock concerts and record stores, boyfriends' and girlfriends' houses, rounding up friends and bringing them back to her house for parties, since her father was gone.

The neighbors began to take notice, but for a time they attributed her behavior to the ever-increasing absence of her father. They thought that once he got a new job and otherwise righted himself, things would return to normal.

Sarah R. also became charitable.

She donated blood to the Red Cross. She volunteered at a pet shelter and learned how to vaccinate the kittens. She volunteered at the rehab hospital in hopes that her father would appear there, but in the meantime, she intoxicated the junkies with the opiate of her charm and the Revolution Dress.

As the days passed, the police and child services department began to take notice. While Sarah R. did an adequate job maintaining the inside of the house, the front lawn did not receive the attention Zachary R. had given it with his mower. Their New England lawn began to grow long and thick and green with blades that grew high as her hips.

Social workers began to visit with greater and greater frequency to inquire about her well-being and about the whereabouts of her father, but Sarah R. was always able to demonstrate the adequacy of her circumstances by showcasing the food in the cupboard, the clean surroundings, and the maintenance of her grades at school.

In this regard, Sarah R. particularly excelled. Sarah R. was no little match girl. She was curious and rapidly lost any semblance of naiveté. She had no problem figuring out how to handle her homework dilemma while at the same time earning extra money to supplement the money she was receiving from her "chauffeur" service.

Sarah R. convinced the owner-proprietor of the local bookstore to hire her and pay her under the table, since she was still without a social security number.

The bookstore owner took an avuncular interest in Sarah and, understanding her circumstances, paid her far too much for the work she did, which was shelving books for a few hours a week.

Sarah R. was curious about many things, one of which was the disturbing thoughts of philosophers. With the help of the bookstore owner, she was able to understand and relate to much of what they had to say.

Sarah R.'s favorite philosopher was Thomas Hobbes.

Solitary, poor, nasty, brutish, and short. These were just about the least sentimental and the truest words she could imagine to describe life. With the help of the bookstore owner, she made the study of Hobbes her hobby. And the bookstore owner paid her well and helped her with her homework, even doing entire algebra assignments if she was really struggling.

Sarah R. wasn't above cheating. She wasn't above mooching. Honing such skills was essential to survival in her Hobbesian world.

85. Deep Depression, Bitter Fool

Zachary R. passed by his house en route to the New Hampshire mountains, too embarrassed to see his daughter in his condition of dirt and fly bites and ratty overcoat. He scoffed at the Cold Angel when she appeared. He lashed out at her for making a fool of him, for her being a figment and a fraud, for deceiving him, for making him quit his job and becoming an embarrassment to his daughter and to himself.

When he passed right by his house, the neighbors didn't recognize him.

Sarah R. saw him coming up the street from the living room window. She went into the kitchen to get cleaning supplies to quickly clean up before he walked through the door. She rearranged the furniture, threw the Revolution Dress into the laundry bin, vacuumed the carpets, washed the dirty dishes, and sponged the walls with mild dish soap.

Sarah R. became so engrossed in her cleaning that before she knew it, an hour had gone by and her father had not walked through the door.

She broke inside.

She grabbed a hammer and began pounding divots into the freshly sponged walls. She busted and pounded until the vicious energy was gone. Then she went into the attic and fell asleep in the dirty and wrinkled Revolution Dress.

Meanwhile, Zachary R. kept heading north toward the New Hampshire mountains. He wanted redemption. He wanted to revisit the picnic grounds where his mother had collapsed on the hard dirt and where the traveler had helped him. He wanted to keep alive his chances to become a Messiah or Rock Star.

But when he arrived, he found that the place held no honest significance. It was dead, indifferent. His life had gone off on this destructive tangent, and it was too late to get back what he had.

Zachary R. crouched under a picnic table and waited for the thud of a falling pine cone.

86. A Moment of Clarity

The Cold Angel sat beside Zachary R. under the picnic table and rubbed his back like winter. Zachary R. felt the shivers bloom inside of him. Acute rattling, acute comfort.

He looked at the Cold Angel and said, "Sometimes the shivers are painful, but you make the shivers feel good. And also, what am I doing here?"

"Service to mankind," she said.

"No," said Zachary R. "That makes no sense. I am here because of the boxcars and the endless train. My mother never recovered from her fall from when I told that story. Even after the traveler and I got her home, she was never the same. She just lay there in bed in that tissue-fiber nightgown and moaned and glared all day long and that fucking parrot and my father who cared only for chess and my pregnant wife and that sleazebag Bernrd Red cheating on my honeymoon.

"I'm here because I want to change the past. Service to mankind has nothing to do with it. Service to mankind is bullshit."

The Cold Angel ran her veil over his scalp and said, "You have been lying to yourself for a long time, but you don't have to suffer anymore. Goodbye, Zachary," she said and disappeared into the fog.

PART XII

87. Leaves of Absence

It looked like Easter clouds on the morning after the Cold Angel, though the New Hampshire trees told him it was autumn. Zachary R. paused and then proclaimed, "Leaves of Absence."

His bites still hurt and his overcoat was still ratty and malodorous, but he felt clean inside and his mind was clear.

He took a quick inventory of his circumstances: The mission was a fraud. He had no job. His adolescent daughter was home alone.

Zachary R. set off on foot toward home thinking, "I like rivers and women."

He arrived home on a thin autumn Monday, only slightly drunk and feeling good about making a new start.

The first thing he noticed as he approached the front door was the condition of the front lawn: green blades high as his hips.

"I'll mow it this Saturday after I get my old job back," he thought.

Zachary R. arrived at the front door of his house expecting to have to knock and wait for his daughter to greet him and let him inside.

To his slight dismay, however, the door was unlocked. He let himself in and announced his presence to ensure that he didn't startle Sarah.

There was no response to his voice. He went room to room searching for Sarah. She was nowhere to be found.

He went into the master bedroom and lay down on the bed. He heard sounds coming from the ceiling. Thuds and squeaks.

He got up and went into the closet with the entrance to the attic. He climbed up the ladder and pushed open the attic door.

Sarah R. screamed. "Dad, what the hell!?"

Zachary R. beheld his daughter. Sarah R. sat cross-legged on the attic floor, head shaved, wearing her mother's burgundy dress, the urn on her left, the cigar box on her right, a copy of

Hobbes' *Leviathan* in her hand, and the words *solitary, poor, nasty, brutish,* and *short* written in melted wax on the attic floor.

Zachary R.'s mind muddied and his insides churned. He felt chilled and nauseated.

Without uttering a sound, he climbed back down the closet ladder and ran for the bathroom. He grabbed the flyswatter and recited the words: forehand, backhand, microphone, guitar, spider on shoulder, cockroach on soap bar slipping, slipping, slipping. One violent dry heave. He grabbed his haunches and moved his knees to his chest.

Sarah R. knelt beside him, placed her hand on his shoulder, collapsed on him, and embraced him until he slept.

* * * * *

Zachary R. awoke in his own bed on Tuesday morning, a breakfast tray on the nightstand: toast, grapefruit, coffee, orange juice.

He was still shaken by the sight of his daughter in the attic, but if she still loved him enough to bring him breakfast in bed, how bad could she be? He cleaned himself up and dressed for his return to work.

Zachary R. drove the Nova downtown to the Law Offices of Miller & Associates, which was located in the fourth-largest skyscraper in Boston.

He rode the elevator to the top floor, where the file room was located, went into the boss's office, and asked for his old job back.

To his mild displeasure, the boss and his two fellow file clerks were happy to have him back, as they had been unable to find a replacement for him who lasted more than a week.

A small part of Zachary R. was relieved that the safety and routine of a day-to-day job had been returned to him, but a larger part of him died inside when he saw those files with their twelve-digit numbering scheme.

He managed to get through Tuesday and Wednesday without too much resistance, but by Thursday morning, thoughts of the Cold Angel and the mission began to stir.

He spent most of Thursday at the photocopier on the floor below daydreaming about his recent adventures, which now didn't seem so onerous. He had forgotten about betraying his daughter's trust and the bad burger in the shed and the vicious greenhead flies and being thrashed about in the freezing ocean tide.

All he could remember was the freedom and the reclamation of his identity as an aspiring Messiah or Rock Star.

By the time of his commute home on Thursday evening, the moment of clarity he had that past weekend had all but vanished. Zachary R. felt agitated and restless. It took every ounce of willpower not to stop inside the bar for seven drinks.

The sight of Sarah when he walked through the door gave him all of five minutes of relief, but her head was still bald and she had not taken off her mother's dress. Zachary R.'s agitation returned. And his nausea. He tried to sleep it off, but dry heaves kept coming all night long. He stuck the handle of the flyswatter down his throat to no avail. Dry heaves. Tap water helped a little, but the retching continued. Pain and fatigue. His entire body began to shake.

It was five o'clock on Friday morning when Zachary R. coughed blood into the toilet and it formed the shape of a rose.

He passed out. Minutes later he was awoken by seven pale girls who had circled him, raising their lockets to cover their giggling faces. One of them, a redhead with black lips, who was somewhat gorgeous, lay down beside him and wrapped her arms around him. Warmth and comfort replaced pain and nausea. He fell back to sleep, peacefully.

The next time Zachary R. woke, the girls vanished. He made his way to the living room and called in sick to his boss.

He spent the whole day on the living room sofa recovering, looking out the window at the tall green blades in the front lawn.

"I will mow tomorrow at halftime," he thought.

88. Committed Revisited

Zachary R. slept well through the night and woke late on Saturday morning.

His stomach felt better. His head was clear. He was very hungry. He went into the kitchen and opened the refrigerator, but it was warm and empty, except for a grapefruit and a Hershey's chocolate bar.

Zachary R. closed the refrigerator and saw a Post-It note from Sarah R. stuck to the door. The note read: "Went to the blood drive. Took the Nova. Unplugged the fridge to save on the electric bill. Feel free to plug it back in since you are back now and we are both working. See you this afternoon. Sarah."

Zachary R. reached behind the refrigerator and plugged it in. His stomach growled and his mind went blank for lack of food.

He went into the living room and turned on the television. College football. Nebraska at Boston College. Early in the first quarter. He stared at the television for a moment, and then made a decision to walk down to the Burger Shack to get a burger to go so he could return and watch the game.

Zachary R. made it to the Burger Shack and back without incident, except for brief flashes and afterimages of the brown bag with the bad burger that he had partially eaten and tossed in disgust onto the hard dirt floor of the abandoned shed on the riverbank. He felt pity for this lonely burger that he had left to rot alone in the shed. The searing mental sun beat down hard through the thin autumn air.

As he sat in the living room of his house, eating the good Burger Shack burger and watching the football game, he began to feel guilty. The desire to care for the bad burger, to restore it to edibility, became unbearably urgent.

Luckily, however, the game reached halftime and he recalled that it was time to mow the front lawn, green blades high as his hips. He forgot about the bad burger once the mowing began.

In fact, his concentration on leveling the lawn was so singular, so intense, that it never wavered, even as the Nova swerved down the street, ran over the curb, and barreled through the front yard. He didn't look up from the mower until he heard the Nova crash through the living room window.

Zachary R. cut the engine and ran inside. Sarah R. had already exited the car and was brushing glass and other debris off herself when Zachary R. entered what was left of the living room.

Love and calm and clarity overwhelmed him.

"What happened, Sarah?" he asked. "Are you all right?"

"I am so sorry, Dad," she cried, visibly shaken and pale. "I was driving home from donating at the Red Cross and all of the blood in my head went to my feet. I must have passed out."

Zachary R. recalled his advice to her about the virtues of donating blood to fight evil men. He felt proud of her and ashamed of himself at the same time. The black sun of empathy shined inside of him and seemed to illuminate the debris in the house.

"It's okay, Sarah," he said softly. "It's okay."

He kissed her and sent her to her room with the grapefruit and the Hershey's from the fridge. Then he set about surrounding the house with orange cones to distract the eyes of the neighbors.

Pitiful thoughts of the bad burger— half-eaten, lonely, and festering in the abandoned shed—returned with merciless ferocity. He wanted to care for it, so he set off on foot saying, "Service to mankind, Service to mankind."

The Goth Girls watched in amazement as Zachary R., with superhuman tenacity and endurance, walked for eight miles, ducking into tenements, ripping numbers off of doors and feeding them, nails and all, into his desperate and bleeding mouth. The tenants screamed and tilted and spoke in tongues as they beheld Zachary R. in his psychotic ecstasy. The Goth Girls clutched their Damien lockets and swooned at the gory sight of it all.

Zachary R. wound up in the hardware store for the third time. The security guard had no choice but to keep his word and hold him for arrest or at least get him to a hospital to care for his bleeding mouth.

A month later, in the asylum, Zachary R. claimed to the Cracked Snail, "I have Neosporin. . . ."

89. Mind of Science Versus Mind of Zachary

The doctors and nurses in the asylum did their best to eradicate the worms, microbes, and malodor in Zachary R.'s mind. "It's like pulling out the innards of a pumpkin," said Zachary R. when the nurses asked him how his treatment was going.

These men and women, this collective mind of science, worked diligently to rehabilitate Zachary R. Psychotherapy, antipsychotics, pain killers, and antidepressants were generously prescribed, dispensed, and administered. Droperidol. Haloperidol. Lorazepam. Diazepam. Paxil. Prozac. And more.

Several forms of occupational therapy were also attempted.

Crossword puzzles met with marginal success.

Jigsaw puzzles saw a slight regression.

Chess necessitated a lockdown of the entire premises as Zachary R. flung the board and the pieces across the room, hitting a paranoid schizophrenic and inciting an all-patient melee. Heavy doses of sedatives and antipsychotics were administered to all.

Finally, it occurred to the mind of science to ask Zachary R. what he liked, to which he responded, "I like rivers and women."

While the doctors were satisfied and the nurses bewitched by this answer, it was not the answer they were looking for. They rephrased the question to, "What kinds of activities do you enjoy?" Zachary R.'s immediate reply was "mowing the lawn."

The mind of science was pleased with this answer. Within two weeks, authority had been given, forms had been signed, and Zachary R. was out on the asylum lawn assisting the gardening staff with mowing duties—which were called privileges—for the rest of his days inside.

90. The Cracked Snail's Portrait

Zachary R. sat in the exact middle of the asylum lawn on a chair that made a pattern on his legs. He knew that if he stared long enough into the grass, he would see a glint in the blades under the searing mental sun and then the Cracked Snail would come into focus.

And each time, without fail, the Cracked Snail would say, "With that level of concentration, you could paint my portrait, which I would like very much." So, one day, Zachary R. brought a box of colored pencils with him onto the asylum lawn and tried to draw the Cracked Snail's portrait.

Using exclusively the yellow pencil, Zachary R. drew the spiral of the snail's shell, including a jagged line to indicate where the crack was.

Each time he showed the drawing to the Cracked Snail, it replied: "Your style is in the manner of the universal minimalists or the minimal universalists. Simplicity and grandiosity,

Messiah and Rock Star, both are conveyed in your work."

Each time Zachary R. heard the Cracked Snail's assessment, he would smile, fold the drawing into eighths, put it into his pocket, and then later shut it inside a drawer in his room.

After thirty-four spirals with jagged lines were drawn, something more began to appear in the portraits. Around the spiral, still with the yellow pencil, Zachary R. drew a tilted triangle. Inside the tilted triangle was a set of double doors, like cellar doors, and reaching to open the double doors, a tall, thin figure with a right-angle chin and eyes that blossomed like sunflowers.

Soon the thirty-four spirals became fifty-five spirals with tilted triangles, which became eighty-nine tilted triangles with double doors, which became one hundred and forty-four tall, thin figures reaching to open the double doors, all in searing yellow pencil folded into eighths and placed inside a drawer in his room.

91. Kittens and Heroin

Stardust in her backpack. Flask in her pocket. Opium in her veins.

In the months after her father was committed to the asylum, Sarah R., in order, stopped going to school, adopted a kitten, and took up heroin.

But she didn't quit her job at the bookstore. Although the bookstore owner was a positive influence on Sarah R. in most respects, he did have his shortcomings, one of which was a burgeoning heroin habit. To his credit, however, he kept his stash hidden from Sarah and didn't catch on that she was the reason his supplies were dwindling more rapidly than normal until he noticed her nodding off in the middle of their discussions on Hobbes.

Having seen this telltale sign, he instantly knew to examine her arms, which were defaced by fledgling needle tracks.

"Trust me, Sarah," he said, "you don't want to develop a junk habit. It'll kill you. It's killing me."

"But it feels so good, like a feather boa or ashes dusting my face, or like I'm Jesus' daughter," she replied.

The bookstore owner smirked. "How Lou Reed of you," he said.

"Sarah," he said with avuncular concern, "I'm afraid you won't be able to work here anymore. I don't want you developing a habit. I couldn't live with myself."

The bookstore owner reached into his desk drawer to retrieve his checkbook. He handed Sarah R. a substantial check as severance.

Sarah R. pocketed the check, hugged the bookstore owner, swiped his stash, ran home, pet the kitten, finished off the bourbon in her flask, shaved her head, climbed the ladder into the attic, jumped into the Revolution Dress, and overdosed.

92. Trick-or-Treating with Foster Parents

The overdose would have ended Sarah R.'s time on Earth had the child services department been less diligent in placing a social worker to drop by regularly until proper foster parents could be found.

Not only did the social worker know CPR, but she also owned a car. The social worker greeted Sarah when she arrived home from the bookstore, saw her climb the ladder into the attic, and felt the music thumping above her.

As the social worker prepared their dinner, she noticed that the CD had begun to skip with machine-like speed and metronomic precision. She waited for the thumping to resume, but five minutes passed and there was no change in sound or feel.

The social worker climbed the ladder into the attic and saw Sarah's motionless body lying limp and heavy on the attic floor next to a spoon, a burner, and a syringe.

She choked with helplessness. She could perform CPR and make all efforts to keep Sarah breathing, but there was no way she could get her down the ladder and into her car to take her to the hospital emergency room.

The social worker revived Sarah R. and turned her on her side, slid down the ladder, sprained both ankles on landing, crawled to the phone, and dialed 911.

The paramedics arrived in seven minutes, revived Sarah R. again, and took her to the emergency room for overnight observation.

The ER doctors believed the overdose was intentional. They intended to admit Sarah to the asylum for observation and counseling, but Sarah, not wanting to be anywhere near her father, convinced them it was a horrible accident, that she was just experimenting with the macabre because of Halloween, which was a week away, and accidentally overdosed.

The doctors didn't find this story believable in the least, but they sent her home anyway because they agreed among themselves that it would not be in her best interest to be anywhere near her father.

Sarah R. stayed overnight in the hospital and was driven home the next afternoon by her new foster parents.

* * * * *

In later years, Sarah R. didn't recall much about her foster parents except that they were kind to her and to her kitten. "Kind people never leave much of an impression," she lamented. She also recalled that they let her be a junkie that Halloween, even though she had just overdosed the week before.

"They laughed at the horrified expressions on the faces of the neighbors when they laid eyes on my junkie makeup and my needle tracks, which were real," she said.

93. The Notorious Dr. Beverly Farworthy

Mostly the mind of science sought Zachary R.'s rehabilitation, but sometimes minds have tumors. One such tumor on the mind of science was the notorious Dr. Beverly Farworthy.

When Zachary R. learned that he had been scheduled for a session with Dr. Farworthy, he asked the other patients in the dayroom about her. The patients complained about Dr. Farworthy's unorthodox methods; about how she would examine patient histories to find their most hideous demons and then, rather than assuage them, she would exploit them. Dr. Farworthy believed this approach worked because, much like an exorcism, the patient's demons were forcibly and immediately brought out into the light where they could be subdued and defeated.

Dr. Farworthy's approach was controversial, yet from time to time it yielded tremendous results. Had she not had the unattractive habit of ingesting high-dose ecstasy before her sessions, she could have become a celebrity doctor.

"Zachary," said Dr. Farworthy, before he even had a chance to sit down, "can you tell me why you didn't respect yourself enough to deal with your cheating wife?" Without time to think of a proper answer, Zachary R. replied, "I was isolating and surviving. I was trying to win."

"Could you repeat that?" asked Dr. Farworthy.

"I was isolating and surviving. I was . . ."

"Trying to win," she said, finishing the thought for him. "Now, tell me about the incident on your honeymoon." Zachary R. spared no details in his description of the events on the day of his betrayal, including the name he saw on the concierge badge, "Bernrd Red." On hearing this name, Dr. Farworthy's eyes lit up. And then the ecstasy took over and the doctor, without giving it a second thought, began to divulge confidential patient information.

"Did you know Bernrd Red was a patient of mine?" she asked. "He came through here thirteen years ago and I was responsible for curing him. What happened on your honeymoon was the tip of the iceberg with Bernrd Red. He was ultraviolent. Not just with his lovers, and not to diminish the pain he caused you, of course," said Dr. Farworthy, rambling on.

Zachary R. turned gray. Still standing, he clutched the back of the analysand chair with such force that the cheap upholstery began to tear.

When Dr. Farworthy proudly showed him the scar Bernrd Red had given her during one of their sessions, Zachary R. went berserk, smashing up her office and attacking her.

A month later, after the investigation had been completed, Dr. Farworthy was summarily dismissed and her license to practice psychiatry revoked. Her last act as a psychiatrist was an act of retaliation. Dr. Farworthy told Zachary R. that he was a violent sleazebag just like Bernrd

Red, and that Zachary R. was sleeping in the same bed in the asylum that Bernrd Red had slept in. She was lying, of course, but Zachary R., of course, believed her.

94. Bernrd Red's Former Bed

Zachary R. sat up in what he believed was Bernrd Red's former bed, unbearably awake because of his honeymoon.

He alternated between talking to himself, remembering chess with his father, and having imaginary quarrels and fistfights with Bernrd Red. All of these were catalyzed by varying dosages of antipsychotics and sedatives and painkillers, which had the following side effects:

Queens and pawns.

Wind chimes and lavender.

Knights and bishops.

Savage splendor.

He imagined that Sarah handed him the urn. He opened it and stared at the ashes, searching for humanity.

95. The Cracked Snail's Opinion

Zachary R. was beside himself after his visit with the notorious Dr. Beverly Farworthy, convinced she was telling the truth that he was sleeping in the same bed that Bernrd Red had slept in.

He wanted confirmation from a known trustworthy source.

Zachary R. sat in the exact middle of the asylum lawn on a chair that made a pattern on his legs, staring urgently into the green blades and hoping to see the Cracked Snail.

He fidgeted and scratched at his arms. He hummed Haydn. His mind buzzed under the searing mental sun like bees in a lavender bush, until at last he fell asleep. He woke an hour later, still seated in his chair, with a neckache and a sunburn, when the Cracked Snail finally appeared.

"I apologize for the delay," said the Cracked Snail. "I'm afraid my wound has been extra painful today and I have overindulged on poison pellets. I must have passed out in the asylum garden."

"Apology accepted," said Zachary R.

"You look anxious," said the Cracked Snail. "What's on your mind?"

"Was there ever a patient here named Bernrd Red?" asked Zachary R.

"Yes," said the Cracked Snail. "He came through here about thirteen years ago. He wore a ruby ring. He made the nurses sweat."

"What was your opinion of him?" asked Zachary R. "Are he and I similar? Dr. Farworthy told me I remind her of him."

"Dr. Farworthy is a liar," said the Cracked Snail. "The only similarity between the two of you is your high intensity. But your high intensity is inspiring and sincere, and his was just stupid and violent. I never cared for Bernrd Red."

Zachary R.'s eyes blossomed like sunflowers. "Thank you," he said.

"Anytime," said the Cracked Snail.

96. The Cracked Snail's Soliloquy

The Cracked Snail slithered among the blades of the asylum lawn, singing this song to the patients:
"There are many worlds in which to live, choose the one with the most to give.
"There are many minds in which to fight, ignore your mind and do what's right."

97. Forgiveness

Zachary R. lay in bed in the asylum feeling unwanted pity for Bernrd Red, who had suffered in this same asylum thirteen years earlier. But no matter what he did, no matter what contradictory and violent thoughts he had for Bernrd, the black sun of empathy refused to dim.

Zachary R. tossed and turned and shivered through the night until, finally, his mind gave out. He heard footsteps coming down the hall and stopping at his door, the door opening. Bernrd Red shined a flashlight at Zachary R. "Can you forgive me?" he asked.

Zachary R. sat up in bed and muttered, "Yes." His eyes blossomed like sunflowers.

"Just kidding," said Bernrd Red. "I'm not asking for your forgiveness. You'll never learn, will you?"

Zachary R. felt the sensation of being hit in the head with a rock. He bull-rushed Bernrd Red and drove him out the door and into the hall.

Then he shoved Bernrd Red down the hall and out onto the asylum lawn, where seven women were waiting in lab coats to escort him off the premises.

PART XIII

98. A Letter

Zachary R. sat in his room examining each of the one hundred and forty-four portraits of the Cracked Snail when an orderly kindly interrupted to inform him that a letter awaited him in the asylum mailroom.

The orderly escorted him through the dayroom, across the asylum lawn in the searing mental sun, and finally past intake and into the mailroom, where the mail attendant handed him an open envelope with a letter from Sarah R. inside.

The orderly unfolded a chair and motioned for Zachary R. to sit and read the letter, which was written in all caps and read like a telegram:

DAD:

HOPE YOU ARE WELL. I'M OKAY. WORN OUT MY WELCOME WITH THE FOSTER PARENTS. DON'T BE ANGRY AT THEM. THEY'RE NICE PEOPLE. SAINTS. I AM TAKING THE URN, MOM'S DRESS, AND

THE NOVA TO LA. I WOULD COME SEE
YOU, BUT IT'S STILL TOO HARD. GET
WELL. DON'T BE TOO HARD ON
YOURSELF.

LOVE, SARAH

P.S. BAD NEWS ABOUT THE HOUSE.
FORECLOSURE.

"Can I keep this?" asked Zachary R.

The mailroom attendant looked at her
supervisor. The supervisor nodded.

Zachary R. put the letter back inside the
envelope, folded the entire apparatus in half, and
put it in his pocket.

Back in his room, Zachary R. emptied the
drawer with the one hundred and forty-four
portraits of the Cracked Snail and put the letter
inside. He slipped the portraits under the
mattress.

99. Dr. Russell Keating

Zachary R.'s behavior began to improve after he read the letter from Sarah, for both heroic and practical reasons. Not only did he want to go on a quest to L.A. in search of his daughter, but also he wanted to try to save his home.

The dismissal of Dr. Farworthy also helped. Her replacement, Dr. Russell Keating, was far more qualified to care for Zachary R., if for no better reason than he sincerely desired Zachary R.'s recovery.

Dr. Keating was the rose to Dr. Farworthy's thorn, the healthy tissue to her tumor on the mind of science. Dr. Keating, for example, understood the healing properties of Zachary R.'s mowing the asylum lawn. A routine had been established whereby Zachary R. would say, "I like rivers and women" and Dr. Keating would grant him permission to mow the asylum lawn. This state of events was agreeable for doctor and patient, as well as for asylum management, which saved on gardening expenses.

Zachary R. had now been in the asylum fourteen months and all indications were that his release was imminent. He took his meds. He attended his sessions with Dr. Keating. He spoke with the Cracked Snail and drew its portrait. He mowed the asylum lawn. And each night before bed, he read the letter from Sarah.

Dr. Keating reported Zachary R.'s progress to the board, specifically noting his affinity for rivers and women. The board agreed with the doctor that Zachary R. was ready to return to society.

100. The Next to Last Night at the House

It looked like Easter clouds on the day of Zachary R.'s release from the asylum. Dr. Keating shook Zachary R.'s hand and pulled him to his bony body for a rickety hug.

Zachary R. packed his clothes, the portraits of the Cracked Snail, and the letter from Sarah. An orderly appeared at the door with a wheelchair and wheeled the whole apparatus, including Zachary R., out of the asylum and back into the world.

The clouds cleared and, though it was winter, the sky seemed hot under the searing mental sun. Zachary R. felt good. His mind was quiet and his resolve was strong. His plan to sell the house and head west to find his daughter was both logical and the right thing to do.

The asylum shuttle service dropped Zachary R. off in the driveway of his house. He was relieved to see that measures had been taken to board up the living room window and that the lawn had been watered and mowed in his absence.

When Zachary R. walked through the front door, which had been left unlocked, he found five envelopes lying in the entryway. The first envelope contained the key to the house. The second envelope contained a note from the neighbors confirming that they had been doing basic upkeep and that the gardener—Annabel R.'s erstwhile paramour—had been maintaining the front lawn. The third envelope was from the U.S. Postal Service, informing him that his mail was being held at the post office. The fourth envelope was from Sarah R., confirming what she had written in her letter, that she had gone to "LA" and that the house was in foreclosure. The fifth envelope was a subscription offer from *Playboy* magazine.

Suddenly Zachary R.'s mind became noisy with worry over home and daughter. He set off on foot to the post office to retrieve his mail, which consisted almost entirely of past-due notices on the house.

He considered the definition of insanity: "to do the same thing over and over and expect different results." He went to the bar anyway.

The bartender immediately recognized Zachary R. and recalled his pattern of behavior, which was to confront the customers with his cryptic statements, such as:

"Cigar boxes and romance novels are the brass knuckles of sex."

Or, "I am nostalgic for the dark-road signature of the skunk."

Or, "Are you lonely as the cello? No, I am lonely as an aisle of concrete in the moonlight."

The bartender firmly pulled Zachary R. aside and explained that Zachary could stay in the bar and drink so long as he kept his mouth shut. Zachary R. promptly agreed to these terms. In the spirit of compromise, the bartender poured Zachary R. three double shots of Wild Turkey and sent him out the back door.

Zachary R. returned home, grabbed his suitcase, and climbed into the attic. He dumped the contents of the suitcase onto the attic floor, scattered the portraits of the Cracked Snail, and passed out.

101. The Last Night at the House Revisited

Zachary R. came to the next afternoon in the sweltering attic, sweating bourbon and shaking violently. His head throbbed and his mouth was dry.

He climbed down from the attic, knowing he would be leaving for good that night. He took a quick inventory of what he would be able to take with him to L.A.

There was no food in the cupboards and the fridge was warm and empty.

No furniture could come, of course.

There were no toiletries in the bathrooms, though the flyswatter still hung from a hook on the wall by the toilet.

Zachary R. carefully removed the flyswatter from its hook and carried it up the ladder into the attic, where he packed his clothes, the letter from Sarah, and the flyswatter. Finally, he gathered the one hundred and forty-four portraits of the Cracked Snail and packed one hundred and forty-three of them in his suitcase. He unfolded the last portrait and placed it in the exact middle of the attic. He took his suitcase and climbed down from the attic for the last time.

Zachary R. dropped the suitcase in the boarded-up living room and slept on the sofa until the sun went down.

When he woke, he took one final pass through the house. Everything seemed to be in order, except for the toilet, which he had forgotten to flush in his drunken stupor. He flushed the toilet and sterilized the seat with a sponge and rubbing alcohol.

Toilet was sterilized. Flyswatter was packed. Fridge was warm and empty. Asylum was in the past.

Zachary R. closed the door of his house for the last time. . . .

102. All the Unlocked Doors

How was it possible,
all the unlocked doors?

Was it the Goth Girls
or unknown others?

Was it a failure of body,
every nerve scraped and startled,
or confusion of mind,

every memory ambiguous and addled?

How was it possible,
all the unlocked doors?

103. A Boxcar Journey to L.A., Part 1

Zachary R. woke the following morning next to a stack of pine logs outside his former house, which now had busted windows in addition to the boarded-up living room window, and new divots pounded into the walls in addition to the divots his daughter had pounded.

He grabbed his suitcase and set off on foot to the hardware store.

Zachary R. was hopeful that the security guard there would take pity on his circumstances and give him bus fare for the trip to L.A.

Zachary R. had no money. He had signed forms in the asylum that gave the relevant authorities the power to pay his bills during his stay. By the time of his release, Zachary R.'s meager savings had been depleted. No money. No house. No car.

The moment Zachary R. walked through the door of the hardware store, he was turned around and escorted out by the familiar security guard, who was clearly a man of his word. Zachary R. didn't even have an opportunity to grunt. Nor did he protest with his fists. Instead, he set off on foot to the Boston rail yard, where he boarded a boxcar and headed west.

104. A Nova Journey to New Orleans

As indicated in her letter, Sarah R. packed the urn and the Revolution Dress and took the Nova to LA. But by "LA," she didn't mean Los Angeles, but rather Louisiana—and specifically, New Orleans.

Sarah knew her father would misinterpret the letter to mean Los Angeles, which meant he would not be able to find her. She also knew she would confuse her foster parents and the child services department. She was determined to start a new life without the false hope of her father recovering.

The Nova held up remarkably well, considering what she had put it through. The engine ran smoothly despite the busted-up grill and the missing headlight, which got her fix-it tickets in New Jersey, West Virginia, and Tennessee.

Each night she slept in the backseat, or rather, she lay awake in the backseat with mixed emotions. On the one hand, she felt shame and confusion. She opened the urn, searching for humanity in her mother's ashes and finding none. She thought about her father and felt ashamed for deceiving him about where she was headed, as well as for the fact that she couldn't muster the strength to be there for him on his release from the asylum. She worried that he would quickly become ill again without his daughter and with his house in foreclosure. On the other hand, she was free—free of the weight of her father's illness, free of the false pity of the neighbors, free of her do-gooder foster parents, free from school.

But she was also free of her kitten, which she gave to the bookstore owner. "Every bookstore needs a cat," he said, reassuring her that he would take care of it. He even named the cat Hobbes, which made her cry.

Sarah R. arrived in New Orleans in early February, on the Wednesday before Mardi Gras.

105. A Boxcar Journey to L.A., Part 2

At last, Zachary R. was onboard an endless train that passed through tunnels in hills with shacks and cigarettes and by pigeons perched majestically on telephone wires, some with human heads, which made him shiver and giggle.

He was onboard the endless train that sent his mother over the edge and onto the hard dirt of the New Hampshire forest and into a tissue-fiber nightgown.

Zachary R. smiled the eyeless smile of eradicated dreams. This was what he wanted all along. And why not?

All aboard!

He introduced the Goth Girls to the Cold Angel. He showed off his portraits of the Cracked Snail. He laughed forgivingly, condescendingly, about his wife and Bernrd Red. He checkmated his father.

After what seemed like a complete and different and better lifetime, the train arrived at the massive rail yard near downtown Los Angeles.

He disembarked and set off on foot toward the soft prison of Hollywood and the grim task of searching for his daughter, whom he had happily forgotten about on the train.

106. A Bus Ride to the Ocean

From Argos

a thousand years

to Bethlehem

from Bethlehem

two thousand years

to Boston

from Boston

a boxcar journey

to Hollywood

from Hollywood

a bus ride

to the ocean

in the searing mental sun

a procession of ghosts

and he joined it

like a raindrop joins

a river.

PART XIV

107. Sea Change

Dr. Farworthy would not have been kept on the asylum staff as long as she was, had it not been for her tremendous success in reforming Bernrd Red, who was diagnosed with paranoia and acute sociopathic tendencies.

A landmark case study was published in the *New England Journal of Medicine*, which demonstrated the efficacy of aggressive combination therapy involving twice-daily private talk therapy coupled with stimulants, which, the study showed, had the paradoxical effect of reducing symptoms and ultimately curing the patient.

The doctor was only too willing to show her colleagues her scar, admonishing them to be vigilant in the early going because stimulation could intensify symptoms.

The case study, of course, was completely bogus. Doctor after doctor got attacked by overstimulated, hyperanalyzed, paranoid, sociopathic patients.

But there was no denying Bernrd Red's transformation.

During his violent sessions with Dr. Farworthy, and for that matter, during his entire stay in the asylum, he heard nothing but Crosby, Stills, Nash & Young's "Carry On" running through his mind over and over and over, which was the reason why he had checked himself in in the first place, and which was the reason why he ultimately put a stop to the carnage. During his final session with Dr. Farworthy, and without explanation, Bernrd Red—rather than continue promoting the sensation of being hit in the head with a rock—kissed the doctor's cheek, stroked her hair, went to his room, and never beat anyone again.

After being discharged from the asylum, Bernrd Red moved to New Orleans, where he lived passive and uneasy, cantankerous and celibate. But the music was good in New Orleans, which made life tolerable.

Bernrd Red loved music.

108. Café Macabre and the Fortune-Teller

Solitary, poor, nasty, brutish, and short.

Sarah R. repeated her Hobbesian mantra for inspiration as she searched for a job in New Orleans, bald head notwithstanding.

Even with Mardi Gras long over, there were abundant positions available in the clubs and bars, most of which would have hired Sarah even though she had only turned sixteen in December. But Sarah instinctively knew she wanted nothing to do with serving rowdy drunks.

She gave Café Du Monde a try. The first week went well enough, serving chicory coffee and beignets to tourists. But when Monday morning arrived after a weekend of drinking in the Dungeon and pondering the empty urn, Sarah R. just couldn't bring herself to go back.

Instead, she spent the day recuperating and then, on Tuesday, four weeks post Mardi Gras, she got a job at Café Macabre, which sold poetry chapbooks and voodoo dolls in addition to coffee and pastries. A fortune-teller was stationed upstairs.

All new hires received a complimentary visit with the fortune-teller, and Sarah visited with him on the night after her first shift ended.

Her first question for the fortune-teller was, "Aren't you supposed to be a woman?"

The fortune-teller replied, "Aren't young women supposed to have hair?"

Sarah R. frowned and then allowed a crack of a smile to creep through. "Never mind my past," she said. "What do you see in my future?"

With the utmost confidence and clarity of voice, the fortune-teller replied, "You tricked your father. Your father is injured. Your father is dying."

109. A Cigarette Break

The string of bells jingled against the glass business door of Café Macabre when Sarah R. stepped outside for her cigarette break.

Freaked out by what the fortune-teller said the night before, she leaned against a pole with chipped paint and faded stickers, and resolved to leave for L.A. first thing tomorrow morning.

She brought flame to paper and smoked her tobacco, flicking ashes into the eyes of the daisies which stayed open anyway and moved like her hair would have—if she weren't bald—in the direction of the wind which swept copper leaves along the dry black street.

Then up came Bernrd Red in flannel pajamas that snagged his sores and made him grimace.

He saw Sarah R. against her pole and said, "Wouldn't it be nice if you had some hair that could blow in the direction of the wind? . . . But carry on, I mean, at least you're not like me. I drink in the morning and sleep until sundown, and then I wake nervous as a bull thinking slow as cheese and I pace in my pajamas in silence except for the pebble in my slipper, which irritates the hell out of me and makes me moan, but at least I'm done beating my lovers and at least I'm done promoting the sensation of being hit in the head with a rock. Hosanna."

He reached into his pocket, grabbed a handful of pennies, and tossed them—along with his pinky ring—into the dry black street.

The string of bells jingled against the glass business door of Café Macabre when Sarah R. stepped back inside.

She said "Benediction" as she dropped the pennies and the ring one by one into her tip jar.

110. News from the Working Parts, Part 2

Zachary R. couldn't be sure how long he had lived in his alley between medium buildings. He couldn't recall what his daughter looked like. He couldn't recall the human details of his life, only the symbols and the figments of his imagination. Or, perhaps, the figments, at some point, became more real to him than the human details. He had crossed over to the other side, as it were.

After all he had been through since his arrival in Hollywood, it was no surprise that his search for Sarah had waned to the point of flat black sky. No moon, no stars. Just the occasional knight, rook, or bishop.

After his release from police custody and the hospital, all he could think about was the pain in his injured hand, which had traveled up his arm, into his shoulders, and finally his brain.

And, to add insult to his injured hand, he also suffered from adult-onset asthma from breathing bus fumes, rotting food, urine, and feces.

He sampled his fingers: semen on the index, beer on the middle, stardom on the ring, asthma on the pinky, murder on the thumb.

He searched along the boulevard, but he couldn't remember why. Pain was all that remained.

His chances for Messiah or Rock Star were gone.

111. The Goth Girls Hold Vigil

Zachary R. lay unconscious in his alley between medium buildings, dreaming about pine trees and leisure, the infection becoming ever more dire.

Seven Goth Girls dressed in lab coats encircled him, each holding a lit candle. The redhead approached him and dripped hot wax onto his forehead, waking him.

"You're somewhat gorgeous," she said. "Chess is nearly impossible."

The dirty, bloodied, wax-stained ice rink of Zachary R.'s face melted. "I love it when you quote the Cracked Snail," he said.

She continued, "I need to look far away to erase your naked image from my mind."

Zachary R. giggled terribly, then slipped back into unconsciousness.

The redhead heard the sound of a plane. She looked at the sky.

112. An Ambulance Journey to the Hospital

The next time Zachary R. regained consciousness was to the sound of the siren of the ambulance that transported him to the hospital. His pain was so severe now that it no longer bothered him.

On the contrary, his pain now induced alternating states of euphoria and lucidity, both of which gave him a sense of well-being.

The nurse in the emergency room hooked Zachary R. up to an IV with antibiotics and shot him full of morphine. He was admitted to the ICU the next morning.

In his lucid moments Zachary R. rang for the nurse to come and listen to him rhapsodize about his daughter. The nurse was kind and tried to reassure him that L.A. was a big city and that Sarah would be there any day now to see him. Zachary R. was kind, too, and agreed with the nurse, even though he knew he would never see his daughter again.

At the end of his second day in the ICU, Zachary R. inquired as to whether the hospital had a courtyard with grass. The nurse confirmed that this was so.

113. A Nova Journey to L.A., Part 1

First thing tomorrow morning arrived and the Nova was packed and ready for the trip west. This wasn't due to the urgency Sarah R. felt to find her father, though she felt plenty. Rather, it was because she had been living in the car since she nearly burned down the bargain motel.

She shaved her head in the rearview mirror, said a prayer for her father, and kissed the ground for her mother, whose body and Revolution Dress were forever ashes in New Orleans.

Then she paid a visit to the Dungeon to say goodbye to the Dungeon Master who doubled as a hot dog vendor, but, sadly, the Dungeon had closed for the morning and there wasn't time to search the streets for the man's hot dog cart. Sarah R. reached into her pocket and breathed a sigh of relief when she felt the familiar edges of his business card scrape against her fingers. She removed the card from her pocket and slipped it in her cleavage, a souvenir, a keepsake, an heirloom to be placed in a future family album.

* * * * *

Sarah R. cashed her final paycheck from Café Macabre, put gas in the Nova, set the empty urn at her side, and headed west on the I-10 in search of her father.

Texas was long and flat with trees scattered in the distance. Sarah R. fell in love with it. She was falling in love in general. She decided to let her hair grow, somehow knowing that her life was blooming as part of some master plan, some benevolent grand scheme.

On night one of her journey, she slept in San Antonio. On night two of her journey, she slept in El Paso. On day three, the day she intended to drive straight through to L.A., she stopped for lunch in Las Cruces, New Mexico, the city in which she would live the rest of her life.

114. Las Cruces

Sarah R. drove into Las Cruces, New Mexico, looking for a café like Café Macabre. The town mainly had Tex-Mex restaurants, but it was also a college town, so there was no shortage of coffee houses.

Interspersed among the Starbucks were some definite possibilities. There was Café Trieste, Café Voltaire, Café Sport, and then she saw Café Hobbes. Sarah R. parked the Nova and navigated her way through a gauntlet of students to get to Café Hobbes. The string of bells jingled against the glass business door when she stepped inside.

Sarah R. walked directly to the cashier, a good-looking youth about eighteen years old, whom she assumed was a college student.

Painted in searing yellow letters on the wall behind the cashier were the words *Solitary, Poor, Nasty, Brutish,* and *Short.* Sarah R. swooned and collapsed onto the counter, where she would have struck her bald head were it not for the lightning-quick and chivalrous hands of the cashier, who caught her head just before impact.

When she came to, she was lying on her back in a long wooden booth with the cashier seated next to her holding a tissue soaked in rubbing alcohol that he had waved under her nose to revive her.

"Are you okay?" asked the cashier. "I often have that effect on girls who see me for the first time. I should have tried to warn you somehow."

Sarah R. rolled her eyes. "I swooned because of Thomas Hobbes, not because of you. He's my favorite philosopher."

"He's a drag," said the cashier.

"You would say that," snorted Sarah R. "You're probably a frat boy with perfect grades, shiny happy parents, and a golden retriever back home. You're a story about a boy and his dog. Solitary, poor, nasty, brutish, and short. That's my mantra."

"You're a runaway, aren't you?" he asked.

"Well, kind of," she said. "More like I was run away from. My mom is dead. I scattered her ashes in New Orleans. And my dad is certified. No lie. He's in L.A. and he's very sick. That's where I'm headed, to L.A."

"I'm sorry to hear that," he said. His tone softened.

"I was a runaway not too long ago. I was planning on running away to Hollywood to become a movie star, but then my mom got this suicide note in the mail written by a runaway in Hollywood."

"That makes no sense at all," said Sarah R. "I'm leaving. Thanks for sparing me a concussion."

"Wait. Let me explain," he said. "My mom processes magazine subscriptions in Boulder, Colorado. That's where I'm from. The runaway mailed his suicide note in a business reply envelope for *Playboy* magazine. My mom made a photocopy of the note and gave it to me to convince me not to run away. It worked. The kid comes across as a narcissistic jerk, which is what I was. I carry the note in my pocket wherever I go. Here, let me read it to you."

The cashier reached into his back pocket and pulled out the suicide note of H. James Branhoover, which read as follows:

"And so I ran away to Hollywood. Bigger moths need bigger flames. I know after I jump off this building, the world will mourn and pandemonium and chaos will reign. For the record, my dad was a good-for-nothing banker and my mom was an abusive whore. Good riddance to them. Didn't they know who I was? Come to think of it, didn't any of you people know who I was? Fuck all of you! No longer yours, H. James Branhoover."

Sarah R. fell silent for a minute and then said, "I've never heard a real suicide note before. It's so sad." Then she allowed herself a small smile. "Bigger moths need bigger flames? What does that mean?"

The cashier laughed. "It's bullshit. Or maybe he thought he was Icarus," he said.

"That's beautiful," said Sarah R. "He was so delusional that he took his own life."

"You're twisted," said the cashier.

"Thank you," said Sarah R.

*　*　*　*　*

Sarah R. awoke the following afternoon on the couch in the cashier's apartment, her head throbbing from the margaritas they had drunk the night before. She went into the bathroom and looked at herself in the mirror. She noticed that her hair had begun to sprout.

The cashier wasn't home, but he did leave her an apple, a poppy seed bagel, and a note, which informed Sarah that he hadn't run away from her, that he had to work the morning shift at Café Hobbes, how she should feel guilty because she got to sleep off her hangover while he had to suffer through his to the sound of café blenders, that he thought she was the most beautiful bald girl he had ever seen, that she should know that his name was Jason Cooper, and that he should know what her name was since he would be waiting for her to return from L.A. He concluded the note with his phone number and address, and drew a blank line for her to fill in her name.

Sarah R.'s heart raced with joy, but joy was quickly replaced by the sobering thought of her ailing father almost a thousand miles away. She scribbled her name on the note and set off in the Nova to L.A. to find Zachary R.

115. On the Third Day

On the third day in the ICU, the nurse secured Zachary R. to the bed on which he had lain immobile since his rescue from the alley. She wheeled the whole apparatus into the hospital courtyard, which had grass of varying lengths.

The long blades were comic lifelines.

The medium blades were tragic lifelines.

The short blades were Hobbesian lifelines.

Drizzle beset Zachary R.'s face. He watched as best he could, a witness of renewal blinking in the pinprick rain.

Strapped down in the bed with only his head exposed, he thought, "I liked rivers and women."

Then he declared, "I am ready to die."

Suddenly Zachary R. stood up in what seemed to be the sky, except there were large double doors, like cellar doors, lit by the black sun of empathy. Zachary R. swung open the doors and returned to where he was in the years before his birth.

116. The Electric Light Dirge for Cello and Organ

After Zachary R.'s return to where he was in the years before his birth, the interested parties in Boston, Los Angeles, and New Orleans converged to arrange for the disposal of his earthly remains.

The hospital nurse from Los Angeles and the hot dog vendor were interviewed, along with asylum staff and various detectives from all three cities. Events were pieced together, and it was determined that Zachary R.'s body would be cremated and his ashes delivered to New Orleans, where they would be scattered in the exact middle of Lake Pontchartrain.

It seemed doubtful, at best, that either Zachary R. or Annabel R. would have wanted to be joined in death, let alone in a shallow, brackish lake at the mouth of the Mississippi that neither had visited during their lifetime. Nevertheless, this seemed to be the best option based on the available information.

Asylum staff in Boston suggested that the Electric Light Dirge for Cello and Organ be played at the funeral, which the hot dog vendor suggested take place in a small church near Café Macabre, because that was where Sarah R. was last seen.

It looked like Easter clouds and smelled like rain, like Annabel R., on the day of the funeral, which took place on the vernal equinox, the day Zachary R. had opened his backpack and showed Annabel R. the small poster ad for the carnival that had staked a patch of earth at the foot of the hill of shacks and cigarettes; the day when she wore the Revolution Dress and parted her hair down the middle; the day Zachary R. wore an indigo T-shirt and sideburns and his eyes blossomed like sunflowers; the day she led him to the photo booth by the fortune-teller and sat him down and drew the curtain; the day they rode the parachutes, fired guns, and burned sage in the name of loneliness; the day it was so warm that the sky seemed to descend and nothing was distant; the day Zachary and Annabel moved through the carnival in such gentle oblivion that gypsy kids had no trouble stealing rolls of tickets from their pockets; the day Sarah R. was conceived.

The funeral was attended by the hot dog vendor and the hospital nurse from Los Angeles. Sarah R. did not attend. Despite a diligent search of most points between New Orleans, Boston, and L.A., she could not be found.

The hot dog vendor and the hospital nurse held hands as the Electric Light Dirge for Cello and Organ began to play, filling the small church and the air just outside the open windows and doors.

Then up came Bernrd Red in flannel pajamas that snagged his sores and made him grimace, and he heard the beautiful dirge out in the street and the music reminded him of a better time with Mozart and the nannies, and he stepped inside the small church and he joined hands with the hospital nurse and the hot dog vendor.

When the ceremony ended, the three of them hugged. The hospital nurse and the hot dog vendor told what they knew about the man whose ashes they held in an urn and were about to scatter across the lake.

"At least his wasn't a story about a boy and his dog," said Bernrd Red.

"Carry on, sir, madam," he said in his best concierge voice, and disappeared down the wet black street humming Crosby, Stills, Nash & Young.

117. A Nova Journey to L.A., Part 2

It was the evening before the vernal equinox when Sarah R. set off in the Nova to L.A. to find Zachary R., whose ashes would be scattered across Lake Pontchartrain the following morning. Sarah R. drove straight through the night and into the morning all the way to L.A., where she walked into a police station, identified herself, and explained to them about her father.

A detective at the police station made a brief investigation and discovered that her father was listed in the previous week's coroner reports.

"We've been looking for you," he said. "Please have a seat."

Sarah R. sat down in the chair that the detective pulled out for her.

"Your father passed away last week at Cedars-Sinai," said the detective, gently. "He had been living in an alley in Hollywood."

Sarah R. closed her eyes and silently repeated her Hobbesian mantra. The detective put his hand on her shoulder.

"Where is he now?" she asked.

"His body was cremated and the ashes were transported to New Orleans," replied the detective.

Sarah R. let out a staccato laugh of shocked disbelief. She sat in silence for several minutes.

"Can someone tell me where the alley is?" she asked.

"Yes," muttered the detective.

* * * * *

Sarah R. returned to the Nova and lay in the backseat, clutching the empty urn and alternating between crying and sleeping. She woke with the rising sun the following morning, bought sunflowers from an immigrant in a busy intersection, parked the Nova in Zachary R.'s stretch of pavement between medium buildings, placed the flowers in the empty urn, and set the arrangement down on the cleanest spot she could find.

Sarah R. stared at the sunflowers in the urn in the alley and found humanity at last. She headed off in the Nova back to Las Cruces.

EPILOGUE

The Goth Girls

When Zachary R.'s ashes were scattered across Lake Pontchartrain, the Goth Girls scattered throughout the twenty-first century, keeping the memory of Zachary R. close to their hearts, which are held within their Damien lockets.

The Goth Girls will gather again in the twenty-second century in the cathedrals, prisons, and streets of the world to select a troubled man to torment and to protect.

The Cold Angel

After the Cold Angel said goodbye to Zachary R. and disappeared into the fog, she had nothing but time to reflect on the outcome of her final mission in service to mankind. She thought about how she had led Zachary R. to his moment of clarity in the New Hampshire mountains, and about how little effect this ultimately had on his fate. She thought about what Zachary R. had said: "Sometimes the shivers are painful, but you make the shivers feel good." Then she recalled her own advice: "You have been lying to yourself for a long time, but you don't have to suffer anymore."

Now the Cold Angel understood that her final mission was as much in service to herself as it was for Zachary R. She thanked God for granting her the wisdom to understand, and then she asked Him to bless what she now knew to be her true calling.

The Cold Angel, complete with veil, hands like winter, and the power to summon and control the movement of fog, visits fever patients around the world and makes their shivers feel good.

The Cracked Snail

The Cracked Snail continues to slither among the blades of the asylum lawn, thinking "Service to mankind," eating poison pellets for the pain, and looking fondly at one of its portraits that Zachary R. drew, portrait number one hundred and forty-five, which had blown across the asylum lawn and lodged in the lavender bush.

The Cracked Snail will continue to talk to asylum patients in the searing mental sun until the asylum closes its gates forever.

Bernrd Red

Bernrd Red still lives passive and uneasy, cantankerous and celibate, in New Orleans. He wanders the streets of the French Quarter, singing "Carry on, love is coming to us all."

Book Two

Trust Fund Baby

PART I

1. Roof Access

Haley James Branhoover, the Branhoovers' second son, sat in his room in the youth hostel and wrote the last words of his life—rancid, buttery words that when he read them back aloud, offended him.

"Trust fund baby," he said.

He couldn't stand the sight of his suicide note sitting so accusingly on the nightstand, so he sealed it in the nearest thing he could find: a business reply envelope for *Playboy* magazine.

He went downstairs to the mailroom and dropped the envelope in the slot. On his way back up, he read the words "Roof Access" around each turn of the staircase.

He walked into the open air on the roof. "Roof Access," he said. He repeated the phrase. It gave him unexpected energy.

He sat down on the edge and dangled his legs over.

The youth hostel was only five stories high. H. James Branhoover thought that might not be high enough to kill him, and he didn't want to wind up crippled and in a wheelchair, so he pondered the optimal way to make the plunge onto the concrete below.

He heard the sounds of a television coming from an open window. "The triple Axel is the most difficult jump in her program," said the announcer. H. James Branhoover let out a burst of sound. A laugh. A sarcastic laugh, certainly, but a laugh nonetheless.

Then more phrases: "Cold beer." "Hot coffee." "Cheeseburger." I want a cheeseburger, he thought.

Then up the street came a homeless man, clutching his mangled hand and humming Haydn. It was the man from the alley who reminded him of Charles Larson. Searchlights crossed overhead. A soft breeze moved his arm hairs. He closed his eyes and pushed himself off the roof.

Several minutes later, the homeless man arrived at the spot where the lifeless body of H. James Branhoover lay. He reached out his injured hand and touched the corpse. "I am afraid to die," he said.

2. Kay Sunday

A strand of Kay Sunday's long blonde hair dangled from the notebook of H. James Branhoover. "Church blonde. Mother hen blonde," it read. "Pretty blonde. Wholesome. Winsome. Helpful." But, like any two people who have known each other for a long time, she had betrayed him, and he had betrayed her.

Kay Sunday was slight of build, had large, pale blue eyes, and the highly unglamorous habit of sniffing gasoline fumes for fun. She hung out with a group of innocents who made you feel your age when in their presence; that your desires were silly and why not try to relax. Sit on a porch and decompress. Do something real and worthwhile, something unpolitical, like planting roses.

Kay Sunday was H. James Branhoover's best friend.

3. Investigation and Notification

Because H. James Branhoover had mailed his suicide note to the subscription processing center for *Playboy* magazine in Boulder, Colorado, the detectives in charge of the investigation of his death were initially unable to rule out accident or homicide.

They placed the strand of Kay Sunday's hair in a plastic bag and scrutinized each entry of his notebook for possible clues.

They questioned the homeless man from the alley who had reminded H. James Branhoover of Charles Larson, as well as one of the boys who fake gayness for the sake of slavery, who saw the homeless man reaching for the body and muttering "I am afraid to die."

It would have taken expert detective work, or even clairvoyance, to uncover the connection the homeless man had to H. James Branhoover. Fortunately for all involved, the detectives did not possess such powers.

Eventually the suicide note was found and the investigation closed. Mrs. Branhoover received the news of her second son's suicide in the comfort of her Colonial mansion in Pittsburgh, where she spends her days beneath the drapes of the living room window, looking at the river below.

PART II

4. The Splendorous Layout of Christmas Morning

Energy shot through the five-year-old body of H. James Branhoover—the second son of H. Charles Branhoover and Chloe Branhoover—as he lay in bed with a nauseated sense of anticipation of what awaited him that Christmas morning.

Jimmy's bedroom was the lone occupied room of six on the second floor of the Branhoovers' two-story, ten-bedroom Colonial mansion located on the summit of one of Pittsburgh's many hills.

Jimmy Branhoover was a little prince living in a castle at the top of the world, the Allegheny River below serving as his moat.

His father, the well-to-do and good-for-nothing banker H. Charles Branhoover, was the aging king, now in his seventies, feeble and mildly ashamed of the totality of his life.

His mother, Mrs. Chloe Branhoover, the unlikely queen, the former roughhouse prostitute Chloe Red, had recently celebrated her fortieth birthday, which meant that mother was as close in age to her second son as she was to her husband.

The Branhoovers' first son, Bernard, of whom Jimmy was entirely unaware, was employed as a concierge in a bed-and-breakfast on a road called Bath in a seaside village out West. Bernard Branhoover, who changed his name to Bernrd Red to promote the sensation of being hit in the head with a rock, had not been in contact with his parents since his father had expelled him from Pittsburgh when Bernrd was eighteen. He was now twenty-five and, like Jimmy, was unaware that he had a brother.

So the home of the ignorant little prince was permeated by the scent of the Christmas tree (a twenty-foot Douglas fir) and the electricity that lit the lights in its branches seemed the same electricity that lit young Jimmy when he opened his bedroom door Christmas morning and beheld the splendorous layout of presents, two dozen, all his, and the lone stocking, also his, hanging directly above the well-mannered fire in the Branhoovers' fireplace.

5. The Negligently Hung Stocking

Jimmy Branhoover rushed down the stairs and fell face-first into the plush carpet of the living room, where all the excitement of Christmas had been arranged.

His parents, who had been awaiting their son's arrival for the past half hour, sprang to their feet in anticipation of their son's crying, which, to their surprise, failed to manifest. The severity of the fall was sufficient to cause a minor concussion, but the boy seemed completely unfazed. The splendor of the two dozen presents, all his, trumped the jolting pain inside his skull.

Jimmy bounced across the carpet with the awkward precision of a pouncing kitten and sat among his presents under the Christmas tree.

His mother, feeling guilty about her violent reign over her first son, doted on Jimmy as her penance, which seemed to explain the boy's exuberant and unassuming disposition.

But Mrs. Chloe Branhoover had also, of late, resumed her role as Chloe Red. Not only was her husband old, but he was also cheap and controlling. As a banker, he believed the only way to keep his young, formerly wayward wife securely in his possession was to restrict her allowance. But tightening his purse strings did nothing but loosen his wife's legs and her attention to detail on this particular Christmas morning.

Mrs. Branhoover had haphazardly wrapped Jimmy's gifts and inconsistently marked the tags. Sure enough, eighteen gifts were marked "To:

Jimmy, From: Santa," but three gifts read "To: Jimmy, From: Chloe," two gifts read "To: Jimmy, From: blank line," and one gift read "To: Bernard, From: Santa."

When Jimmy read "To: Bernard," his faced twisted mildly, but then he burst out laughing. "Look, Mom and Dad," he said, pointing at the tag. "Santa accidentally gave one of this kid Bernard's presents to me!"

Then, just as H. James Branhoover, the Branhoovers' second son, began tearing into the wrapping paper of their first son's present, the overstuffed stocking above the fireplace, which Chloe Red had negligently hung with a piece of masking tape, dropped onto the hearth below, scattering the contents into the fire, which began to rage with the new fuel of Jimmy's toys. Now their son seemed finally to notice the pain inside his skull and began to cry inconsolably. Mother and father looked at each other with accusatory eyes and then descended upon their five-year-old boy, smothering him with the overzealous

affection of secretive and lying parents whose
consciences had condemned them long ago.

6. You Think This Is Real, but It Isn't Real at All

Jimmy Branhoover was still a pouncing kitten
the following fall, when he entered kindergarten
at the very private, formerly traditional, and now
progressive Carden School.

While some of the children cried and clung to
their parents on the first day of school, this was
not the case for Jimmy or the slight, blonde girl,
Kay Sunday, who, even at the age of five, had
otherworldly eyes that said she knew something
you didn't.

The Carden School, from day one, employed
its newfangled approach to education and sat
"like with like" rather than "name with name,"

which meant that it was possible for a "B" to sit next to an "S," which meant that Jimmy and Kay, whom the teacher determined to be like with like, were seated next to each other.

While the two children's personalities weren't exactly alike, there was no disputing their mutual affection.

By the third day of school, the entire class had been arranged according to the teacher's intuition. The exuberant and unassuming Jimmy and the alien Kay were already best friends who shared everything, including the same palette for their finger paints, which Jimmy, without hesitation or reservation, ran through Kay's hair.

Kay Sunday's hair looked like a hallucination, with purple, red, and green streaks to complement her natural blonde.

The teacher, Mrs. Germany, Deirdre to her husband and the other teachers, upon seeing Kay's hair, momentarily forgot her forward-looking ideology and grabbed Jimmy by the arm.

"Jimmy!" she exclaimed. "Don't ever paint Kay's hair again! Understand?"

Jimmy Branhoover was stunned silent by his teacher's sudden rage, but not Kay Sunday. Little Kay looked directly at Mrs. Germany with her otherworldly eyes and said, "You think this is real, but it isn't real at all." Then Kay ran her hand through her painted hair, smeared it on Jimmy's shirt and then her own shirt.

The paint seemed real enough to Mrs. Germany.

7. What's the Idea of Peeing in Our Tub

By the time Halloween came around, Jimmy Branhoover and Kay Sunday were inseparable, inasmuch as is possible for a couple of kindergarteners to be.

Mrs. Germany, the progressive kindergarten teacher, was so charmed by the two children—and by her self-satisfaction that she and her pedagogical philosophy had been responsible for bringing them together—that she suggested to Jimmy's and Kay's parents at the October PTA meeting that the two should spend the night together, which she promptly restated as "they should have a sleepover" when Mrs. Branhoover slapped her across the face.

Mr. and Mrs. Sunday, who, unlike the Branhoovers, were accustomed to being and doing everything together, including sharing their unlikely family business as spiritual consultants and amateur astronomers, selling God and telescopes, immediately assented to the idea, volunteering the Branhoovers' mansion for the occasion.

Mrs. Branhoover, unaccompanied by her septuagenarian husband, glared at the Sundays and vowed to hate them and their dubious business forever. "Will this Saturday night be good for Kay?" she muttered. "Saturday is Halloween."

Mr. and Mrs. Sunday looked at each other, their eyes beaming vacuously, yet infectiously, and then they looked at the sullen Mrs. Branhoover and blurted out in unison, "Oh, how you shine."

Now Mrs. Branhoover was beside herself. "Bring Kay over by three o'clock so we can dress them up for Halloween," she said, and then quickly turned and walked away.

* * * * *

The Sundays arrived at the Branhoovers' door at 3:25 that Saturday. Kay had her costume curled up in both arms. It was a bee costume, complete with two bee wings, six bee legs, and black and gold bee makeup.

Mrs. Branhoover let Kay inside and pointed toward the living room. "Go wait in that room and I'll get Jimmy," she said. Then she looked at Mr. and Mrs. Sunday and instructed them to

326

return the next morning at ten to pick up their daughter.

By the time Mrs. Branhoover had closed the front door and turned around, Jimmy had found Kay.

Jimmy was already in costume. Mrs. Branhoover, as an experiment, had picked three superhero costumes: Superman, Batman, and Wonder Woman. Jimmy immediately picked Batman. While she was alarmed that her son chose the Dark Knight (yet not really that surprised, given who his father and brother were), at least he didn't choose Wonder Woman, which pacified her fear that she had given birth to a sissy, what with him palling around with a girl and all.

Batman and the bumblebee frolicked in the living room smearing the gold bee makeup on each other, while Mrs. Branhoover looked on without an inkling of concern or amusement.

As for Mr. Branhoover, he chose to remain in his bedroom, too tired to contend with the frenetic energy of two children on Halloween.

At six o'clock Mrs. Branhoover took the kids trick-or-treating and by seven had them back and preparing for bed.

Jimmy bathed first and was already in bed. Mr. Branhoover, having forgotten that there were two children in his home that night, opened the bathroom door and was shocked to see little Kay sitting in a bathtub of golden water.

Mr. Branhoover blurted out, "What's the idea of peeing in our tub?!" To which Kay, giggling, responded, "It's not my pee. It's bee pee."

Mr. Branhoover slammed the door shut and returned to his bedroom. As he laid his head on his pillow, he allowed a barely audible, breathy chuckle to escape his old lungs.

8. Cow with Braces

Kindergarten for Jimmy and Kay went by in a timeless hallucination of finger paint. Timeless in the sense that time, and the dread that comes with its passing, had no influence on the two children.

So the school year came to an end and the summer passed by, too, which meant it was the autumn of first grade.

Jimmy thought the first-grade classroom smelled like a pumpkin cloud and resembled the big kids' classrooms because it had cursive letters written on the blackboard.

Jimmy and Kay's first-grade teacher was the same as their kindergarten teacher—Mrs. Germany.

Mrs. Germany was pleased to see that Jimmy and Kay were still friends with the same enthusiasm as the previous year. She knew firsthand how a summer together (or a summer apart) can change the dynamic of a friendship.

329

She looked out the window, thinking wistful thoughts of friendships come and gone and of the heartbreak of change.

Then, in the way that only a mature adult can do, she banished the memories of a lifetime and returned her focus to her responsibility: the twenty-two children waiting for first grade to begin.

Mrs. Germany faced the class, smiled purposefully, and asked, "Do any of my returning students notice anything different about me this year?" Kay Sunday thrust her hand high above her head, waving in that same hand a large piece of construction paper, which Mrs. Germany took from the girl and examined.

Then, in the way that only a mature adult can do, Mrs. Germany banished her hurt feelings and held up the drawing that Kay had produced in her first minutes in the first grade: a cow with braces.

Mrs. Germany grinned widely and the classroom burst out laughing. "That's right, Kay Sunday. I got braces this summer," she said.

Kay was proud of her achievement, but she was perplexed by the laughter. Mrs. Germany could see that Kay honestly meant no harm, and so laughed herself.

9. Clayton Mulder

With the exception of the straightening of Mrs. Germany's crooked teeth, the eight seasons of the first and second grades came and went with few perceptible changes. The same twenty-two students progressed through their lessons at the expected rates, and the relationships established in kindergarten persisted.

But then came the autumn of the third grade, and with it the arrival of a twenty-third student: Clayton Mulder.

Clay Mulder had moved to Pittsburgh from Santa Cruz, California, on account of his father's procuring a lucrative administrative position at the Presbyterian hospital.

Clay had spent the first eight years of his life on a boogie board in the chilly, shark-infested water of Northern California, and among the redwoods and deadheads who were his parents' friends. As such, he was an affable, willing, and fearless boy, and a natural to become friends with Kay and Jimmy.

Clay deflected with charm and ease Kay and Jimmy's early and obvious attempt to make fun of his name, which he said he planned to change as soon as the law permitted. When Kay asked him what he was going to change it to, he jokingly said Millicent. All three of them laughed, and then Jimmy, who had misheard him, asked,

"Why would you want to be called Innocent?" They all laughed again.

Kay seemed to go into a trance. "I like it," she said. "I really like it. I'm going to start calling you that now, if you don't mind. I mean, my real last name is Sutter, so it's no big deal."

"I'm good with that," said Clay Mulder. "Kay Sunday and the Innocents. That would be a cool band name."

"Definitely," said Jimmy.

"Jimmy, you could be Innocent #1, and I'll be Innocent #2," said Clay, who walked over to the supply cabinet, removed a bottle of rubber cement, unscrewed the lid, and took a deep whiff. "Let's celebrate," he said, passing the bottle to Jimmy, who glanced at it and then passed it to Kay, who, to Jimmy's surprise, also took a deep whiff.

"It's so strange you did that," said Kay to Innocent #2. "I found a gas can on my porch at home, and I really like the smell of the gas," she said.

"We should partake of the gasoline fumes after school," said Innocent #2. "That'll be the start of Kay Sunday and the Innocents."

"Yes!" exclaimed Kay. "There's some stuff I'd like to get off my chest about my parents' church, and this could be perfect for that."

Jimmy nodded, trying his best to muster enthusiasm.

"When do we convene the first session?" asked Innocent #2.

"Let's meet after school next Monday," said Kay. "There are some preparations I'd like to make, so we are sure to do this right."

"Sounds good to me," said Innocent #2.

"Me too," said Jimmy, reluctantly.

10. High Octane

The following Monday afternoon, Kay Sunday, Jimmy Branhoover, and Innocent #2 convened on Kay's porch for the inaugural meeting of Kay Sunday and the Innocents.

Kay had gone to great lengths to prepare the porch in a manner consistent with the principles of her parents' religion. She had placed three wicker chairs facing each other in a triangular formation and the gas can in the exact center of the triangle. Forming a circle around the triangle of chairs was a wreath of potted roses. The three of them sat in their assigned chairs, and then Kay spoke:

"The nature of these sessions is likely to be political, involving unfortunate truths of human controversy. For this reason, I have surrounded us with roses and placed the healing fumes of gasoline within easy reach. Upon commencement of each session, I suggest that we pass the can around twice, and then testify fearlessly and

335

honestly about the matters that concern us. Innocent #1, I understand your reluctance to inhale the fumes, so there will be no judgment or reprisal should you decide to refrain. Do either of you have any questions?"

Neither boy spoke.

"Okay," said Kay. "For this inaugural session, I recommend that we sit in silence and consider the roses surrounding us, how they are just as real and worthwhile—and perhaps more humane— than any human controversy."

Kay Sunday and the Innocents sat in silence for five minutes, and then Kay adjourned the meeting.

Jimmy spent that evening in his bedroom, feeling uneasy about the new ritual of the high-octane sessions and anxious about the changing dynamic of his friendship with Kay Sunday.

PART III

11. On Earth as It Is in Heaven

The Sundays (legally, the Sutters), Mr. and Mrs., Kristov and Kristina, Kris and Kris, were spiritual consultants and amateur astronomers, selling God and telescopes. Their slogan was "On earth as it is in heaven." And, to illustrate their point, they would often say, "A hurricane is more than a hurricane. A galaxy is less than a galaxy."

The Sundays were poor. Then they were rich. Then they were poor again. But their daughter, Kay, was bright and happy, and she believed in her parents' brand of religion wholeheartedly, never a question asked. It was as if Kay were the living proof of the veracity of their vision. The Sundays believed in intelligent design and that there was consistency throughout the universe. "On earth as it is in heaven" and "what you loose on earth is loosed in heaven."

The Sundays took this literally and as their primary directive. Their one-room church on the outskirts of Pittsburgh (near an Amish community, which thought the Sundays were members of some kind of cult) had a wooden cross on the roof, but that was already there when the Sundays bought the property. Mr. Sunday had painted the church a spacey, deep purple. The outside west wall had a perfectly rendered solar system painted on it, while the outside east wall had the Milky Way galaxy on one half and a hurricane on the other half.

The roof was partially retractable because the Sundays' church was more an observatory than a house of worship. On clear nights the roof would open and the Sundays' prize possession, a NASA-quality telescope—which nearly plunged them into bankruptcy—would announce its presence.

The Sundays got many converts, but most were not religious zealots. Rather, they were fledgling astronomers who quickly wearied of the whole God angle.

A pattern was established: new converts in; then a month of preaching and stargazing would pass, with the converts becoming ever more annoyed by the preaching. Some would quit the congregation. Mr. Sunday would attempt to convince the remaining converts to stay, his faith never wavering. His appeal would usually go something like this: "If you read into Maya, ancient Egypt, and ancient Greek history and their knowledge of astronomy, you'll find that life on earth has a symbiotic relationship with the cosmos. For example, the birth of Jesus with the brightest star. What I'm trying to impart is that God is in the distant cosmos. This is true. Also true: You are the distant cosmos and God is in you. Hear the good news!"

The Sundays' spacey church would soon be empty, except for the telescope.

12. The Heavy Scent of Patchouli

Kay Sunday and the Innocents sniffed high-octane fumes and testified.

Kay: A thin man in a short-sleeved, button-up shirt was handing out Jesus brochures. I didn't see them, but I knew they were Jesus brochures because the heavy scent of patchouli preceded the man. That's the way things work, in case you didn't know. True knowledge comes naturally like that. The knowledge that comes from reason, have you ever noticed how it always winds up being disproved?

Innocent #2: Rings so true that Jesus must have struck the bell himself from the brightest star!

Kay: Testify, Innocent #2.

Innocent #2: I saw that same thin man the other day. I was on my skateboard and I was in a hurry. I had a determined expression on my face, which the man must have found inspiring. When

I rolled by him, he clapped his hands and said, "God bless you." So I said, "Shut up."

Kay: Good for you, Innocent #2. Now, I believe in Jesus as much as the next man, but that was just meddlesome.

13. The Life of a Hurricane

Mrs. Sunday wrote a sermon, which she recited at the beginning of every service. It went like this:

Summertime arrives in the tropics. The air warms over the water. The sea creatures also pick up the pace, diving down, darting up, and round and round the schools go the sharks. Water spouts swirl and the spiral forms. Category One has just been born.

Category Two, the adolescent storm, cocky, unstable, unsure of itself, drifts rebellious over the sea and soon becomes a Category Three.

Category Four: Ladies, fat and loud, gossip around the rotund table. Let them go. Don't be proud.

Category Five: The Wall of Sound.

Denouement: It's raining in Arkansas.

The congregation would just sit there, dumbfounded, thinking, There is a cross on the roof of this church, isn't there?

14. Rooster Man

Kay Sunday and the Innocents sniffed high-octane fumes and testified.

Kay: A rooster man came strutting down the street in a fancy suit. He cut across the park with folks in shorts and T-shirts sitting in the green grass with picnic baskets, and I thought, A man's got no business walking through a park in a fancy suit unless he's a preacher. And I've never met a rooster man who was a preacher, at least not a respectable preacher transmitting Jesus from the cosmos. A man strutting in a fancy suit must have something to hide.

Innocent #1: God bless you, Kay Sunday.

Innocent #2: I saw that same rooster man the other day up to the same no-good thing, and I thought, You come into this world and you don't know a thing, and then one day—or over a week, maybe—you figure out about death, and once you've done that, once you understand that the day will come when you no longer know the back of your own hand, you know there's just no good reason to be strutting around like a rooster in a fancy suit.

Kay: Innocent #2, you are transmitting!

Innocent #1: God bless you, Innocent #2.

15. Religious Education

Despite the secular philosophy of the Carden School, Jimmy was receiving a thorough religious education as a result of his close relationship with the Sundays, the high-octane sessions with Kay and Innocent #2, and through his mother, who was unwittingly exposing her son to the Book of Revelation.

When Jimmy turned eight, Chloe Branhoover, worn down by her life as a roughhouse prostitute and her sham of a marriage, discovered the televangelists, whom she watched in a room on the second floor across from Jimmy's room after her husband went to bed.

Chloe Red was usually able to muster a half hour of attention before falling asleep on the sofa.

The televangelists preached all night long until the morning news came on at six, which meant that the family member who received the message was young Jimmy, who drifted in and out of consciousness, hearing verses such as "I am the Alpha and the Omega, who is, and who was, and who is come, the Almighty" and "He will rule them with an iron scepter; he will dash them to pieces like pottery" and "Behold, I come like a thief! Blessed is he who stays awake and keeps his clothes with him, so that he may not go naked and be shamefully exposed." In summary, the message he received was this: Forces are aligning and the end is near, cryptic and terrifying.

The profound impact that such a message can have on an eight-year-old who recently had the characteristics of a pouncing kitten cannot be underestimated.

Over the span of a single month, Jimmy Branhoover the pouncing kitten became Jimmy Branhoover the brooding Christian with Book of Revelation doomsday scenarios running through his mind day and night.

Chloe Branhoover, whom Jimmy began to think of as Babylon the Great, panicked over the abrupt change in her son's personality. She brought him to a psychiatrist, who dubiously recommended that he also speak with a priest. The hope was that a religious man would be able to shed light on the meaning of the final book of the Bible. And that is exactly what the priest did, which made Jimmy even more of a true believer.

Suddenly Mrs. Branhoover missed her first son. She could comprehend Bernrd Red promoting the sensation of being hit in the head with a rock. She was utterly perplexed by her second son, the eight-year-old doomsday preacher.

16. Yin/Yang on a Wigwam

Kay Sunday and the Innocents sniffed high-octane fumes and testified.

Kay: A heretic wearing a gold watch and stinking of patchouli oil bought an acre across the road from my parents' church. I saw the man sitting on a brand-new tree stump, a hot chainsaw resting on his lap and a newly fallen pine lying in the green on his left, its spirit hovering in the dust. And do you know what that man was doing?

Innocent #1: Testify, Kay Sunday.

Kay: He was wiggling his leg, that's what he was doing.

Innocent #1: Only a pervert wiggles his leg.

Innocent #2: I saw that leg-wiggling pervert the other day. I saw him on his acre painting a yin/yang symbol on a wigwam.

Innocent #1: Only a heretic would paint a yin/yang on a wigwam.

Kay: What a charlatan that man is! The Reverend Patchouli Goldwatch! That's what his name is. I don't care what he says otherwise.

17. Fancy Clothes and Suffocating Perfume

Kay Sunday and the Innocents sniffed high-octane fumes and testified.

Kay: The overwhelming scent of patchouli blew with the breeze across the road and invaded our church, so I went to have a chat with the Reverend Patchouli Goldwatch.

Innocent #1: Set him straight, Kay Sunday!

Kay: When I looked him in the eye, I recognized him as the meddlesome thin man handing out Jesus brochures and interfering with Innocent #2's skateboard, and also as the rooster man in a fancy suit strutting across the park, ruining picnics. I looked him in the eye, and he said, "My name is Vander Stevenson. I am a man of God."

Innocent #2: The first words out of the man's mouth are a lie!

Kay: That's the truth, Innocent #2. He's all fancy clothes and suffocating perfume, but he's not a man of God.

Innocent #2: I'll bet he was wiggling his leg while he was looking you in the eye and lying.

Kay: I should have known to look, but I didn't. That would've given him away for sure.

18. The Rows of Destitute Men

When H. James Branhoover was alone in his room reading the Book of Revelation, his ideas were big and his thoughts profound. He grew fortified in his biblical solitude. He constructed entire world-changing sermons in his head with words so powerful that he feared for the lives of those who might hear them, thrust from the comfort (or discomfort) of their daily existences and into prophecy-fulfilling action.

He vowed late at night that the next morning he would rise up in the light and save a man or two out in the street.

He would walk down to the Salvation Army thrift store, where the men stood fidgeting in filthy rows, and his eyes would fall upon them with a mixture of compassion, pity, and condescension. His mind and heart would swell with anxious fury as he searched for the words that seemed so true and large in the safety of his bedroom, but now seemed shamefully small against the intimidating faces of the day.

H. James Branhoover would walk past the rows of destitute men in silence and wind up over at Kay Sunday's, where, as Innocent #1, he would continue to be silent except when he praised Kay and Innocent #2 for their high-octane outbursts—which he knew were not as important as his nocturnes—and all the attendant humiliation of knowing that he was bringing his Kay and Innocent #2 together.

19. How Can You Fail to Acknowledge the Miracle?

Every day for a week, Jimmy walked down the hill to the Salvation Army thrift store, where he passed by the rows of destitute men. He felt on the verge of saying something profound to them, but he intuitively understood the more days that passed, the less likely he would be to say anything at all.

After the third time Jimmy came into their realm, the men began to talk to one another about the boy who carried the burgundy Bible.

The honest man, whose only vices were Rolling Rock and Tanqueray, thought Jimmy was some sort of delirium tremens angel and hoped he wouldn't ever speak and shatter the illusion.

The quiet man with the permanent scowl— the kind of man who shuns his mother because she brought him into the world—thought Jimmy was put there by the FBI as bait, though he would never get into specifics. The quiet man muttered "Damien Freakshow" whenever Jimmy passed by.

And then there was the self-proclaimed "inveterate grifter," whom the quiet man, under his breath, called the "inveterate incompetent." This man thought Jimmy smelled of wealthy parents and began to plot a way to get him to bring money along with his Bible.

* * * * *

So late at night the young H. James Branhoover studied the Book of Revelation and rehearsed his sermons for the rows of destitute men down at the Salvation Army thrift store.

After several trips down the hill, Jimmy had completely lost his nerve and had begun to use the time to consider other, less risky, forms of service to God and mankind.

Nevertheless, he walked again among the intimidating faces, but this time the quiet man with the permanent scowl nudged Jimmy hard enough to knock the Bible out of his grasp and onto the concrete. As Jimmy bent down to pick it up, the quiet man blurted out "Damien Freakshow!"

The inveterate grifter's tongue darted in and out of his tight lips and he wrung his hands.

The honest man cringed and backed up against the wall.

Meanwhile, the quiet man again knocked the Bible out of Jimmy's grasp, but this time Jimmy stared the man down and shouted, "How can you fail to acknowledge the miracle?" The quiet man withered as if he had been doused in holy water, and the honest man came off the wall laughing and applauding his angel.

20. Babylon the Great

The Holy Spirit had moved H. James Branhoover. There was no other plausible explanation. He pored over all of his sermons and his notes when he returned home, and nowhere did he find that preemptive strike of a question: "How can you fail to acknowledge the miracle?" He relived the moment over and over in his bedroom—evil had withered and good had blossomed because he was there and had spoken the truth: "How can you fail to acknowledge the miracle?"

Just then his mother burst into his room, a john in tow. "Jimmy, this is Clarence," she said. "Clarence owes us money, so he's going to take us in your father's car to Target to buy us some things."

Neither of the two young men spoke as H. Charles Branhoover's BMW wound its way down the hill and out into the suburbs to Target, where the irritated Chloe Red yanked a shopping cart from the back of the shopping cart train and thrust it in the direction of Clarence the john, who pushed the cart up and down the aisles while Chloe tossed items into the cart with one hand and crushed her son's bicep with the other hand.

Clarence couldn't help but notice Jimmy wincing in pain. "Hey, no need to take this out on the boy," he said. "It's not his fault I was short. I could've sworn I had another hundred in my wallet."

"You probably did, Clarence," said Jimmy. "My mom's a hooker, you know. She probably rifled through your pants and took it when you weren't paying attention."

Chloe Red smacked her son across the face and dragged him out of the store, leaving Clarence with the cart and wondering about his money.

* * * * *

The next morning, Chloe Branhoover wasted no time in removing Jimmy from the Carden School. She wanted to punish him twofold: by separating him from Kay Sunday and by homeschooling him in the manner of her first son, Bernard.

PART IV

21. Chloe Abadie Reynaud

Unlike most orphans, Chloe Abadie Reynaud was a noisy, active child, easy to laugh and to make others laugh. She was extroverted and rough. Girls were intimidated by her energy and her fearlessness around bugs and animals, and later around older boys and men.

And, like most forces of nature, Chloe Abadie Reynaud produced a wide swath of destruction. She seemed a victim of her own energy, to wit:

Chloe was fond of playing "smear the queer" with the boys during recess, a brutal and exhilarating kind of football involving a dozen or so boys (and Chloe), in which the object was to give the ball to one boy and for this boy to run for his life as the other boys tried to tackle him.

Smear the queer was a difficult game for the teachers to comprehend, and they often broke it up thinking a fight had started.

But for the boys in Chloe's age group, running and hitting and being hit was a thrilling and mandatory antidote to stultifying school.

One morning, shortly after her tenth birthday, Chloe woke with stomach cramps. All she could think about was 10:30 recess, when she could take out her suffering on the boys on the field.

The 10:30 bell rang and Chloe ran to the ball bin, grabbed the football and dashed out onto the grass, where she taunted the boys, whom she somehow knew would never have to suffer the way she was suffering now.

The boys charged onto the playground, but Chloe, rather than elude them, picked the biggest boy and ran directly at him. The ensuing collision was life-altering for both children.

Chloe dropped as if she had collided with a gorilla. Worse, she began to sob as the menstrual blood trickled down her thighs.

The biggest boy initially thought Chloe had been mortally wounded and began waving at the teachers for help. Chloe leapt to her feet and slammed the biggest boy's chest. "Stop it!" she yelled.

The bell rang. As the children dispersed, murmurs of "Chloe Blood" could be heard on the playground and in the halls.

22. From Chloe Blood to Chloe Red

The evolution from Chloe Blood to Chloe Red was a predictable one. By the time grade school came to an end, Chloe had no friends, but that didn't diminish her noise or energy, which she redirected toward the more challenging demographic of older boys and men.

Her grades, which were never spectacular in grade school, began to suffer all the more when, at the age of fourteen, she unhesitatingly agreed to enter into an agreement with an enterprising high school boy whereby Chloe would let the boy touch

her in increasingly dangerous places in exchange
for increasing sums of money.

The arrangement proved so successful for
Chloe that she mysteriously began to attract older
and older, richer and richer clients, the oldest and
richest of whom, fifty-one-year-old H. Charles
Branhoover, touched Chloe Red in the most
dangerous of places, so dangerous, in fact, that
the sum of money required in compensation set
up Chloe and her offspring for life.

23. A Satisfied Man

From the age of three, H. Charles Branhoover
was a satisfied man. Never a child. Never given to
boyish whims. Shrewd. Self-centered. Never too
short. Never too tall. Always stronger than
average. An aggressive dog. A bloodhound.
Always in the lead without the slightest pity or

compunction for the weak creatures of the world, including his wife and two sons, whom he took care of (financed and kept hidden) strictly out of utilitarian self-interest.

He really couldn't be bothered with what he considered to be the by-product of his lust, which was prodigious.

H. Charles Branhoover carried himself with dignity, had aristocratic mores, and because he was utterly amoral, had a nose for money like a bloodhound has a nose for fox. H. Charles Branhoover was an ideal American.

It wasn't until he attained seventy years, when his mind and body finally weakened, that he began to exhibit that most un-American of character traits—self-reflection.

This new self-reflection was the direct and proximate cause of his new feebleness and his mild shame over the totality of his life.

He began to notice churches, for example. He began to visit cemeteries.

He began to wonder about the whereabouts of his first son, Bernard, or perhaps more accurately, whether Bernard was real or a figment of his fledgling imagination.

24. Moneybags and Milady

H. Charles Branhoover and his wife raised Jimmy like a prince, but while a princely upbringing is filled with physical comfort and ease, and the occasional anonymous servant, the mental aspect is less certain.

Outside of his relationship with Kay Sunday, Jimmy had little in the way of human companionship. When he wasn't at school, Jimmy was lonely and frightened, spending most of his home life trying to stay out of the way of his parents.

With his father, this really wasn't so difficult. Father and son spent most of their days sequestered in their rooms, which were on different floors of the mansion, and when the two did cross each other's paths, Mr. Branhoover looked at Jimmy like he was someone he should know but couldn't place the name with the face.

Jimmy's mother was more of a challenge.

Mr. Branhoover was essentially a wraith haunting the halls of the mansion, which was less than satisfying for Mrs. Branhoover, who continued to entertain gentleman visitors. Jimmy was forced to vie for his mother's attention with the dregs of humanity, white-collar types with high incomes and low scruples.

Jimmy was frustrated by his mother's distance and her darting eyes. He despised his mother's clientele, who had three reactions to his presence: overfriendly, outright dismissive, or oddly mortified by him, as if he were some sort of fatal microbe. Jimmy despised them, but he also took their behavior to heart and, on occasion, unintentionally disrespected himself by showing them his good report cards and school artwork. To their credit, most of these men were one-time customers, their desperate horniness trumped by shameful compassion for the little boy.

Worse for Jimmy than his encounters with his mother's guests, however, were his encounters with his parents on those rare occasions when the three of them were together in the same room. The antipathy mother and father had for each other was palpable. Jimmy noticed that they rarely called each other by their real names, but by made-up names that he could tell they disliked. Mr. Branhoover, when perturbed, called Mrs. Branhoover "Milady," and Mrs. Branhoover, with an utter lack of art, called her husband "Moneybags." When the perturbation was particularly acute, Mr. Branhoover would say, "Once a whore, always a whore," to which Mrs. Branhoover would respond, "Look who's talking."

PART V

25. The Devil Himself

Kay Sunday and the Innocents sniffed high-octane fumes and testified.

Kay: Vander Stevenson, aka meddlesome thin man, aka death-dissing, leg-wiggling, picnic-ruining, yin/yang-painting, land-grabbing, church-stealing rooster man, aka the Reverend Patchouli Goldwatch, needs to be straightened out.

Innocent #1: Testify, Kay Sunday.

Kay: The godless reverend has been attending my parents' services on the sly. He's been mocking our faith right inside the doors of our church. He snickered at my mom's sermon on the topic of hurricanes. The man wants nothing less than our parishioners, our land, our church, and our telescope.

Innocent #2: Patchouli Goldwatch is the Devil himself!

Kay: Amen, Innocent #2. [Kay embraces Innocent #2. Innocent #1 frowns.]

Kay: Innocent #1, are you okay? This is good news. We've identified the Devil in our midst.

Innocent #1: Bless you, Kay Sunday. Let's bring the Devil down.

Kay looked at the gas can, wondering at the efficacy of its contents.

26. Three New Friends

Devastated by Kay's enthusiastic embrace of Innocent #2, H. James Branhoover did not go home that night.

Instead, he walked down to the Salvation Army thrift store in search of his three new friends.

He walked recklessly along the filthy row, not quite able to make out the faces in the dark.

"Hey, Damien Freakshow, where's your Bible?" asked the quiet man, breaking the silence.

Jimmy shrugged and replied, "I must have left it next to the gas can."

"You weren't going to burn it, were you, Angel?" asked the honest man.

"I didn't have a lighter," replied Jimmy.

The inveterate grifter giggled through his tight lips and darting tongue.

"How can you fail to acknowledge the miracle?" said the quiet man.

Jimmy laughed and joined them. The honest man carefully wrapped his angel with a wool blanket.

* * * * *

Several hours passed in silence and sound, in wakefulness and unconsciousness, under the sun and the moon, for the new young man and his three new friends.

For the first time in his eleven years, H. James Branhoover had mentally accepted an adverse truth: Kay Sunday didn't love him, even though she knew he loved her.

He sat with his three friends, similarly unloved, and felt simultaneously burgeoning camaraderie and creeping bitterness.

This was different from his parents not loving him. He was okay with that because he didn't really care for them either. There was, in fact, a certain security in their mutual lack of affection.

But this was different. Jimmy accepted that Kay didn't love him, but he didn't accept that he couldn't change her mind.

The sermons in H. James Branhoover's notebook would now have to share space with strategies for winning back Kay Sunday.

27. Another Adverse Truth

H. James Branhoover didn't arrive home until late the next afternoon, which meant he had missed school, which meant his mother had actually noticed his absence, since she was his new teacher.

It would be unfair, however, to say that Chloe Red didn't love her boy. She did. And she was determined to demonstrate her love when she saw him stumble through the front door, the telltale scent of "the night before" in his clothes.

"Jimmy," said Chloe Branhoover to her second son as he began the dazed ascent to his bedroom. He twitched and, without turning, continued climbing.

"Haley James Branhoover!" she yelled. "Get back down here this instant."

For a brief moment, Jimmy wondered if he had wandered into the wrong house, or his house but in an alternate universe.

His mother had never used his full name before, and Jimmy thought it odd that he sort of liked hearing it said this way. He'd heard other parents (including Kay's parents) call their children by their whole names when he was at the Carden School, but never his own mother. Maybe she's finally grown up, he thought, then shook his head, comprehending the strangeness of such a thought for an eleven-year-old boy to have of his mother.

Jimmy turned and descended the stairs. His mother, pleased and somewhat surprised by her boy's obedience, softened her tone.

"James, I'm not going to interrogate you about where you were all last night," she said.

"Okay," said Jimmy.

"I'm actually very proud of you for being able to handle yourself out there. I think this means you're all grown up," she said.

Jimmy stood there in silence, marveling at the strangeness of the conversation.

"Young man," she continued, "I have something to tell you that I didn't think you'd be ready to hear until you were mature enough."

Chloe Branhoover led her son from the foyer to the living room, where they sat down near the hearth.

"Do you remember the Christmas when you were five years old and we sat right here and you were opening presents, and one of the presents said 'To: Bernard, From: Santa.' "

"Yes," said Jimmy.

"And you thought Santa had made a mistake," said Chloe.

"Yes," said Jimmy, semi-laughing.

"It wasn't exactly a mistake, James," she said. "Bernard is a real boy. He is your older brother."

Jimmy was silent.

"You have an older brother, James. His name is Bernard. He is thirty-one years old now. He left for Las Vegas when he was eighteen, before you were born," she said.

"Way before I was born," said Jimmy, stoically.

"I'm sorry, James, I should have told you then, when you were five. And I shouldn't have taken you away from your friends at school. I'll take you back tomorrow and reenroll you," said Mrs. Branhoover.

"That's okay, Mom," said Jimmy. "I don't want to go back there anyway."

28. A Case of Mistaken Identity

H. Charles Branhoover experienced a curious (and perhaps ironic) side effect to his septuagenarian dementia: he began to notice and take an interest in things other than himself. He wandered the halls and rooms of his home during all hours of the days and nights, occasionally encountering his wife ("Hello, Milady," he would say) and his second son, whom he mistook for his first son.

"Bernard," he said to Jimmy, "we need to talk about your behavior. You can't be throwing rocks with angry letters attached through my office window. Now, I love you, son, so I'm not going to punish you. Instead I'm going to give you an opportunity. What do you know about Las Vegas?"

As luck would have it, Chloe's confession to Jimmy about his older brother had occurred the previous day, so Jimmy understood immediately that his elderly father thought he was speaking to Jimmy's mysterious older brother and didn't actually intend to send the eleven-year-old away to Las Vegas.

"You've mistaken me for Bernard," said Jimmy. "He doesn't live here anymore. I'm James, your second son."

H. Charles Branhoover examined the features of his second son's face for what seemed like an eternity to Jimmy. And then, finally convinced of the veracity of the boy's assertion, H. Charles Branhoover said, "And so you are. Delighted to meet you, James."

Father and son shook hands and went their separate ways.

29. My Name Is Vander Stevenson. I Am a Man of God.

As was customary and right, and as always, Mrs. Sunday arrived at the pulpit in her family's church and opened the service with her sermon, "The Life of a Hurricane."

Then Mr. Sunday joined his wife and proclaimed, "God is in the distant cosmos. This is true. Also true: You are the distant cosmos and God is in you. Hear the good news!"

The congregation might have thought good news was preceded by the scent of patchouli, because just as Mr. Sunday had uttered the words "good news," the man Kay Sunday had dubbed the Reverend Patchouli Goldwatch stood up and announced: "My name is Vander Stevenson. I am a man of God." Then he fired a precision strike of theological missiles at the Sundays, who simply lacked the moxie to respond in kind.

The man of God concluded by offering the congregation an alternative to what he called "far-out astrology."

"My church is literally across the road," he said, "and I promise my services will be light-years closer to your hearts and souls than the Sundays' well-intentioned but misguided lunacy."

Many in the congregation began to chuckle under their breaths. The Reverend Patchouli Goldwatch wiggled his leg when he heard their laughter.

30. Bon Voyage

Kay Sunday and the Innocents sniffed high-octane fumes and testified.

Kay: You know what today is?

Innocent #2: Tuesday?

Kay: That's right. Which means it was just two days ago when the Devil himself, the Reverend Patchouli Goldwatch, mustered enough nerve in his cowardly thin body to stand up in my parents' church and mock our faith.

Innocent #2: He's going straight to Hell!

Kay: Which means it was just yesterday when my parents sat me down on this very porch and informed me that they have been planning a mission to Cambodia and that they are going to finance it by selling our church and telescope. Can you guess who the buyer is?

Innocent #2: No!?

Kay: Yes. Vander Stevenson. Man of God. The Devil himself.

Innocent #2: We can't let this happen.

Kay: It's too late. The Sundays are moving to Cambodia.

Innocent #2: What about your house?

Kay: We rent it.

Innocent #2: How could they sell out so easily?

Kay: You know my parents. They see everything as a sign. Plus, they said Goldwatch made a generous offer.

Innocent #2: I'm not surprised. Innocent #1, don't you have anything to say about this?

Innocent #1: Bon voyage, Kay.

[Innocent #2 lunges at Innocent #1. The two boys fight feebly.]

Kay: Stop it, right now! Jimmy, go home. We don't want you here anymore.

Innocent #2: Yeah, get the fuck out of here.

Innocent #1: I've got better places to be anyway.

Jimmy picked up the gas can and hurled it off the porch, drenching the Sundays' lawn. He gave

Innocent #2 a final shove and walked off in the direction of the rows of destitute men.

31. Street Reflection

The Salvation Army thrift store was eight miles from the Sundays' front porch. This meant Jimmy had several hours of street reflection, which differs from the various forms of sedentary reflection in the same way that a stream differs from a pond.

Pond reflection tends toward the serene, with placid resolutions that grow stagnant and mossy if not acted upon. Street reflection leads to immediate, vigorous action, the consequences of which often become corrosive or destructive.

For eight miles Jimmy walked the streets of Pittsburgh, reflecting on the events of his recent past.

Those whom he had trusted, or perhaps more accurately, those whom he had relied upon in the years closest to his birth—his mom, his dad, and Kay—had each let him down in a uniquely monumental way.

He tried hard to understand how his mom could withhold from him the fact of his older brother for the first eleven years of his life. He considered the physical characteristics of every thirtyish male who passed by and wondered if his brother might be dead. This thought made him squirm with helplessness.

Then he considered the haplessness of his father when he mistook Jimmy for his possibly deceased older brother. His father: a spiritual wastrel festering in his own money and lust, in his trivial American success, for seventy years. That Jimmy was a product of these artificial ingredients was the second-most demoralizing aspect of his first eleven years.

Most demoralizing was the deterioration of his friendship with Kay Sunday. For all her otherworldly charm, Kay was maddeningly mercurial. Jimmy imagined her favorite shot in billiards would be the break, the colorful spheres scattering and bumping off the cushions and each other and occasionally dropping into the pockets by chance. This was the only plausible explanation for Kay's affection for Innocent #2. The colorful sphere that was Kay had randomly bumped around the pool table of Pittsburgh and dropped into a side pocket with the colorful sphere of Innocent #2.

For eight miles H. James Branhoover walked the streets of Pittsburgh reflecting on his parents, his brother, and Kay.

The strain on his mind produced an unusual thought: that the Salvation Army thrift store was more his home and his homeless acquaintances more his friends than were his actual home and so-called friends.

In the moving stream of his street reflection, Jimmy decided that he would spend an entire week with his three new friends, standing alongside the rows of destitute men and sorting out his religion in his notebook.

32. The Rising Sun

Jimmy arrived with the rising sun at the Salvation Army thrift store. He walked eagerly along the filthy row like a boy at an airport searching the faces for his long-lost brothers.

The men were mostly gathered in clusters, so it was difficult to distinguish one face from another. Then he noticed isolated at the far end of the row the wool blanket the honest man had given him on his previous visit. Next to the wool blanket lay the bruised, scraped, and bloodied body of the honest man and the green shards of Tanqueray and Rolling Rock bottles, the myriad facets of which glittered in the bright morning light.

Despite all the awful news that had recently befallen him, Jimmy reacted with the tranquility and patience of a triage nurse in coming to the aid of his friend. He carefully removed his notebook from his coat pocket and used it to sweep away the shards of glass.

Next, because he didn't know the honest man's name, he identified himself by the name the honest man had given him.

"Sir, it's Angel. Are you okay? I'm here to help you," said Jimmy.

"Angel? Is it really you?" asked the honest man, unable to open his eyes.

"Yes," said Jimmy. "Who did this to you? What happened?"

"I can't stop drinking," said the honest man. "Could you sit with me until this passes?"

"That's why I'm here," said Jimmy.

Jimmy sat down next to the honest man and rested his back against the thrift store wall. He opened his notebook, clicked open the ballpoint pen that served as a bookmark, jotted down a few lines, and promptly fell asleep.

By the time Jimmy woke, the sun was in the western sky. His face and lips were sunburned, and his sinuses ached from hours of incessant snoring.

The honest man was also awake now, sitting next to Jimmy like a bloodied watchdog. He had managed to remain conscious despite his injuries and hangover in order to watch over the sleeping Jimmy, who was also being watched by the inveterate grifter from one of the clusters of loitering men.

It took the inveterate grifter until dusk to concoct a scheme for separating Jimmy from his money. He approached the honest man and his angel, and addressed the honest man first.

"Rough night, eh?" said the inveterate grifter. "I'll withhold the embarrassing details."

"Unless I committed a crime, you know I'd prefer to be spared further humiliation," the honest man replied.

"You didn't do anything nefarious that I saw. Well, except what you did to yourself. It's a shame; it truly is. I know you're a good man. And I've already forgotten what you called me," said the inveterate grifter.

"Oh, dear," said the honest man. "You know I didn't mean it, whatever it was."

"Now that raises the age-old question going all the way back to Bible times: Do we believe the drunk in his sober remorse, or do we believe the drunk when he's drunk?"

The honest man grimaced and slumped against the thrift store wall.

The inveterate grifter then turned his attention toward Jimmy.

"What does the Bible have to say about drinking and drunks, young man?" he asked. "Have you written anything down in that notebook of yours that might be of use? Is there a miracle we have failed to acknowledge?"

Jimmy thought for a moment. Then he leafed through his notebook and read aloud: "Proverbs

23:20-21. 'Do not join those who drink too much wine or gorge themselves on meat, for drunkards and gluttons become poor, and drowsiness clothes them in rags.' And Proverbs 23:31-35. 'Do not gaze at wine when it is red, when it sparkles in the cup, when it goes down smoothly! In the end it bites like a snake and poisons like a viper. Your eyes will see strange sights and your mind imagine confusing things. You will be like one sleeping on the high seas, lying on top of the rigging. "They hit me," you will say, "but I'm not hurt! They beat me, but I don't feel it! When will I wake up so I can find another drink?" ' "

The honest man nodded and groaned.

"Oh, those Proverbs are as wise as they are pretty to hear," said the inveterate grifter. "And what does the Bible have to say about charity?"

While Jimmy scanned his mind for chapter and verse, the quiet man emerged from a cluster of men and joined Jimmy and the other two.

"What has the inveterate incompetent been saying to you, Freakshow?" asked the quiet man.

393

"I've been keeping an eye on him since he swooped down on you."

"He just asked me what the Bible says about charity," said Jimmy.

The quiet man made a sound like an air brake on a truck.

"No he didn't, Freakshow," said the quiet man. "What he asked you over many convoluted words and sentences was 'Can I have your money?' "

The honest man managed to smile through his battered face.

"Maybe he's starving but too proud to just come out and say it," said Jimmy, who reached into his pocket, pulled out five 20-dollar bills, and handed one of them to the inveterate grifter.

"Put those away, Freakshow," whispered the quiet man.

"He's right, Angel," said the honest man. "You mustn't do that around here."

But H. James Branhoover wasn't done handing out twenties. He handed one to the quiet man, who accepted it in spite of himself, and he slipped two in the honest man's shirt pocket, which left Jimmy with one twenty-dollar bill, which meant he wouldn't be able to stay for a week.

"I'll need this one for my ride home," said Jimmy, putting the money back into his pocket, rising from the Salvation Army thrift store wall, and walking off in search of a cab, utterly unaware of the force with which he had insulted these men.

33. Heavy Drapes

Chloe Branhoover had pulled back the heavy drapes from the living room window and watched the street all through the night before, when her son had walked eight miles along the streets of Pittsburgh.

When he didn't arrive home, she went upstairs and tried to find comfort in the televangelists, which meant she wanted to fall asleep.

But because the words of the televangelists are specifically fashioned to infiltrate the hearts of the vulnerable, Chloe Branhoover, like her son when he listened from his bedroom, remained rapt until morning.

She finally succumbed to sleep when the *Today* show came on and was still unconscious when Jimmy arrived home. She was dreaming about smear the queer when the sound of Jimmy's bedroom door clicking shut roused her. She spent several minutes thinking about how she would confront her son, but instead of entering his bedroom, she went downstairs and climbed into bed with her husband, who (unknown to her) had passed away about the time when Jimmy was giving away his father's money to the three homeless men.

34. Trust Fund Baby

Mrs. Chloe Branhoover stretched her arm across her husband's cold chest under the covers. Several minutes passed before she understood that he was gone.

First she thought about the heavy drapes. Then she thought about her son. Then, in the way that only a mature adult can do, she banished her own pain and went upstairs to tell her boy of this latest adverse truth.

Jimmy was writing in his notebook when his mother entered his bedroom. Once again she had that calm, kind, and loving expression that Jimmy was coming to dread as the inevitable harbinger of terrible news.

Chloe sat at the foot of her son's bed.

"What are you writing about?" she asked.

"I'm writing a letter to Kay," he said.

"Oh," she exclaimed, with both genuine and pleasant surprise that she wouldn't be forced to feign interest in his latest religious zealotry.

"Kay's a special girl," said Chloe, "but I wouldn't get too close to her. She's fickle."

Jimmy, who had rarely done so before, even as an infant, began to sob. His mother, who had rarely done so before, embraced him with genuine vigor, as if she had just been told for the first time that this boy was her son.

Jimmy explained to her about the high-octane sessions on Kay's porch and how Kay had changed since the better days of Mrs. Germany and the Carden School. All Mrs. Branhoover could do was nod with compassion and comprehension, which was all Jimmy needed to fortify himself for the latest bad news he knew his mother was preparing to impart to him.

"What happened, Mom?" asked Jimmy.

"I'm just going to tell you everything, okay?" said Chloe.

Jimmy nodded.

"Your father is dead, Jimmy. He passed last night in his sleep."

Jimmy nodded again.

"We are a wealthy family," she said.

Jimmy rolled his eyes. "I know that, Mom. I'm not two," he said warmly.

"Well, what I mean to convey is that your father was frugal with our money, but that's going to change now, Jimmy."

"Okay," he said.

"He set up a trust for you that I now have control over until you turn eighteen. I want you to take responsibility for your own decisions, so whenever you need money, just let me know and I'll get it for you, no questions asked," she said.

"Really? How much money is in the trust?"

"I'm not sure of the exact amount, but it's in the neighborhood of ten million dollars," Chloe said.

H. James Branhoover, the Branhoovers' second son, let out a staccato laugh of shocked disbelief.

"Ten million?" he repeated.

Chloe Branhoover laughed brightly. "You're a millionaire," she said.

"Any more bad news?" asked Jimmy.

"There is one more thing," she said. "Kristina Sunday called yesterday. She said that she and her husband sold their church to a more persuasive man of God."

"You mean the Devil?" said Jimmy, restraining a grin.

Mrs. Branhoover did her best to maintain a neutral expression.

"She said the Sundays are moving to Cambodia."

Jimmy shrugged with unconvincing nonchalance.

"Anything else?"

PART VI

35. Bright Red Swastika

Vander Stevenson, aka the Reverend Patchouli Goldwatch, took immediate steps to obliterate the eccentric art on the Sundays' former church.

Initially remaining true to his promise of offering an alternative to the Sundays' "far-out astrology," Stevenson painted the exterior of the structure Southern Baptist white, and he put the telescope in storage.

Attendance began to drop almost immediately. The congregation was having a difficult time reconciling Southern Baptist white with the man who painted a yin/yang symbol on a wigwam.

Goldwatch understood that he needed to divert the negative attention away from him and put it back on the Sundays, as he had done so successfully before.

He thought about all the ways he could defame the Sundays. There were so many. Then he said, "Kristov, Kristina, Kay. KKK."

He went to his new church late on Saturday evening and worked all through the night so that come Sunday morning the congregation would arrive to see a bright red swastika painted on the side of the building.

36. Proper Swastika

For the first time in the history of the church, there was an overflow line (stretching several yards out the door) to attend a Sunday service. Goldwatch remained inside until he could hear the line begin to hum like a mob. Then he rose in the pulpit and called for the entire congregation to gather outside.

Standing in front of his new creation, Goldwatch explained the long history and true spiritual significance of the swastika prior to the Nazis' misappropriation of it.

He explained how the swastika symbolizes good luck, protection, circular movement and rebirth, and how his swastika's arms faced left and not right like the Nazis'.

Then he turned his attention to the Sundays. He announced with authority the initials of their names—KKK—and how their quirky brand of religion, seemingly benign, was actually deliberately designed to distract true Christians from the teachings and message of Christ.

Half of the congregation—the credulous half—applauded the Reverend and began to move toward the entrance. The other half of the congregation—the skeptics and the amateur astronomers—grumbled and began to disperse, including Innocent #2, who shouted to anyone with ears within a square mile of the church: "Charlatan!"

405

37. Reconciliation of the Innocents

In the early days of the high-octane sessions on Kay Sunday's porch, Jimmy and Innocent #2 had exchanged phone numbers under the pretense of becoming friends and the tacit understanding—which was also plain to Kay, though the boys didn't acknowledge it—that neither boy had any intention whatsoever of calling the other.

All three children were students at the Carden School, with the established dynamic of Kay and Jimmy as best friends and Innocent #2 as a willing sidekick, though shorter and not as handsome as Jimmy, who had the good fortune of inheriting his father's looks.

Jimmy was certainly surprised when Innocent #2 called him to apologize for putting him on the spot at Kay Sunday's, as well as to confide in him about his feelings for her and about Goldwatch defaming the Sundays with his swastika stunt.

Jimmy was equally surprised by his own reaction to the call. He couldn't abide the words coming out of his mouth:

"Apology accepted," he said, regarding their confrontation on Kay's porch.

"Let's come up with a plan to get Goldwatch out of the Sundays' church," he said, shocked to hear himself suggest that they work together.

But worst of all: "Kay has feelings for you, too. I think you would make a good couple."

Mercifully, Jimmy eventually found the courage to hang up, but not before he invited Innocent #2 over to discuss the Goldwatch situation.

After he hung up, he opened his notebook to a blank page and stared at it until his shame had subsided enough for him to reflect on what motivated him to say such deplorable things.

Ultimately, he concluded that his responses were not cowardly but perfectly brave, and probably the surest way to win Kay back. Remaining magnanimous toward Innocent #2 clearly seemed to be Jimmy's best option under the circumstances. He would prove to Kay once and for all that he was not jealous of Innocent #2 and was, in fact, more desirable than his adversary. Why shouldn't he be magnanimous? Compared to Innocent #2, he was smarter, taller, better-looking, had known Kay longer and was her best friend, and would take the initiative in getting the Sundays' church back from Goldwatch.

He was also much wealthier than Innocent #2, though he didn't include this item in his mental list.

38. No Octane

Innocent #1 and Innocent #2, sans Kay Sunday, met on the Sundays' former porch to plot the overthrow of Vander Stevenson, aka the Reverend Patchouli Goldwatch.

Jimmy: I saw the swastika on the Sundays' church. I can't believe there wasn't a riot.

Innocent #2: He attracted a crowd and then he blamed the swastika on the Sundays' first names. He connected them with the Ku Klux Klan and said that his "correct" swastika would purify the building.

Jimmy: And the people believed him?

Innocent #2: It didn't matter. Don't you see? The people weren't thinking about Goldwatch anymore. They were thinking about the Sundays and the KKK.

Jimmy: Hey, man, I get it. Don't talk to me like that.

Innocent #2: Like what?

Jimmy: Look, you little punk, I'm Kay's best friend. I'm the one who's going to get their church back for them. Not you.

Innocent #2: You don't get it. Kay doesn't like you the way she likes me, even if you do buy her church back from Goldwatch.

Jimmy: What do you mean, "buy" it?

Innocent #2: I'm sorry, Jimmy, I think you mean well, but you're deluded. You're totally sheltered and your parents are completely messed up. Kay and I feel sorry for you. I mean, you don't even go to school anymore.

Jimmy: You have no idea who I am, where I've been, what I've done, or who I've helped. You're just the short little sidekick who sniffs gasoline fumes with her and says something funny every now and then. That's the only reason Kay likes you. There's no threat of anything real, and that appeals to her because she's shallow.

Innocent #2: Then why do you like her so much?

Jimmy either had no answer to this question or didn't have the energy to explain it. He picked up his pen and notebook, and walked off the porch in the direction of the rows of destitute men.

39. Ten Thousand Dollars

H. James Branhoover was barely off the Sundays' former property when he determined there was no way he was going to suffer another eight-mile trudge through the less desirable neighborhoods of Pittsburgh. He found a convenience store and phoned his mother.

"I need ten thousand dollars to take down to skid row," he said.

"Okay, James," she said, already regretting her promise to him. "I'll phone the bank now."

"Thanks, Mom," said Jimmy, and he hung up the phone.

Jimmy took a cab to the bank, which presented only one obstacle to his attainment of ten thousand dollars: another quick call to his mother so that she could identify her son's voice. And that was that. The teller counted out ninety 100 dollar bills and fifty 20s, zipped them up neatly in a relatively easy-to-carry pouch, and handed it to the twelve-year-old boy across the counter.

Jimmy felt nauseated when he climbed back into the cab and headed off to see his three friends at the Salvation Army thrift store.

In the backseat of the cab, he sat holding his pouch of money and ruminating on his latest confrontation with Innocent #2.

He couldn't understand why he couldn't control his temper and remain magnanimous, even under the circumstances.

He couldn't understand why he didn't sock the little punk in the nose.

"Kay and I feel sorry for you." What a joke. They're the ones who sniff gasoline fumes, not me, he thought.

Mercifully, this inner debate concluded when the cab pulled up at the Salvation Army thrift store and Jimmy saw the honest man waiting for him with clear eyes and clean clothes.

"Hello, young man," said the honest man when Jimmy stepped out of the cab.

Jimmy instinctively reached out his right hand, which the honest man instinctively grabbed and shook, the entire apparatus of the transaction slightly embarrassing the two of them.

"What happened?" asked Jimmy. "I'm sorry, it's just that you look completely different. I mean, you look better."

"I got religion," said the honest man. "I'm going to AA meetings and am looking into the jobs program over at Goodwill."

"Why? What changed?" asked Jimmy.

"Now don't let this go to your head, but it was you. Your commitment to God and your notebook and 'how can you fail to acknowledge the miracle' and all that," said the honest man. "Hey, listen, I don't believe I know your name, unless your name is Angel," he said, laughing.

"Haley James Branhoover," said Jimmy, surprised to hear himself announce his full name and to hear the authoritative tone of his voice. "But I go by Jimmy or James," he continued.

"It's a pleasure to meet you, James," said the honest man. "My name is Charles Larson." The two of them were unable to resist the urge to shake hands again.

"Charles was my father's name," said Jimmy. "He passed away recently."

"I'm sorry to hear that, Angel," said Charles Larson.

"Thanks," said Jimmy, and quickly changed the subject. "I brought something for you and your friends," he said, unzipping the pouch and showing the honest man the ten thousand dollars.

"Put that away!" said Charles. "You mustn't do that. You're going to get yourself robbed and killed. And those two aren't my friends. Come to think of it, they're not your friends either. They wanted to hurt you when you shoved your money in their faces the last time. You mustn't ever do that again, James."

"Then I want you to have all of it," said Jimmy. "Get yourself an apartment and some clothes for your new job. Charles—my dad—was loaded. I've got millions more where this came from. I want you to take this."

The honest man took the pouch, shoved it down the front of his pants, and then covered it up with his untucked shirt.

"Thank you, Angel," said Charles Larson, clean and sober and floating on a pink cloud, all because he acknowledged the miracle that Haley James Branhoover brought to the rows of destitute men.

40. Pink Cloud, Red Paint

H. James Branhoover was so overwhelmed by what he had just done—no one, not Innocent #2 or Kay Sunday, his dead father, or even the quiet man or the inveterate grifter, could deny that he had saved a man's life—that he wept in the cab on the way home.

Surely this was what the late-night televangelists were trying to tell him from the room across the hall while his mother tried desperately to sleep.

Surely Jimmy had been entrusted with the boon of his father's inheritance because he had the God-given desire to change people's lives. The money was simply an enabling tool. How could he fail to acknowledge the miracle?

He thought gently about his father—how God had designed him to be a ruthless, self-absorbed, philandering banker so that his fortune could be passed down to his God-fearing son, who would put the money to good use.

If Jimmy and his wisdom and his money could restore Charles Larson—a hopeless skid row alcoholic—to sanity, then what else could Jimmy do and who else could he save?

He opened his notebook to a blank page, stared at it for less than a minute, closed it, and told the cab driver to wait for him as the cab pulled into the Branhoovers' driveway.

Jimmy ran into the garage, grabbed a can of red spray paint, and then jumped back into the cab while his mother watched from the living room window under the weight of the drapes.

The next stop for the cab was the Sundays' former church, where Jimmy casually and conspicuously strolled up to Goldwatch's correct swastika, spray-painted over it, and then next to it painted a bright red 666 and the following prayer:

Lord Satan, make me an instrument of Thy chaos. Where there is hatred, let me be called among the haters; where there is injury, let

*my wrath be the cause; where there is doubt,
let me be the spreader of lies; where there is
despair, let me extinguish the faltering flame;
where there is darkness, let my sullenness be
the cause; where there is sadness, let my mirth
twist and tear like a dagger. O Divine
Master, grant that I may not so much seek to
console as to be consoled, to understand as to
be understood, to love as to be loved. For it is
in receiving that we truly give, in being
pardoned for our transgressions that justice is
truly served, and in dying that we are truly
dead.*

—*Vander Stevenson, Antichrist*

Jimmy stepped back and admired his work for a moment, then he turned and tossed the spray can as far as he could and began walking back toward the cab, which was no longer there, in its place a police car, and instead of a cab driver, two police officers.

"Is that your artwork on that church?" asked the first officer.

"I don't know what you're talking about," said Jimmy.

The second officer then grabbed Jimmy's hands and turned them palms up.

Jimmy grinned. "Looks like I've been caught red-handed," he said.

41. Smug Jimmy

H. James Branhoover sat in the police station with a smug expression while the officers tried to scare him with high-end cost estimates for the property damage and the damage his stunt would do to his reputation in the community.

To the latter Jimmy reminded them that he was a minor, so his identity was off-limits; to the former he said nothing, confident in his new knowledge that his money could absolve him of the consequences of his antics.

Eventually the officers lost interest in the young perp and let him make his phone call. When Jimmy told his mother where he was and what he had done, she began to cry.

Jimmy couldn't believe it. What is going on with her? he thought.

When Jimmy and Chloe arrived home after she picked him up at the station, Chloe hugged Jimmy and said, "I hope you don't turn out like your brother, though I could hardly blame you if you did."

42. Top Jimmy

First thing the following morning was the first time H. James Branhoover had been the one to retrieve the newspaper from the front porch of his home.

And there it was. The headline on page one of the local section of the *Pittsburgh Post-Gazette* read "Precocious Minor Defaces Swastika Church with Anti-Simple Prayer."

Jimmy read the article from beginning to end half a dozen times before he showed it to his mom. Chloe Branhoover read the headline aloud to her son, and though she tried to muster enthusiasm for the phrase "Precocious Minor," her worried expression belied her obsession with the notion that her second boy was going to turn out like her first boy.

"I'm proud of you, James," she said. "You're a creative and intelligent young man. But what you did was a crime. Do you understand that? What you did harmed someone."

"What I did was expose the devil that swindled the Sundays and took their church," said Jimmy.

Mrs. Branhoover took a moment of thoughtful silence. "I know how much you like Kay Sunday, but she's not the one for you, James," she said. "You could pull off a hundred more of these quixotic triumphs, but it won't make a difference where Kay is concerned. She's made up her mind about you and that will never change."

"With all due respect, Mom, I find it difficult to take relationship advice from you," said Jimmy. "And besides, that's not why I painted the church."

"Okay, James," she said, and walked into the living room to resume her post at the window.

* * * * *

Jimmy couldn't contain his excitement. He needed to talk to someone who would truly appreciate what he had done. He picked up the phone and dialed Innocent #2.

"Brilliant, Jimmy. Absolutely inspired," said Innocent #2, who had already read the article even more times than Jimmy had. "What are the cops going to do to you?"

"I don't know," said Jimmy. "Some kind of restitution, I'm sure. But who cares, right? I can pay it however much it is," he said, laughing.

"Trust fund baby!" exclaimed Innocent #2. "Send the devil Goldwatch running! Hey, I'm going to write Kay and tell her the good news."

The fireflies in Jimmy's head promptly transformed into a lead weight, which dropped into the pit of his stomach.

"Definitely," said Jimmy, trying to revive the good insects now moldering in his abdomen. "Hey, I've got to go. My mom's calling me," said Jimmy.

"Cool," said Innocent #2. "I'll write the letter to Kay and drop it in the mail first thing tomorrow."

Jimmy hung up the phone, slammed the newspaper against the wall, and called a cab to take him to find Charles Larson.

43. Charles Larson

"Skid row?" asked the cab driver when Jimmy slid into the back of the cab. He looked into the rearview mirror and examined the cabby's eyes, which were mirthful and eager to make sport of him.

Jimmy forced a neutral expression and extinguished the light in his eyes.

"Goodwill," he said. Not another word was spoken between the two of them.

At Goodwill, Jimmy walked directly to the reception desk and asked for Charles Larson.

"Are you his son?" asked the receptionist.

"No, just a friend," said Jimmy, trying to conceal his shock.

"He's not scheduled today, but you can try tomorrow. He's due in at ten o'clock," she said.

"Can you call him and tell him James is here to see him?" asked Jimmy.

The receptionist shrugged. "Sure," she said, and dialed the number.

"Mr. Larson?" she said. "It's Darla at Goodwill. There's a boy called James here to visit you . . . I don't know, let me ask him."

"James, would you mind seeing Mr. Larson at his apartment?"

"Not at all," said Jimmy.

The excitement in his voice startled Darla, who gave Jimmy Mr. Larson's address, which was less than a mile away.

"James!" exclaimed Charles Larson, opening the door before Jimmy could even knock.

The two gentlemen shook hands for the third time, and Charles Larson took Jimmy on a thorough, five-minute tour of his sparsely furnished, yet tidy, studio apartment.

Jimmy sat down on Larson's Murphy bed, so overwhelmed by the positive outcome of his charity that he laughed and wept simultaneously.

Charles Larson sat next to Jimmy and stroked his leg. "It's all because of you, Angel," he said.

Jimmy leapt to his feet. "What the hell are you doing?!" he exclaimed.

"Nothing, Angel," said Charles Larson. "I'm just a tactile person when I'm happy."

Jimmy took a moment to calm himself. "Okay," he said. "It's just . . . can you please stop calling me Angel?"

"Of course, James. You're a decent young man and your name is James. I respect you and I apologize," said Charles Larson. "Anyway, I'm doing well. I am still sober since we last spoke and my plan is to do janitorial work to put myself through school. My goal is to become a nurse, James," he said.

"That's great," said Jimmy, still deflated by what he considered a violation of his person. "Well, I'd better get going. I'm sure my mom's looking out the window wondering where I am," he said, trying to mask his fear with a feeble smile.

"Of course, of course," said Charles Larson. "You mustn't worry your mother."

The two gentlemen shook hands again and Jimmy walked out the door and back to Goodwill, where he called a cab and went directly home, his eyes downcast and wide, and his pride shaken.

44. Every Maternal Nerve

Chloe Branhoover was so pleased to see the cab arrive in her driveway on the same day as its departure that she had to catch her breath before her son walked in the door.

H. James Branhoover embraced his mother tightly and then explained how his work on skid row was complete.

Every maternal nerve in Chloe's body comprehended that something had happened to her boy down there, but every maternal instinct told her now was not the time to press him on it.

"I'm so glad you accomplished your goal, Jimmy, but I'm even happier that I don't have to worry about you getting hurt down there," she said, with equal parts nervousness and relief in her voice.

"I'm sorry, Mom," said Jimmy. "I promise I won't go down there anymore."

"Thank you, James," she said. "Oh, your friend, um, Innocent #2 called. He wants you to call him back about the Reverend Patchouli Goldwatch. Does that make sense?"

Jimmy laughed. "Believe it or not, it does," he said and walked upstairs to his bedroom, where he fell asleep within minutes.

45. It Can't Be That Dire

Jimmy spent the first several hours of the following morning preparing his nerves and his patience for the phone call, promising himself that he wouldn't get angry. He was so intensely focused on his mock conversations with Innocent #2 that he didn't hear the phone ring.

"James," said his mother from downstairs, "um, Innocent #2 is on the phone for you."

Jimmy was immediately annoyed, but he forced himself to mind his emotions before he picked up the receiver.

"Hello?" said H. James Branhoover.

"Jimmy, hey!" exclaimed Innocent #2. "You'll never guess who I just talked to."

"I don't know . . . Kay," he said flatly.

"No, no," he said. "Goldwatch! You're not even going to believe me, but he says he might be willing to give the Sundays their church back."

"Are you serious?" said Jimmy. "Did you threaten to kill him or something?"

Both boys laughed.

"Nah, nothing like that, but I'll store the thought away for later," said Innocent #2.

"What did you say?" asked Jimmy.

"I told him you were willing to buy him out," said Innocent #2. "I told him you are loaded."

Jimmy exploded. "You little punk!" he screamed, and then he remembered his precall pep talk, set the receiver down, and walked away for a moment.

When he picked up the phone again, he heard a dial tone.

Mrs. Branhoover tried to comfort her second son. "Are you okay, sweetheart?"

"I'm fine, Mom," said Jimmy, again surprised and pleased by her compassion.

"Does this have something to do with Kay Sunday?" she asked. "I understand how painful this must be, James, but I promise that someday you'll meet a girl who won't make you feel so angry and confused."

"It's not about Kay," said Jimmy. "It's about what I'm willing to pay for right over wrong."

"It can't be that dire, sweetheart, you're just a boy," she said.

46. Strong First Impression, but Not a Lasting One

Jimmy stayed awake into the early hours of the morning in an attempt to honestly appraise his motives should he decide, against all better instinct, to meet with Goldwatch to buy back the Sundays' church.

Was it as simple as his mom had insisted? That he was trying to impress Kay? Or was it truly as dire a matter as right versus wrong, or even good versus evil?

Jimmy stared at a blank page in his notebook considering these questions, ultimately concluding that impressing Kay Sunday would be nothing more than a collateral reward for doing what was right, and that, like his work with the rows of destitute men, his true motives were righteousness and redemption. How could he fail to acknowledge the miracle of Charles Larson? If his mom knew about Charles Larson, surely she would agree that there was more at stake than impressing a girl.

That settled it. H. James Branhoover was going to buy back the Sundays' church, and his motive for doing so was, if not pure, at least right enough.

* * * * *

Jimmy called Innocent #2 the moment he awoke the next day.

"I thought about it all last night, and I think buying the church back from Goldwatch is the right thing to do," he said.

"I think so, too," said Innocent #2.

"But when I meet with him, I don't want you to be there," said Jimmy, unconcerned by his bluntness.

"I understand," said Innocent #2, who then gave Goldwatch's phone number to Jimmy and hung up without saying goodbye.

* * * * *

Jimmy put the receiver in its holder and immediately picked it up again before he could think about chickening out. He dialed Goldwatch's number.

"Vander Stevenson," said the voice on the other end, which for a split second caused Jimmy to think he had dialed the wrong number.

"Hello?" said Goldwatch.

"Sir," said Jimmy, "my name is Haley James Branhoover. I'm the one who . . ."

Goldwatch let out a screwball laugh that put Jimmy at ease.

"You're the clever boy who painted the anti-Simple Prayer on the side of my church," said Goldwatch.

433

"Sorry about that," said Jimmy.

"Don't be sorry, Haley. I'm not sorry you did it. In fact, I'm glad you did it, and now let me tell you why," said Goldwatch.

"You can call me James," said Jimmy.

"And you can call me Vander . . . or Mr. Stevenson, if you think it strange to call an adult by his first name," said Goldwatch.

"Mr. Stevenson it is," said Jimmy.

"That's fine, James," said Goldwatch. "James," he said, "I'm a man who makes a strong first impression but doesn't leave a lasting one. That's why I'm glad you did what you did and am insisting that any charges or restitution be dropped. Now hear me out, James. You see, I'm not a man of God, necessarily. I'm more of a businessman. And from what Innocent #2 tells me—and forgive me for saying so, but that boy is contemptible—you have the means to purchase the church back for the Sundays, and I would get a tidy profit in return," said Goldwatch.

"That sounds about right," said Jimmy, pleased to hear that charges would likely be dropped and that Stevenson held the same low opinion of Innocent #2 that he did. "And what exactly do you mean you make a strong first impression but don't leave a lasting one?"

"As early as I can remember, people have been drawn to me and my screwball stunts. It's the damnedest thing, James," said Goldwatch. "Now hear me out. Take the swastika stunt, for example. It doesn't get more screwball than that, but people bought it, James, and I'll admit I am addicted to the power of my own charisma, how it gets me what I want with such little resistance. But, and it's the damnedest thing, the same people I can charm so quickly are the same people who turn on me equally quick. I like to get in and out as fast as possible, and that's why I am willing to accept any reasonable offer you make for the purchase of the property."

"Well, okay then," said Jimmy. "I think $200,000 over what you paid for the property is reasonable. Do you agree?"

"I think that is beyond reasonable, James. In fact, I think it is downright generous. I accept your offer," said Stevenson.

"Great," said Jimmy. "That wasn't so bad at all."

"Not bad at all. Pleasant even," said Stevenson.

"What next? I'll call Innocent #2 with the good news, and he can write the Sundays to let them know I'm giving them the money to buy back their church," said Jimmy.

"Oh, they are going to be thrilled," said Stevenson. "Until next time."

"Until then," said Jimmy.

47. A Telegram

Innocent #2 sent a telegram to the Sundays in Cambodia, which read as follows:

DEAR KRISTOV, KRISTINA, AND KAY: UNDER MY DIRECTION, JIMMY BRANHOOVER PAINTED ANTI-SIMPLE PRAYER ON GOLDWATCH'S CHURCH. GOLDWATCH LOST SUPPORT OF CONGREGATION AND AGREED TO SELL CHURCH BACK TO YOU. JIMMY BRANHOOVER WILL GIFT YOU THE FUNDS FOR THE REPURCHASE.
YOURS, INNOCENT #2

Kris and Kris were shocked and thrilled by the news. The people of Cambodia had been kind, if unreceptive, to the Sundays' brand of religion, though they enjoyed Mrs. Sunday's hurricane sermon, which she called "The Life of a Typhoon."

Kay, however, was sullen, which her parents found incomprehensible. Mrs. Sunday pleaded with her daughter. "But you hate it here, Kay," she said. "Your father and I are getting our church back from the preacher you hated so much, and you get to go home to your boyfriend and see your old friend Jimmy, too. What an unbelievably generous thing for Jimmy to do. He is turning into a remarkable young man."

"The only thing remarkable about Jimmy is his money, and it's not even his, really, it's his rotten old man's," said Kay. "Did you read the telegram? This wasn't even his idea, it was my boyfriend's. Jimmy thinks he can buy me, but he's just a friend, and he's not even that anymore."

"Honestly, Kay!" exclaimed Mrs. Sunday. "Such hateful things to say about Jimmy Branhoover. You should be grateful, and nothing else, for what he has done. If you want to know the truth, James is a finer young man than your boyfriend."

"H. James Branhoover is a dope, Mom," said Kay Sunday, who then silenced her furious mother with a hug and the long, deep stare of her otherworldly eyes.

PART VII

48. Two Letters

The Sundays needed approximately one month to wind up and dissolve their operation in Cambodia, during which time Kay sent Jimmy the following letter:

> *Dear Jimmy:*
>
> *I'm going to come straight to the point: You can't buy me. Your money means nothing. Innocent #2 is my boyfriend, and I know this whole thing was his idea. You wouldn't have had the guts to do any of this on your own. You were mostly silent concerning Goldwatch during the high-octane sessions, and you barely took part in the ritual of the fumes.*
>
> *–Kay*

And Jimmy sent the following reply:

Dear Kay:

You know damned well it wasn't his idea to paint the anti-Simple Prayer on your church. He doesn't even know who St. Francis of Assisi is. I'm giving your parents the money to get their church back and am sending the Devil packing. I have no desire to "buy" you or otherwise take anything from you, so you might as well start being nice. Also, I'd like to resume the high-octane sessions when you return. I can promise you, I won't be mostly silent.

Sincerely,

Jimmy

49. Clever and Full of Grace

Kay Sunday and the Innocents sniffed high-octane fumes and testified.

Kay: Now I'm just going to come right out and say it. Jimmy Branhoover, you barely pass that gas can under your nose, let alone inhale as much as we do.

Jimmy: You can't be serious. We're sitting here on your brand-new porch in your fancy new home, you never have to go back to Cambodia for as long as you live, your parents got their church back, you got your boyfriend back, the Reverend Patchouli Goldwatch—the Devil himself—is gone for good, and all you can do is give me grief for not wanting to give myself brain damage just for the sake of some idiotic ritual.

Kay: Look who's the rooster man now, all proud of that stupid anti-prayer he got lucky and painted, and his rotten old man's money that he used to buy my family.

Jimmy: You know you're just talking now, Kay. You know that's not true. How could someone so clever and full of grace be so shallow?

Kay: Well, now, that's got to be the most interesting thing you've ever said. But it's too little, too late. You're nothing but a trust fund baby, H. James Branhoover. No one will ever respect you. Your opinion doesn't count.

Not another word was spoken. Jimmy picked up his notebook and quietly left the property, while Kay buried her face in her hands and sobbed. Innocent #2 sat staring at the ground, the handle of the gas can dangling from his index finger.

50. Aftermath

Jimmy Branhoover spent the first month after his falling-out with Kay Sunday in isolation in his room, reading his Bible and making entries in his notebook.

He noticed in his time of trouble that he was less and less interested in the Book of Revelation and more interested in the Psalms, Gospels, Ecclesiastes, and Epistles.

He used the Bible as a sort of Magic Eight Ball. He would ask it questions, open the Book, and then turn the pages until he found the answers he needed. He was especially interested in passages that his eyes tried to skip over because they made him uncomfortable. For example, "But love your enemies, and do good, and lend, expecting nothing back," and "Again I tell you, it is easier for a camel to go through the eye of a needle than for a rich man to enter the kingdom of God."

These verses made him squirm over his never-ending inability to reconcile his true motive for giving the Sundays the money to buy back their church. To make matters worse, from time to time he could hear his mother downstairs on the telephone talking to Kristina Sunday. They were becoming close friends. Jimmy couldn't believe how insensitive this was. If Jimmy were the father and Chloe were his daughter who had just suffered a falling-out with an acquaintance's son, there is no way he would be on the phone with the son's parent trying to become friends.

When Jimmy confronted her on this, Mrs. Branhoover said it wasn't what Jimmy was thinking at all. In fact, she said "Mrs. Sunday advocates on your behalf. She reminds Kay what a remarkable young man you are and tells her you would be better for her than Innocent #2." To which Jimmy grinned sarcastically and responded, "I'm sure that's really helping my cause."

"I remind Mrs. Sunday that Kay isn't the right girl for you," Chloe said.

The more Jimmy heard his mom say these words, the better, the lighter, he began to feel.

He started to think about the future. He wondered about Charles Larson.

51. A Scrubs-Clad Woman

Despite all the adverse truths in his first dozen years—his mom being an on-again-off-again prostitute; the death of his well-to-do and good-for-nothing father; his hitherto unknown and now absent older brother; his withdrawal from the Carden School; his confrontations with the quiet man, the inveterate grifter, and Vander Stevenson aka the Reverend Patchouli Goldwatch; his being arrested for spray-painting a church; and his falling-out with Kay Sunday—H. James

Branhoover was feeling pretty good about the way things were going.

I remind Mrs. Sunday that Kay isn't the right girl for you, Jimmy repeated in his mind. Chloe Branhoover had stuck up for her son and subtly implied to Mrs. Sunday that her daughter wasn't good enough for him. The otherworldly Kay, for all her grace and charm and wit, was ultimately a shallow girl, while Jimmy, a sheltered, mostly silent, undereducated trust fund baby, was ultimately a serious young man, learned in Bible verses and had led a hapless alcoholic away from skid row and into sobriety, possibly even into nursing school.

Jimmy began to fixate less on Kay Sunday and more on Charles Larson.

Still concerned about the thigh-stroking incident, Jimmy spent the first months of his fixation monitoring Charles Larson from the safety of taxi cabs. He would pass by Larson's apartment at different times on different days of the week.

Jimmy didn't always see Larson on these drive-bys, but when he did, Larson always appeared well-dressed (though in secondhand clothes) and sober, and always alone.

Jimmy made detailed entries in his notebook each time there was a sighting.

After a year went by, Jimmy noted a change in Larson's dress. He now wore scrubs as often as he did street clothes. And then something even more remarkable: every Tuesday and Thursday, Charles Larson would arrive home at noon in a car driven by a scrubs-clad woman. They would disappear behind Larson's apartment door for an hour and then they would reappear—always smiling and sometimes laughing—and drive off in the woman's car.

This was the evidence Jimmy was waiting for. He was no longer concerned about the thigh-stroking incident. He made entries in his notebook concerning the optimal time to reintroduce himself to the honest man and to introduce himself for the first time to the honest man's girlfriend.

52. Fifteenth Birthday

Chloe Branhoover had made good on her promise to allow her second son to make his own decisions with little or no maternal interference. This even included his birthdays.

On all of Jimmy's birthdays since the death of his father, Mrs. Branhoover would purchase a card and a modest gift—usually a new pen or the most luminous writings on religion she could find—and then she would give Jimmy his gift and kindly ask him his plans for the day.

On his fifteenth birthday, as on his recent birthdays, Jimmy graciously thanked his mother for pen/luminous religious work; but unlike the past few birthdays, he then informed her that he was going to drop in on an old friend for lunch.

"Not Kay Sunday?" said Mrs. Branhoover.

"No, Mom, not Kay. Someone you don't know, but I may introduce you to him someday. He's just an old friend."

"An old friend?" said Mrs. Branhoover. "You're only fifteen, James. You're too young to have an old friend that I don't know about. Is he from school?"

"No, he's not from school, but please don't worry. You'll meet him soon, I promise," said Jimmy, who picked up the telephone and called a cab.

* * * * *

The woman's car was already parked outside of Larson's apartment when Jimmy arrived via cab. He hastily paid the cab driver and jogged up to Larson's door.

"James!" exclaimed Larson, "so good to see you. I was wondering when you were going to

453

visit again. All those cab rides must be getting expensive." He winked at Jimmy.

Jimmy blushed. "Well, I'm sure they weren't *all* me," he said. "Only four out of every five or so."

"I completely understand," said Larson. "I had to regain your trust. Please, come in. We're about to sit down for lunch."

The honest man escorted Jimmy to the kitchen table, making sure not to touch him in any way.

"James, I'd like to introduce you to my good friend and fellow nurse, Betsy Sullivan."

"Nice to meet you, Betsy Sullivan. My name is Haley James Branhoover," said Jimmy, surprised by the regal tone of his voice.

"Branhoover?" blurted Betsy. "I dated your brother in high school. Bernard or . . . Bernrd, whatever his name is. Ha! He used to call me 'fussy wet salami.' We were in love. How is he doing, James?"

The color exited Jimmy's face, and he grabbed the back of a kitchen chair.

"Um, I've never met my brother," said Jimmy, meekly.

"Well then, it looks like we've got something to talk about," said Betsy, trying to conceal any indication of shock or pity.

"You never told me you had a brother, James," said Charles Larson.

"I didn't even know about him until a couple of years ago," said Jimmy.

"I'm sorry, Angel," said Charles Larson.

"Let me tell you about Bernrd Red!" Betsy Sullivan interjected, exhibiting clear hostility toward soft emotions outside of the hospital setting.

"Bernrd Red? You must be mistaken. My brother's name is Bernard Branhoover."

"Who knows what he's calling himself these days. Could be anything," said Betsy. "Ha! When we were an item, he went by Bernrd Red. He deliberately removed the 'a' from 'Bernard' to irritate the teachers. And it worked! He was clever that way. He irritated me, too, at first. I socked him in the forehead at recess way back in elementary school. He hit me back, the bastard. That's how we were introduced. We were real troublemakers, but we were creative about it. Not like kids today."

"How old are you?" asked Jimmy.

"It's not polite to ask a woman her age," said Charles Larson.

"Thirty-five," said Betsy.

"Same age as my brother," said Jimmy.

"Yeah, sure," said Betsy. "And how old are you, young man?"

"Today is my fifteenth birthday," said Jimmy.

"Happy birthday, Angel!" shouted the honest man.

"Thanks," said Jimmy, thinking for a moment that in some better, alternate universe Charles Larson and Betsy Sullivan were his parents.

53. Harmonious Enough

The first months of Kay Sunday's post-Jimmy Branhoover years were harmonious enough. Her parents had resumed their rightful role as spiritual consultants and amateur astronomers, their spacey church with its telescope having been returned to them. She continued to charm and excel at the Carden School. And she and Innocent #2 were free at last to pursue to the fullest extent the triumph of the high-octane sessions—their relationship—without the perceived need to conceal it for the sake of Jimmy's feelings.

But for Kay "harmonious enough" was precisely the problem. She began to miss Jimmy, or, perhaps more accurately, she began to miss the thrill of the tension between Jimmy and Innocent #2, or, perhaps most accurately, she couldn't stand the idea that Jimmy had gotten over her, or worse, simply forgotten her.

After their falling-out, Kay had expected Jimmy to send an angry letter or two, or, at a minimum, make several angry phone calls with the obligatory threats toward Innocent #2. But Jimmy had given her no satisfaction whatsoever. He simply disappeared.

And even worse, her mom and Jimmy's mom had become friends, and Mrs. Sunday preferred Jimmy to her boyfriend and had no problem telling her so.

Innocent #2, for his trouble, had no better option than to detach as Kay became more and more distant. The high-octane sessions fizzled out and left them on the porch lying on separate sofas, staring aimlessly with headaches.

* * * * *

Kay Sunday had had enough harmony. She rose from her sofa, went inside, picked up the phone, and dialed the Branhoovers' number.

Chloe Branhoover answered.

"Hi, Mrs. Branhoover. This is Kay. Is Jimmy there?"

"Oh hello, Kay. My goodness, how have you been? It's been so long," said Chloe Branhoover, looking over her shoulder, hoping her son didn't hear her.

"Not so well," said Kay. "I miss Jimmy. Is he there?"

Though Chloe desperately wanted to lie, she did not. "One moment," she said like a maid, and went to fetch her son.

"Hello?" said Jimmy, with forced nonchalance.

"I miss you, Jimmy," Kay blurted out. "What are you doing? I want to see you."

Kay's directness eviscerated Jimmy's resolve. "Okay," said Jimmy, "let's go hang out with my new friends Charles and Betsy."

Just as he uttered the words "new friends," he heard the voice of Innocent #2 say, "Are you talking to Jimmy Branhoover?" His ears heard the voice, clear and true, but his eyes weren't there to see Innocent #2 shrug and exit out the front door of the Sundays' house.

"You guys must be really bored with each other if the most interesting thing you can come up with is to fuck with me three years later."

"He just left, Jimmy. We're through. We broke up. I want to put on a nice dress and go with you to meet Charles and Betsy."

"I'm sorry, Kay, but I don't believe you. Or I do believe you, but you'll just change your mind tomorrow or an hour from now. Please don't call me again," said Jimmy, and he hung up the phone.

54. Her Son's Intensity

"James, I'm so proud of you," said Chloe Branhoover, who had eavesdropped on the entire phone call.

"You were listening?" asked Jimmy, doing his best to conceal the agony of denying himself the thing he wanted even more than saving a drunkard's life.

His mother hugged him while his mind repeated the words "I want to put on a nice dress and go with you to meet Charles and Betsy," which seemed to knock the wind out of him.

"Thanks," he said, and pulled away from her embrace. "Does the name Betsy Sullivan sound familiar?"

Chloe Branhoover paused, her eyes searching the space in front of her and inside of her.

"Why do I feel that it should?" she said.

"Because Betsy Sullivan dated my brother in high school," said Jimmy. "And now she's dating my old friend you haven't met. They're both nurses."

"Oh, of course. What was I thinking?" said Chloe, laughing with the intention of defusing her son's intensity.

Jimmy laughed in reply. Then he spoke at length about the rows of destitute men, how his old friend had once been a nameless skid row alcoholic, how he had called Jimmy "Angel," how Jimmy had saved him, how he now had a name (Charles Larson) and a job (nurse) and a girlfriend (Betsy Sullivan), and how Jimmy had spent his fifteenth birthday in their company.

"You really got to know this man, then," said Mrs. Branhoover. She was relieved to finally know the whole truth but was nevertheless alarmed. "Well, I suppose I should tell you that I've been corresponding with your brother since your father died. He would like to meet you, James," she said.

"Where is he? Is he here? In Pittsburgh?" asked Jimmy.

"He lives in New Orleans. Let's go buy you a car so you can visit him," said Chloe with gritty excitement in her voice.

55. A New Car

H. James Branhoover introduced his mother to Charles Larson aka the honest man, and reintroduced her to Betsy Sullivan. The two women sat in the front seat of Betsy's car exchanging war stories about the teenage Bernard Branhoover aka Bernrd Red, while Betsy drove the four of them to the Mercedes dealer.

Jimmy and Charles sat in the backseat in silence, both of them feeling grateful and holy.

In the troubled lives of these four people— Charles Larson the skid row bum, Betsy Sullivan the fussy wet salami, Chloe Red the roughhouse prostitute, and H. James Branhoover the trust fund baby—their morning at the Mercedes dealer was blissfully devoid of adverse truths.

They slid in and out of a dozen or so automobiles and, thanks to the late H. Charles Branhoover, didn't concern themselves with the formidable sticker prices.

Jimmy ultimately decided on a white S500, which his mother purchased in her own name and with her own inheritance.

Charles Larson wept joyously in the backseat of the new car as Mrs. Branhoover drove the four of them off the lot and back to their lives.

56. Lunch with the Branhoovers

Charles Larson looked as though he had just arrived on the summit of Mount Olympus as Jimmy's new Mercedes pulled into the Branhoovers' driveway. He walked to the edge of the property and watched the Allegheny River move through the city, while Jimmy, Chloe, and Betsy went inside to prepare a late lunch. He shivered when he thought about how the quiet man and the inveterate grifter were still down there, either along the rows of destitute men or dead. He recalled how Jimmy had sat with him through his last hangover and how he had not taken a drink since. Then he turned and walked into his angel's mansion to join his friends for lunch.

The conversation focused exclusively on Jimmy's pending trip to New Orleans to meet his brother for the first time.

Chloe Branhoover guaranteed her son that she would teach him all he would need to know about how to drive his new car, and she displayed a refreshingly cavalier attitude about Jimmy being too young to drive and not being able to get a driver's license.

Charles and Betsy were similarly optimistic in this regard, and were positively joyous over the prospect of Jimmy finally meeting his brother.

But then, as if she were sitting at the table, Jimmy heard Kay's voice: "I want to put on a nice dress and go with you to meet your brother."

"I'm thinking about inviting Kay Sunday," Jimmy announced.

Mrs. Branhoover grimaced. "James, how many times do I have to remind you that Kay . . ."

"Ha! I knew you had a girlfriend," said Betsy Sullivan. "Kay what? 'Sunday' did you say? That's kind of odd. Sounds made-up."

"It is made-up," said Jimmy, pleased that Betsy had interrupted his mother. "Her parents are on the eccentric side. Their real last name is Sutter."

"This day just keeps on getting better and better," said Charles Larson. "Of course you must invite her, Angel."

"You sly devil," said Betsy Sullivan.

Chloe Branhoover smiled, rose from her chair, brought her plate into the kitchen, dropped it in the sink, and then returned to the table to announce that lunch was over and how nice it was to have spent the day with Jimmy's wonderful friends.

"Uh-oh," said Betsy.

"Oh, it's not that," said Chloe. "It's just that I am exhausted. I'd love to spend more time with both of you," she said, sincerely.

"This is one of the finest days I can remember," said Charles Larson, rising from his chair, "and it's been a pleasure to spend it in your company."

By now, all four of them were standing. They walked together out to Betsy's car and said goodbye.

57. An Invitation

"James," said Chloe Branhoover as they stepped back inside the house, "if you want to invite Kay to go with you to meet Bernard, then I support you. Anyway, it'll be safer to have company on such a long trip."

Jimmy stared at her for several seconds, still surprised by how different she seemed. "I appreciate that, thanks," he said, and then he picked up the phone and called the Sundays.

"Hello?" said Kay Sunday. The good fireflies stirred to life inside Jimmy's stomach.

"Hi, Kay. It's Jimmy Branhoover. I haven't stopped thinking about you since we last spoke. I'd like to invite you to go with me to New Orleans to meet my big brother. I have a brand-new car and everything. It's a Mercedes S500. White. I just bought it today," he said, laughing nervously.

Kay began to cry. "You've always been such a sweet boy, and I'm sorry for all the times I've been mean to you," she said. "We were childhood friends, and I'll never forget you. I heard how you helped the homeless man. I think you're going to be important, Jimmy. No. You already are important. I love you and I'll never forget you. Goodbye." And she hung up before Jimmy could reply.

He instinctively redialed the number but hung up before it rang.

Kay was right. They were childhood friends and the time of their relationship was over.

Jimmy walked slowly to his bedroom and lay down on the bed. How can I fail to acknowledge the miracle? he thought.

58. A Cryptic Message

At four o'clock in the morning, the Branhoovers' phone rang. Both Chloe and Jimmy thought it was Kay Sunday, but each reacted differently: the irritated Chloe rolled over in bed and covered her ears with a pillow, while the pouncing kitten in Jimmy returned. He sprang upon the phone with childish exuberance, but it was too late. The machine had picked up the call.

Jimmy looked at the clock on the wall and waited five minutes before he lifted the receiver to check messages.

"You have one new message and no saved messages," reported the voicemail service. "To listen to your message, press one."

H. James Branhoover pressed the button.

"First new message . . ."

"Hello, James. This is Vander Stevenson. You've been on my mind a lot lately, which is unusual, believe me. Usually I'm what's on my mind. Ha-ha! You're a good and powerful young man, James. In my experience, those two traits rarely go together. Now, hear me out. Don't ask how—you mustn't ask how—but I know about all of the good and powerful things you've done. Not just for the Sundays, but all of the other things, too. You can do so much more, James. Bigger moths need bigger flames. I think you should leave Pittsburgh. Go somewhere bigger. New York or Chicago. Or Hollywood! Think of the good you could do in Hollywood. You could be famous, James. Bigger moths need bigger flames."

"To delete this message, press seven. To save it, press nine," reported the voicemail service.

Jimmy pressed nine, then replayed the message the number of times it took him to transcribe it verbatim in his notebook.

He returned to his room and lay awake well into the morning, reminiscing about Kay and adjusting the itinerary of his pending trip to include Hollywood.

59. An Inconsequential Lie

"Was that Kay who called at four in the morning?" asked Mrs. Branhoover, carrying a breakfast tray into her son's room.

"Yeah," answered Jimmy. "She said she wanted to tell me she loved me before I left on my trip."

"At that hour? Well, she certainly is beguiling," said Mrs. Branhoover, without irony.

"Oh, now you see it," said Jimmy, laughing. "I'm getting really excited about my trip, Mom, but I'm nervous about meeting Bernard. What if he doesn't like me?"

"Honestly, James, he probably won't like you but if he kicks you out, you've got lots of money and a brand-new car to bring you back home."

"How long will it take to learn how to drive?" asked Jimmy.

"Probably a week or two," said Mrs. Branhoover.

PART VIII

60. From the Ohio to the Mississippi

Eleven days later, H. James Branhoover was—in his mother's estimation—properly trained and ready for his trip. She helped him pack and load the trunk and backseat of the Mercedes, and she hugged him goodbye with a lightness that suggested she expected to see him again soon.

Jimmy took a leisurely five days following the Ohio River west to the Mississippi River and the Mississippi River south to New Orleans, driving cautiously and expertly, and drawing exactly no attention from state troopers from Pennsylvania to Louisiana.

When he arrived in New Orleans, he booked a room in the Riverfront Hilton, where he stayed for a week going on sightseeing tours and walking the streets of the French Quarter, deliberately passing by his brother's address on Toulouse several times.

On the eighth day, he passed by just before sunset and saw a thirty-five-year-old version of himself step out onto his front porch in pajamas, a benign scowl on his face.

61. You Must Be James

"Come here, bro. Let me get a closer look at you," said the scowling man in pajamas.

Jimmy pointed at himself, looking sheepishly to and fro.

"Yes, you," said the scowling man.

Jimmy felt himself scowl a bit as he approached the man directly.

"Blond hair, brown eyes, regal nose. All the traits of a Branhoover. You must be James," said the man.

Jimmy smiled. "And you must be Hugh What's-His-Name? Hefner," he said, trying to break the ice.

"No, I'm his cantankerous and celibate brother, Bernrd," said Bernrd Red, breaking it once and for all.

"BERN-erd? Not BernARD?"

"Didn't Mom tell you? I removed the 'a' from my name," said the Branhoovers' firstborn.

"Yeah, but that was, what, twenty years ago? I thought things might have changed since Pittsburgh," said Jimmy, surprised by his own brazenness.

"You're lucky I'm on my meds," said Bernrd Red, laughing. "Otherwise I'd probably clock you."

Suddenly Jimmy became aware of the music emanating from his brother's apartment, and how it seemed responsible for his cavalier attitude.

"What's that music?" he asked.

"That's Professor Longhair. Why don't you come inside and have a beer with me, James."

477

"I'd love to," said Jimmy.

The two brothers spent the rest of the evening and into the early morning hours of the next day getting acquainted through music and beer, the latter of which Jimmy liked so much, it made him sick.

62. Much Better Than Gasoline Fumes

The following afternoon, Bernrd Red—wearing the same pajamas as the day before—stumbled into the bathroom and discovered his little brother curled up in his underwear next to the toilet. He prodded Jimmy with his foot to see if the boy was still capable of movement. Jimmy squirmed and rolled over, banging his knees against the bathtub with enough force to startle him awake and into a sitting position.

"It's alive!" said Bernrd Red.

Jimmy managed a weary grin.

"Well, if it turns out everything else about you is contemptible, at least I know you like good beer."

"It's much better than gasoline fumes," Jimmy replied, "but I'm never drinking that much again."

"Ha!" exclaimed Bernrd Red. "Once an alcoholic, always an alcoholic."

"What did you say? 'Ha!?' That reminds me of your ex-girlfriend," said Jimmy.

"I haven't had an *ex*-girlfriend since high school," said Bernrd Red.

"Right," said Jimmy. "Her name is Betsy Sullivan. And I'm not an alcoholic. I do know one, though. I helped him off skid row. Actually, he's Betsy's new boyfriend. They're both nurses."

"Whoa, whoa, stop it, Mother Teresa. Quit being such a bore. I think I like you better when you're drunk."

Jimmy closed his eyes and rubbed his temples, feeling wounded by his brother's failure to be impressed. "Sorry, man. I feel like shit," he said.

"You need something to eat," said Bernrd Red. "Do you like cheeseburgers?"

"I love cheeseburgers," said Jimmy.

So Branhoover the elder escorted Branhoover the younger into the kitchen for microwaved sliders, Pepsi, and a shot of bourbon, and then sent him to bed to sleep off his first hangover.

63. The Worst Thing You've Ever Done

Jimmy woke the following morning feeling much better about everything. His hangover was gone, and his brother wasn't such a bad guy after all— or at least he wasn't as evil as Betsy and his mom had made him out to be.

In fact, even as Jimmy was thinking benevolent thoughts about his brother, Bernrd Red was in the kitchen frying up bacon, eggs, and hash browns for the two of them.

"Breakfast is served, James," the elder Branhoover announced from the stove.

Jimmy met him at the dining room table, where he was surprised to see that the breakfast beverage wasn't tea or orange juice, but beer.

"That's how we do it in New Orleans," said Bernrd Red, reading the concerned expression on Jimmy's face.

"Cool," said Jimmy, taking a healthy swig as a pledge of allegiance to his brother's city.

"Doubtless, Mom has told you some terrible things about me," said Bernrd Red. "Let me assure you that everything she told you is true, and that any of the more far-fetched rumors can be more or less substantiated."

"What's the worst thing you've ever done?" asked Jimmy, without flinching.

481

"Ha!" exclaimed Bernrd Red. "I definitely like you better when you're drunk."

"I'm not drunk," said Jimmy.

"That's what you think," said Bernrd Red. "Worst thing I've ever done is sleep with a pregnant woman during her honeymoon with another man. Even worse, she wanted me to rough her up and I indulged her."

"Holy crap, you're going to burn in Hell," said Jimmy, laughing.

"What about you, kiddo?" said Bernrd Red.

"Kiddo? I think you need another beer. And you don't have to call me James, either. I know we're Branhoovers and all, but you can call me Jimmy."

"I'll call you whatever I please, Jimmy," said Bernrd Red, wild-eyed and grinning. "And what's the worst thing you've ever done, little brother?"

"I spray-painted the side of a church once," said Jimmy, sheepishly.

"Not bad," said Bernrd Red, confident that he had reestablished his dominance. "What did it say, Jimmy?"

"It was the anti-Simple Prayer. I took St. Francis of Assisi's Simple Prayer, and I made it say the opposite. For example: 'Lord Satan, make me an instrument of Thy chaos. Where there is hatred, let me be called among the haters; where there is injury, let my wrath be the cause; where there is doubt, let me be the spreader of lies,' and so on. I got caught and had to spend the night in jail."

Bernrd Red laughed respectfully. "That's actually pretty twisted," he said.

"Now it's my turn again," said Jimmy. "I've been wondering where you got that ring. Is that a real ruby?"

"It is indeed a real ruby. Do you like it? Of course you do. The ring was a gift. The owner of the Golden Horseshoe in Las Vegas gave it to me for my services as a cooler. Do you know what a cooler is, Jimmy?"

"Uh-uh," said the younger Branhoover, cracking open another beer.

"A cooler is someone who can make a lucky person's good luck turn sour," said Bernrd Red.

Jimmy's mind flashed to the sourness he felt when his brother had called him a bore for helping Charles Larson. Then he thought about Vander Stevenson aka the Reverend Patchouli Goldwatch.

"Oh, crap," said Jimmy. "I've got to check out of my hotel room. I completely forgot about it. I'll come back tonight, if that's okay with you."

"Ha! Forgets he's renting a luxury hotel room. Such a trust fund baby. You're welcome to stay here as long as you want, Jimmy. You're my brother."

Jimmy guzzled the rest of his beer and walked out the door toward the Riverfront Hilton.

64. The Best Thing That Ever Happened to Me

In true brotherly fashion, a week went by before Jimmy showed up again at Bernrd Red's apartment. Also befitting of brothers, Bernrd Red was utterly unconcerned by Jimmy's failure to return and made absolutely no effort to contact him.

H. James Branhoover arrived at his brother's apartment on a Wednesday night carrying a twelve-pack and under the mistaken impression that Bernrd Red had a job and might not want to drink beers with him on a work night.

"A job?" Bernrd Red snorted, again in pajamas. "Why would I have a job? Do you want to know the best thing that ever happened to me . . . to us?"

"What's that?" asked Jimmy.

"That Dad died and made us rich, that's what. You get to drive down here in a new

485

Mercedes-Benz to hang out with your independently wealthy, happily unemployed, pajama-wearing brother, and we get to sit around and do whatever we please. I mean, you're not even in school, are you?"

"No," said Jimmy, embarrassed.

"Hey, we've got nothing to be ashamed of. You've got your whole life to go to school, if that's what you want. But you get to do it on your own time and not because you need a degree to get some lame job. So let's hang out."

Jimmy handed his brother a beer out of the twelve-pack, opened one for himself, and stepped inside his brother's apartment.

"I don't want to go to school," said Jimmy.

"Good for you, kiddo," said Bernrd Red, challenging his brother to respond.

Jimmy winced. The word "cooler" flashed in his mind, but he managed to stay on topic.

"I'm going to Hollywood," he said.

"Now you're talking," said Bernrd Red. "You're going to be a famous actor, bro."

"Nothing like that," replied Jimmy. "I'm going to help drunks get off skid row. I seem to have a knack for it, and it makes me feel good."

"It's just one drunk talking to another drunk. Isn't that the cliché?"

"You *are* a fucking cooler," said Jimmy.

"Hey, man, if you can't handle the beer, then you're going to have to leave," said Bernrd Red, calmly and condescendingly.

"That's okay by me," said Jimmy. "It was good meeting you."

"Well, at least this isn't a story about a boy and his dog," said the elder Branhoover, who stood and showed his little brother to the door.

65. An Inconsequential Lie

Jimmy returned to his room at the Riverfront Hilton and wrote the following letter:

Dear Mom:

The trip to New Orleans was a success. "BERNrd" is difficult, just like you said he would be. I think he's some kind of ruby-ring voodoo priest in pajamas. But he didn't kick me out until tonight.

I have decided to head to Hollywood to try acting. Please don't worry. The idea was mine, not Bernrd's, and I promise to stay away from skid row.

The car is running great. I miss you and hope you are doing well.

–Jimmy

P.S. Say "Hi" to Charles and Betsy if you see them.

PART IX

66. From the Riverfront Hilton to the Beverly Hilton

Jimmy's 1,900-mile journey from New Orleans to Los Angeles after his falling-out with Bernrd Red reminded him of his eight-mile walk from the Sundays' porch to the rows of destitute men after his falling-out with Kay Sunday.

For 1,900 miles Jimmy drove expertly in his Mercedes-Benz, reflecting on the events of his recent past.

The more time and distance away from his brother, the more disturbing he found their visit to be. Bernrd Red seemed to possess a pernicious energy that was best gotten away from. Maybe he *was* a voodoo priest.

And what of the cryptic message left by Vander Stevenson aka the Reverend Patchouli Goldwatch? Jimmy had transcribed the message verbatim, but part of him wondered whether the call was real or a figment of his four-in-the-morning imagination. Maybe it *was* just a late-night hang-up. Or maybe Kay was right and Goldwatch was the Devil himself.

And what of Kay Sunday? The more time and distance away from Kay, the more his mind focused on her attractive aspects and disregarded the rest: "You've always been such a sweet boy, and I'm sorry for all the times I've been mean to you" and "We were childhood friends, and I'll never forget you" and "You already are important. I love you and I'll never forget you." Jimmy couldn't help but wonder how different things might be if she were sitting next to him now.

And what of his mother? Chloe Red the roughhouse prostitute had accomplished what the vast majority of human beings are incapable of or otherwise flat-out refuse to do: she had changed for the better. In fact, Jimmy wondered at the wisdom of her allowing him to make his own decisions. Shouldn't he be in school? Shouldn't he have waited until he was of legal age before driving across the country? Shouldn't he be afraid to lie to her? Jimmy's answer to each of these questions was yes. He vowed that he would never lie to her again.

* * * * *

While his trip from Pittsburgh to New Orleans took a leisurely five days (probably out of fear of meeting his brother), his journey to Los Angeles was decidedly more urgent.

H. James Branhoover traveled from the Riverfront Hilton to the Beverly Hilton in four days. He checked into his top-floor suite, showered, wrapped himself in the Beverly Hilton's signature bathrobe, laughed because it reminded him of his brother in his pajamas, took it off, lay on the king-size bed, and fell asleep on top of the comforter with the lights on.

67. A Successful Bribe

The next afternoon, H. James Branhoover discovered Trader Vic's. He planted himself in a booth and successfully bribed the waitress to serve him mai tais.

He heard his brother's voice: "Once an alcoholic, always an alcoholic." He dismissed it as more pernicious voodoo. How could a fifteen-year-old be an alcoholic? Charles Larson—now he was an alcoholic. And what of it? If all alcoholics were like me and Charles Larson, then there should be more of us, he thought.

He ordered another mai tai, his fifth, and thought fond thoughts about everybody and everything. Then he curled up in the booth and passed out. The waitress revived him and snuck him outside.

Jimmy awoke in his bed at two in the morning, the day's events erased completely from his mind.

68. A Confession

Jimmy sat in his suite in the Beverly Hilton and wrote the following letter:

Dear Mom:

I have arrived safely in Los Angeles. I'm staying at the Beverly Hilton. I confess that I have lied to you twice.

The first time was when the phone rang at four in the morning. It wasn't Kay Sunday on the line. It was Vander Stevenson, the man who bought the Sundays' church. And actually, now that I have some distance between now and then, I'm not sure it was him either. The message he left for me was so strange that I can't help but wonder if my imagination got the best of me at that early hour. It could be that I was just very stressed about meeting Bernrd, and the call was nothing but a hang-up. Please don't be alarmed. I don't mean to scare you with this news, though I can understand if you find it troubling.

The second time was when I told you I was coming to Hollywood to try acting and that I would stay away from skid row. The truth is that I have no interest in acting, and the real reason I came here is to volunteer at the homeless shelters and missions on, well, skid row. You met Charles Larson. He was a skid row bum, and I helped him get out of there. I'm not pursuing an education—at least not yet—so for now I think this is what I'm supposed to do.

I apologize for telling you these lies. I understand that you have entrusted me to make my own decisions and that you're being lenient with me because you don't want me to wind up like Bernrd. So, no more lies from me.

–Jimmy

69. A Living Entry

As Jimmy tore the page containing the letter from his notebook, he discovered a strand of Kay Sunday's long blonde hair among the pages, no doubt from the time of the high-octane sessions.

This is a living entry, he thought. Then he wrote the following words: "Church blonde. Mother hen blonde. Pretty blonde. Wholesome. Winsome. Helpful."

Jimmy stared at his entry vis-à-vis Kay's hair for a good long minute, feeling perplexed and nostalgic. He closed the notebook on the page of this entry using the strand as a sort of bookmark.

This calls for a mai tai, he thought. He dressed himself accordingly and went down to Trader Vic's, where he was promptly informed by management that he had been eighty-sixed from the premises and that, thanks to him, the waitress who served him had been fired.

And so went the next two years, in a haze of mai tais and blackouts and beers, never setting foot on the rotting pavement of skid row, but often opening his notebook to look at the living entry.

70. Eighteenth Birthday

Around the time of his eighteenth birthday, Jimmy received a card and a letter signed by his mom, Charles Larson, and Betsy Sullivan, wishing him a happy birthday, reminding him that he was now old enough to vote, saying that all was well in the city of Pittsburgh, hoping that his work with the homeless in Los Angeles was going as well as it did in his hometown, and announcing that Charles and Betsy were moving in together.

This was Jimmy's first experience with that troubling phenomenon of time—how two years can slip away unnoticed, how they can get behind you and sneak out the back door with your plans, goals, dreams, and best intentions.

The birthday letter shocked Jimmy into action. He began cruising the streets of downtown Los Angeles in his Mercedes, ten thousand dollars in the glove box, scanning the faces of the destitute men and women in search of an apt beneficiary.

Several days passed without result, and Jimmy began to grow impatient. He needed something to report back home, but he no longer seemed to have the will or, perhaps more accurately, the desperation, to interact with down-and-out and often mentally unstable human beings.

So, on a late afternoon approximately two weeks after his eighteenth birthday, H. James Branhoover drank several beers and promised himself that this would be the day he changed someone's life.

He drove east on Wilshire Boulevard into downtown Los Angeles, which quickly disintegrates into skid row. He scanned the faces of the men and women fidgeting in filthy rows, looking into their eyes for an indication that they had not abandoned God.

Finally, he saw a man who reminded him of Charles Larson, though much older and far weaker. He leapt out of the car, put the ten thousand dollars into the bewildered man's coat pocket, and mumbled something about jobs through Goodwill and getting an apartment. Then he returned to the car, drove straight ahead for several blocks, made a U-turn, and headed back to the spot of his philanthropy.

The elderly man whose eyes had not abandoned God lay coatless and dead in an expanding pool of his own blood. Jimmy instinctively kept driving west through downtown, onto Wilshire Boulevard, and eventually back to his suite in the Beverly Hilton, his body seemingly on the verge of total organ failure.

He lay in bed for what could've been two hours or two days with the singular and unrelenting thought that the only way he could ever find relief would be to kill himself.

71. Divorced

Sometime later in his changed days, H. James Branhoover packed his belongings and checked out of the Beverly Hilton. He drove and lived in his car, divorced from the city and in a black state of mind.

Every moment of his life preceding the skid row incident had been erased. His mother and father, Kay Sunday, Innocent #2 and the Reverend Patchouli Goldwatch, Mrs. Germany, Charles Larson and Betsy Sullivan, the quiet man and the inveterate grifter, his brother, the anti-

Simple Prayer: all gone. He was no longer among the living, but he was not yet among the dead.

Eventually, the living intruded.

The Mercedes had been parked for two days on Santa Monica Boulevard near Cherokee Avenue in Hollywood. This caught the attention of the boys who fake gayness for the sake of slavery, who tapped on the windshield to get Jimmy's attention.

For reasons of youth, ignorance, or otherwise, Jimmy had never been what most people would consider scared during his days with the rows of destitute men. The sight of these three boys, however, none older than fifteen, with stray cat physiques and the fearlessness that comes with a lack of respect for life, terrified him. He pretended to be asleep, but the tapping only grew louder.

"We're not going to hurt you," said the first boy, a practiced effeminacy in his voice.

"Unless you don't talk to us," said the second boy. All three of them laughed.

The laughter flipped a switch in Jimmy's mind. If these three imps jacked his car and left him for dead, the ordeal would be over. This world would no longer concern him. He turned the key in the ignition and rolled down all four windows.

"What do you sweet little boys want?" said Jimmy, tauntingly.

"You!" said the third boy, flashing a mean grin.

"Good, get in then, and let's go," said Jimmy.

The boys glanced at one another, shrugged, and then slid onto the plush leather seats of the Mercedes.

"Do you boys like beer?" asked Jimmy.

"Are you going to get me drunk?" asked the first boy, flirtatiously.

"I'm going to get all of us drunk, and I'm going to pay each of you two thousand dollars for the privilege," said Jimmy.

"Oh, fuck yeah!" said the third boy.

"Where do you boys live?" asked Jimmy.

"Youth hostel on Highland, near the Bowl,"
said the second boy. "And there's a liquor store
just down the street."

72. Six-Thousand-Dollar Promise

H. James Branhoover and the three street boys
arrived at the youth hostel with two cases of beer
in tow. Jimmy procured a room for himself, good
for a year, and invited the boys to join him.

The four of them drank the first case within
an hour or two, but no quantity of alcohol could
erase Jimmy's six-thousand-dollar promise from
the boys' minds.

"So where's our money?" asked the first boy.

This could be it, thought Jimmy. "What
money?" he asked.

"You bitch," said the first boy, clearly acting as spokesman for the other two. "The two thousand for each of us."

"Oh, that was a lie. I thought you were savvy enough to know better," said Jimmy, wincing in anticipation of extreme violence.

To Jimmy's surprise, however, the boys seemed to lose their impish quality. Now they very much appeared as they truly were: frightened teenage runaways. The mood in Jimmy's new room changed entirely.

"I'm sorry," said Jimmy, reaching into the second case and tossing each boy a fresh beer. "I was kind of hoping to die tonight and thought you might be able to help me."

"Nah, we're not killers," said the second boy.

"We're trying to die too," said the third boy, still grinning.

"What's the worst thing you've ever done?" asked Jimmy, on the brink of telling the boys about the skid row incident.

"Let's get out of here," said the first boy.

"Yeah, let's go," said the second boy.

All three boys stood, downed their beers, and tossed the cans to the floor.

"Aren't you coming with us?" asked the third boy, still grinning.

And the four new acquaintances walked out of the youth hostel and into the heart of Hollywood, drunk and trying to forget the worst things they'd ever done.

73. Dimmed the Light in Their Eyes

Jimmy spent the next several months in the company of the three street boys, though they never progressed from acquaintances to friends. They couldn't. Living in the youth hostel in the soft prison of Hollywood forbade it and dimmed the light in their eyes.

And Jimmy's participation in the rituals of their acquaintanceship was limited, much as it was during the high-octane sessions with Kay Sunday and Innocent #2. Where the street boys found temporary relief in shoplifting trinkets, conning tourists, and harassing fellow runaways and the homeless, Jimmy found none. His body was present, but he didn't participate. Where Kay and Innocent #2 took comfort in the ritual of inhaling gasoline fumes, Jimmy barely passed the can under his nose.

The alienation he felt on Kay Sunday's porch was nothing compared to that he felt in Hollywood. In Hollywood, he was trying to die. The further in the past the skid row incident, the greater the magnitude of his guilt.

To the boys' delight and amusement, Jimmy became agitated whenever they harassed a homeless man. So much so, in fact, that this became the boys' primary nocturnal activity.

Jimmy saw at least one aspect of the man from the skid row incident in all of the men and women the boys harassed: the style, depth, and character of the skin; the condition of cuts, scrapes, and bruises; the wildness of the hair; the way the eyes had not abandoned God.

But Jimmy didn't protest any amount of taunting, prodding, or other bullying until the night the boys looked down a stretch of pavement between medium buildings just off the Walk of Fame and spotted a man who—like the man downtown—reminded Jimmy of Charles Larson.

The boys pushed up their sleeves, pursed their lips, and started down the alley to do their impish worst, when Jimmy let his head and back thud against the building and his body slide into a seated position on the sidewalk. He covered his eyes with his hands and wept with such force that the boys were compelled to pay attention.

"Whatever is the matter, dear James?" asked the first boy, his voice already locked in feminine mode.

"Please leave that man alone," mumbled Jimmy. "At least when I'm here. Please."

"Look at that!" exclaimed the second boy. "He's finally having a breakdown."

"It's about time," said the third boy, still grinning. "We were starting to think you were some kind of psychopath."

"Sure, we'll leave him alone. Whatever you want, James," said the first boy.

"Hey, let's get some beers and get wasted in Jimmy's room," said the second boy.

Jimmy did his best to compose himself. "Nah, I'm just going to crash tonight," he said, rising from the huddled mass of himself and walking back to his room in the youth hostel, knowing for certain he would never see these boys again.

74. An Adverse Truth and an Inconsequential Lie

Jimmy sequestered himself in his room, seeing no one and going outside only for beer and fast food. Sitting uncomfortably among grease-stained wrappers and twelve-pack carcasses, he composed two letters: one to Charles Larson and the other to his mother.

> *Dear Charles:*
>
> *I know it's been a long time since we've talked, but that doesn't mean I don't think about you. I was delighted to hear that you and Betsy have moved in together. Could marriage be far off?*
>
> *As for me, things are not going well at all. I got a man killed, Charles. I gave him ten grand down on skid row and someone must have seen me do it, because when I returned, his coat was gone and he was dead. I have started thinking about the martyrs, and I*

think I understand how they find the courage to do what they must.

And to make matters even worse, I can't stop drinking. I'm not sure I want to anyway. When I'm wasted, I look in my notebook. But I don't read the words. I know this is probably the epitome of pathetic, but I found a strand of Kay Sunday's hair among the pages, and I just sit there and look at it. It brings me more comfort than the words.

Yours always,

Haley James Branhoover

Dear Mom:

Things aren't going quite as I'd expected here in terms of helping on skid row, but I haven't given up. Also, I've moved out of the Hilton and into a youth hostel. The hotel just seemed like a waste of Dad's money, and I've got some new friends who live a few doors down from me. It's a really good arrangement.

Isn't it wonderful that Charles and Betsy
have moved in together? If they get married,
I'm definitely coming home for the wedding.
Anyway, I just want to say thank you for
being such a great mom and for trusting me to
make my own decisions.
Love,
James

75. Rancid Words

On a winter evening in his nineteenth year, Haley
James Branhoover, the Branhoovers' second son,
stared at the suicide note he had dashed off
moments earlier on the heels of a week of heavy
drinking, no company, and sporadic sleep.

A part of him wished his final words could
have been the letters he had just sent to Charles
Larson and his mom. But it was too late for those.
He needed to record his final words here, but he

couldn't wait for proper inspiration to strike, because he had the courage to do this now.

He picked the note up off the nightstand and read it aloud:

And so I ran away to Hollywood. Bigger moths need bigger flames. I know after I jump off this building, the world will mourn and pandemonium and chaos will reign. For the record, my dad was a good-for-nothing banker and my mom was an abusive whore. Good riddance to them. Didn't they know who I was? Come to think of it, didn't any of you people know who I was? Fuck all of you!
No longer yours,
H. James Branhoover

The words were rancid. They reeked of pernicious voodoo.

"Trust fund baby," he said.

He set the note back on the nightstand and stared at it again. He couldn't stand the sight of it, so he sealed it in the nearest thing he could find: a business reply envelope for *Playboy* magazine.

He went downstairs to the mailroom and dropped the envelope in the slot. On his way back up, he read the words "Roof Access" around each turn of the staircase.

He walked into the open air on the roof. "Roof Access," he said. He repeated the phrase. It gave him unexpected energy.

He sat down on the edge and dangled his legs over.

76. Dear Angel

On the last day of Jimmy's life, a letter arrived in the mailroom of the Beverly Hilton.

Dear James:

First, the good news. Your kind letter inspired me to propose to Betsy. I had been considering it for months, and then I received your letter. James, she said yes! I'll inform you immediately of the wedding date, and not only do I hope you'll attend, but I would be honored if you would be my best man. Please consider it, James.

And now the further good news. You did not get a man killed. I don't care what the circumstances were. His murder is the fault of those who murdered him, and no one else's. Please don't blame yourself. You are a good man, James, and what you did for that poor soul was even more than good. It was holy.

Oh, dear Angel, how can you fail to acknowledge the miracle?

Yours always,

Charles Larson

Book Three

Kay Sutter Through the Ages

PART I

1. Eulogy

"Of the x number of ways to commit suicide, the outcome for leapers is among the best. The suicide's body hits the pavement, grit, or other hard surface, but the suicide himself feels only the resistance of water— a clear lake of a depth equal to the body's height cubed, typically between one hundred twenty-five and two hundred sixteen feet. Clear water, cloudless sky, full moon, partial view of the galaxy, dragonflies and cedars along the shore, a raft at the end of a wooden dock. In an air temperature of seventy-five degrees Fahrenheit, the suicide waits for sunrise, which never comes."

Kay Sunday looked up from the single page she held with both hands and analyzed the faces of the attendees at the funeral of her childhood friend H. James Branhoover, who had leapt to his death from the roof of a youth hostel in Hollywood, California.

The expressions on their faces seemed to contain the full realm of extreme human emotion, since the deceased's ashes were to be scattered across the Pennsylvania lake that morning and this was to be followed by his good friend Charles Larson's wedding, at which the deceased was to be best man in absentia. But now that Kay had clarified that James wouldn't be available until night, no one knew quite how to behave, and so their faces had to do the work.

The only face that was sympathetic to Kay's eulogy was Mrs. Chloe Branhoover's. Though she was mildly distressed that her son would never see the sun again, except via the secondhand light of the moon, she was relieved to learn that he didn't suffer in his transition to the next world and that his present circumstances were more or less agreeable.

Kay, meanwhile, remained frozen before the mourners because she had planned to close her portion of the ceremony by fixing a photo of James inside a heart-shaped locket, which had just cost her two-thirds of her meager life savings. But the pronounced reactions to her eulogy— which she genuinely did not expect and which made her mind return to the first day of first grade, when she proudly held up a drawing of her teacher as a cow with braces and all the kids laughed—caused her to make quick work of the gesture before she stepped down and assumed a position near Mrs. Branhoover like an elephant calf standing under its mother.

Kay's own mother, Kris, stared at the ground contemplating nature versus nurture, while Mr. Sunday, also Kris, was mesmerized by the ring on the pinky of the deceased's brother, Bernrd Red.

"Like what you see?" asked Bernrd Red, irritated that this man was more interested in the ruby on his finger than in the consequences of his daughter's bizarre eulogy.

"Your ruby is like a red giant star, cooling and dying, consuming every planet in its orbit," said Mr. Sunday. "Did you wear it when James was in your presence?"

"That's right, the ring did it," said Bernrd Red.

Mr. Sunday nodded.

Meanwhile, the man James and Charles Larson had called "the quiet man" during their time along the rows of destitute men approached Kay. He looked into her otherworldly eyes for the first time, hoping to glimpse the alien inside.

Kay returned his gaze with her own, and with an equal amount of suspicion.

"So you're the reason Jimmy found religion and brought his money down to skid row," said the quiet man.

Mrs. Branhoover glared at him. Kay didn't flinch.

"It's okay," he said. "Nobody here hates you. In fact, they all accept what you say without question like they're in a trance or under a spell. And what did you put inside your locket? Can I see it?"

Kay Sunday's eyes switched from inscrutable spy to inquisitive scientist. She unclasped the chain and handed the locket to the quiet man. He opened it and examined the photo of James.

"Damien Freakshow," he mumbled.

"Damien What?" asked Kay.

"Freakshow," said the quiet man. "That's what we . . . I used to call Jimmy when he stalked us bums with his Bible."

"Hmm. I don't like it. It doesn't suit James at all."

"Well, if you put it that way, I don't either," said the quiet man, feigning a trance. "Anyway, I guess what I really wanted to ask is, are you some kind of witch?"

"Through the ages," said Kay Sunday, glancing at the ground and then scanning the sky in search of the source of her reply.

While Kay Sunday searched the heavens, the rest of the wedding guests were left to fidget in the prisons of their bodies until the bride, Betsy Sullivan, announced that in light of the new circumstances, the ceremony would be postponed until that evening so the best man could attend.

As the guests dispersed, Mrs. Branhoover walked to her son's former car, where she retrieved the container with his ashes and then carried it out to the end of the wooden dock on Loyalhanna Lake, her thoughts alternating between the strange comfort of Kay's words and the unbearable image, as she stood at the edge of the dock, of her second son sitting on the edge of the roof of the youth hostel, hopeless, trapped, and believing himself out of options. She felt her body give out from under her, and with it, her son's ashes, which plunged into the water, container and all.

The bride and groom rushed to her aid and escorted her off the dock and back onto the shore, the truth of a boy's short life, tragic death, and his mother's grief made plain once and for all.

2. Intermission

In times of suspended animation in the long lives of a certain ilk of people (people who aren't to be easily let off the hook), such as the hours between a morning funeral and an afternoon wedding moved to the evening on account of the convincing eulogy of a putative witch, the petty animosities imagined in prior solitary hours are forced into abeyance and, in their place, compelled by the mere proximity of the others and sympathy for the grieving mother, a silent acknowledgment of mutual weakness, and something approaching understanding.

3. Wedding

When evening arrived on the lake, the bride and groom were pleased to see that all but one of the twenty-odd funeral guests had remained for the wedding. The quiet man had disappeared to who-knows-where in the hour after Mrs. Branhoover had spilled James' ashes into the water.

The chaplain of the Presbyterian hospital, where both bride and groom worked as nurses, officiated the brief ceremony, which took place in the same setting and under identical weather conditions as Kay had described in her eulogy, which further amplified Mrs. Sunday's shame, especially considering that a winter evening on the lake hadn't been this balmy since the warm spell of 1950.

A helicopter flew over the ceremony and drowned out Charles Larson's voice while he recited his vows, which made the bride laugh, and her laughter caused Mrs. Branhoover to smile, and Mrs. Branhoover's smile restored everybody's well-being, such as it was.

When the noise of the chopper abated, Charles Larson scanned the guests' faces and, noticing their heightened receptivity, removed a piece of paper from the inside pocket of his tux and began to read.

"It is customary at weddings for the best man to say a few—or several drunken—words about his relationship with the groom, share an amusing or embarrassing anecdote or two, and then wish the newlyweds the best of luck."

The guests chuckled politely.

"Well, at this wedding the bride and groom have determined to start a more enlightened tradition and spare our best man the ordeal."

These words once again made the guests uncomfortably aware of their bodies.

"I first met Haley James Branhoover on skid row, which I regret was my former residence. For reasons that are still mysterious to me, James visited us down there when he was just a boy. We had no knowledge of his identity or his circumstances, and during the first several times in our presence he didn't say a word, which made me wonder whether he was some sort of apparition or figment. I theorized that he must be an angel because, again for mysterious reasons, nobody harmed him, even though I knew there were plenty who wanted to. My theory was proved beyond a doubt on the day when his Bible was knocked out of his hand, but instead of shrinking or running, he stared down his assailant and said, 'How can you fail to acknowledge the miracle?'

"When James uttered these words, I knew something important was happening that I didn't understand, and that I needed to get good and drunk to deal with it."

The guests laughed loud enough for Charles Larson to look up from his paper and meet their eyes. He made sure to smile at Kay and then continued.

"You've probably figured out that I'm an alcoholic. I knew what I was and I knew that it put me on skid row and I knew that I didn't care until I met James. On the day I took my last drink, I said to James, 'I can't stop drinking, could you sit with me until this passes?' and he said, 'That's why I'm here.' I believed him, and he kept his word. He couldn't have been more than eleven years old. It's still hard for me to comprehend.

"As I'm sure most of you are aware, James helped me financially as well, but I won't go into that. I'll close by telling you that James confided to me in a letter that he believed he got a man killed in Los Angeles. It was a man on skid row, just like I had been. I wasn't sure I was going to tell you this, but I think it's important you know the reason why James did what he did in ending his life.

"He was a gifted young man and I believe he knew he was loved, but his guilt—wrong as it was

531

for him to blame himself—was too much for him."

With that, Charles Larson refolded the paper and slid it back into his tux.

4. Reception

The quiet man hadn't disappeared to who-knows-where for the reason Charles Larson had thought—that he despised love and its rituals. And "who-knows-where" was much closer than anyone would have guessed.

The quiet man had merely wandered off into the dense forest surrounding the lake because he felt he needed solitude to attempt to grasp Kay Sunday's response to his question.

"Are you a witch?"

"Through the ages."

These three words did no less than cause him to question his entire philosophy of life, which he might also have described in three words: "This is it."

The quiet man had long ago banished any notion that there is anything beyond what the five senses can perceive. He had scoffed at Charles Larson's drunken delusion that Jimmy Branhoover was some kind of angel.

But Kay's "through the ages" had come from somewhere else. Kay herself had scanned the heavens in search of its source, and he had witnessed her do it. If anyone has a foolproof bullshit detector, it's me, he thought, leaning against a cedar.

Then he considered her eulogy vis-à-vis the lake and the day's weather, and concluded that he owed it to himself to return for the reception. And besides, they would have free booze and where else did he have to go?

As the quiet man made his way back to the reception, he found himself looking at the trees along the lakeshore in a new way. The idea that he must return to skid row after this night was over seemed ridiculous at best. I can go anywhere I want, he thought, and considered the ways he could ask Charles Larson for bus fare to someplace warmer than Pittsburgh: Phoenix, San Diego, Miami, New Orleans, or even L.A. He could visit the building Jimmy Branhoover had leapt from. No. He would wash his hands of this bunch once and for all. Miami. He would ask Charles Larson for bus fare to Miami.

When the guests came into view, the quiet man saw the bride and groom speaking with Kay and Mrs. Branhoover, and Mr. and Mrs. Sunday speaking with Bernrd Red.

Mr. Sunday continued to harp on the dying star on Bernrd Red's pinky finger, insinuating that James' mere presence in the stone's orbit was the reason for the souring of his luck and had probably led to his death.

Bernrd Red shrugged and explained that in Vegas he was a cooler "so tell me something I don't already know," but Mr. Sunday had planted the seed in Bernrd Red's mind that Bernrd had contributed to his brother's suicide. The roots of contrition began to take hold and spread inside his skull, parasitic tendrils that would alter the very coding of his DNA and shake up the foundation of his violent upbringing, and against which he would be forced into internal combat for the rest of his days.

The quiet man walked right past Bernrd Red, oblivious to his fledgling metamorphosis, and joined Kay, Mrs. Branhoover, and the new Mr. and Mrs. Larson.

Charles, Betsy, and Mrs. Branhoover were telling Kay about the day they took James to get the Mercedes, how nice a day it was for all of them, and how James had later wondered aloud to his mother whether he should invite Kay to go with him on his journey.

In other words, the three of them were attempting—and failing miserably—to divert Kay's attention from the rough day she was having, so when the quiet man joined them and Kay seemed relieved, or even happy, to see him, the quiet man embraced her while visions of white sand beaches, clear blue ocean, and palm trees moved behind his eyes.

The newlyweds let out a burst of sound, a "Baahh!" which was their version of the sound of joyous disbelief.

"I've never seen you hug anyone in my life," said Charles Larson to the quiet man.

The quiet man promptly withdrew, as did the idyllic visions in his mind, which were replaced with blue words and insults for Charles Larson, which he kept to himself out of respect for his new outlook. In fact, once he saw the look of contrition in Charles Larson's eyes, he knew his day in the sun would be forthcoming.

"You don't know the half of it," said the quiet man. "Ms. S... Ms. ..., I'm sorry, Kay, what is your last name again?"

"Sutter," Kay replied, to the surprise of herself, Charles, Betsy, and Mrs. Branhoover, who had expected to hear "Sunday."

"Ms. Sutter's unique perspective has made me question my own. Charles, I'm just going to come right out and ask: Can I have bus fare to Miami?"

"You see, Kay, there's the proof. People think they're confounded by you, but really it's inspiration. Of course you may have bus fare," said Charles Larson, who removed his wallet from his back pocket and handed the quiet man five hundred dollars.

"Please, just take all of this before you can say no."

"I wasn't going to say no," said the quiet man, who calmly folded the five bills, slid them into his front pocket, turned, and departed without saying another word.

"Bastard," muttered Charles Larson.

This transaction reminded Mrs. Branhoover that she had something to give Kay. She grabbed Kay's bicep and led her to James' former car. She opened the trunk and pulled out his notebook. "I want you to have this, Ms. Sutter," she said.

Though Kay imagined a horrified expression on Jimmy's face, she simply lacked the energy to refuse Mrs. Branhoover.

Most of the guests were utterly exhausted now and took the quiet man's leaving as their cue to pay their final respects to the deceased, offer their final congratulations to the bride and groom, and make their way home, confused and with a new lifetime memory.

5. Notebook

Kay Sutter shut herself in her bedroom for a week, coming out only for essentials, to escape from the funeral and the wedding, and to attempt to understand her supposed witchiness.

She looked at the photo of James in her locket. Heard the name "Damien Freakshow" in the quiet man's voice.

She read James' notebook cover to cover. It was thick: two hundred pages. And every line was filled with text. Kay wasn't surprised by the topics that captured James' attention—herself, his parents, the homeless men, all vis-à-vis religion—but she couldn't help being impressed by the depth and precision of his observations.

She plucked a hair and deliberately placed it in the notebook on the page marked "Living Entry," replacing the hair that had fallen there of its own volition.

There is so much more to people than we ever care to know, she thought. But maybe we should care.

Her mind returned to the last time she saw James, the final high-octane session on her porch, when he had said to her, "How could someone so clever and full of grace be so shallow?" And she had replied with the meanest possible words she could conjure on the spot and under the influence of gasoline fumes. They were hurtful words and they cut to the core, but she couldn't recall exactly what they were.

She closed the notebook and directed her mind to the first days of her friendship with James, Mrs. Germany's kindergarten class at the Carden School.

She wondered why nobody had seemed to notice the depth of James' intellect, when it was clear from his notebook entries that he possessed intelligence, while, conversely, everybody had exalted her abilities, when—she had to admit— what she had mostly demonstrated were flourishes of eccentricity. The best she could come up with was that James' enthusiasm and lack of guile concealed his more thoughtful aspect. People are so easily swindled, she thought. People like to be charmed and swindled. Her mind flashed to the Reverend Patchouli Goldwatch.

She reopened the notebook to the page with her newly plucked hair and began working her way backward to the entries where James had just left New Orleans and had made his way to L.A.

She was surprised by how easily James had succumbed to drinking, considering how vehemently opposed he was to inhaling gasoline fumes. She found it terrifying that James seemed to think his brother was responsible for his addiction and the overall souring of his luck. She was fascinated by his relationship with the street boys, how in his desperation he had managed to find the guile necessary to fool them, and once they had found him out, how they had become vulnerable in James' presence. James had won over these hardened runaways and had become friends with them.

Then she considered the possibility that Jimmy had concocted these stories to assuage his drunken loneliness and the guilt he felt over the skid row incident.

"Are any of the entries from his final days real?" she wondered aloud. "Am I really a witch?"

In her isolation, Kay Sutter concluded that the answer to the former would reveal the answer to the latter.

6. Four Cars in the Driveway

Kay Sutter arrived unannounced at the Branhoovers' mansion. She parked her parents' Volvo next to the late H. James Branhoover's Mercedes, which was parked next to the late H. Charles Branhoover's BMW, which was parked next to a car Kay didn't recognize: a Mustang GT.

She reached for James' notebook and recalled the entries describing Mrs. Branhoover's gentleman visitors. "She must love her work," she said. Then she recalled the woman who was so distraught over her son's suicide that she had collapsed and nearly fallen into the lake.

"What should I do, Jimmy?" she asked.

As she sat waiting for his reply, the front doors of the mansion opened, and out walked Mrs. Branhoover and Bernrd Red. She shut the notebook in the glove compartment and stepped out of the car to greet them. Bernrd Red seemed to smirk and recoil simultaneously when he saw

543

Kay, while Mrs. Branhoover stretched out both arms in welcome.

Kay's mind returned to the Halloween when she and James were kindergarteners and Mr. Branhoover had mistaken Kay's yellow bee makeup for urine when he had walked in on her taking a bath, forgetting in his old age that there was a little girl in his home that night.

Kay allowed Mrs. Branhoover to embrace her, and the three of them went directly to the dining room, where Kay noticed Bernrd's ruby ring on the table. She recalled that her father had mentioned the ring on the drive home after the funeral and wedding, how he had compared the ruby to a red giant star, how he had asked Bernrd whether he wore the ring in James' presence, and how he fully understood what he was insinuating to James' older brother.

Kay couldn't recall her father ever being that mean to anyone, but then James did buy back their church from Goldwatch, so she understood her father's need to blame someone to reconcile the worldly injustice of a good man dying so young, and, knowing her father's point of view, not just a good man but a holy man.

Now the ring lay on the table. Kay considered Bernrd Red's expression when he saw her, Mr. Sunday's daughter, step out of her car, so she determined not to mention it, not only to keep the peace but also to prevent a potentially incendiary digression from her purpose there.

"I like your car," said Kay to the obviously distracted Bernrd Red.

"It's a rental," he replied and then looked at his ring for a good long time to elicit discomfort.

Kay maintained a neutral expression, pulled out the chair closest to the ring, and sat down with provocative obliviousness.

Mrs. Branhoover smiled with kindness at her surviving son and sat down, but Bernrd Red remained standing.

It was witch versus voodoo priest in the Branhoovers' dining room, mediated by a former prostitute.

"Did you get a chance to read James' notebook?" asked Mrs. Branhoover.

"That's why I'm here," said Kay. "I'd like to go to L.A. to meet the boys from the youth hostel to get their perspective on what happened to James."

"Oh, would you?" questioned Mrs. Branhoover.

"I would," said Kay.

"And please, take the Mercedes. James would be delighted to know you were driving it."

At this, Bernrd Red scoffed. "Yeah, and why don't you take my ring while you're at it."

"No, thank you," said Kay, refusing to acknowledge its presence directly under her nose.

As Kay drove down the hill in James' former car, she pondered how she didn't even have to ask if she could borrow it.

7. Winding Down the Hill

As Kay wound down the hill and back into the city in James' former car, she resumed her conversation with him.

"I like to think of you being at the lake," she said. "And maybe I'd like to be at the lake with you. I don't understand why everyone was so upset about it."

She opened her locket and glanced at the photo of James. It was the last photo Mrs. Branhoover had taken of him. She had snapped it the day before James left to visit his brother in New Orleans. He looked thoughtful, all grown up, a little scared. And like the notebook and the car, Mrs. Branhoover wanted Kay to have the photo.

Kay was moved and perplexed by Mrs. Branhoover's generosity toward her. She wondered again about her supposed witchiness. Then she wondered about her parents' Volvo, which she had left behind in the Branhoovers' driveway.

Bernrd Red's thoughts were also on the Sundays' Volvo. He had put the ring back on his finger where it belonged, walked onto the driveway with his bags, opened the door of the Volvo, and sat down behind the wheel ready to return to New Orleans. He twisted the ring around his finger, and while it spun around his skin, slightly burning, the parasitic tendrils inside his skull bore deeper into his brain. He saw his brother's face and another face he hadn't considered in years, the face of the pregnant woman's husband whom he had cuckolded in the honeymoon suite of the bed-and-breakfast. Then he opened the glove compartment and saw his brother's notebook.

Bernrd Red leapt out of the Volvo, tossed his bags into the backseat of the Mustang, wound down the hill, and headed to the airport, acquiring a speeding ticket on the way.

8. Silent Partner

Kay Sutter drove right past her parents' house and onto the interstate. "My mom is disappointed with me, James," she said. "She thought so highly of you, and she thinks I'm an idiot for rejecting you. She doesn't realize that I tried to be your friend again, but you said no. And good for you for saying no to me, James. Good for you."

The late H. James Branhoover was becoming fast friends with Kay, her confidante, her silent partner, patient and kind and forgiving.

"How strange and wonderful that you can be at the lake and here with me at the same time," she said.

"Do you think I'm a witch, James? Your friend from skid row thinks I am. And your mom is being so nice to me. It really doesn't make sense. Maybe I am a witch. Maybe I don't have a choice . . .

"So, what else is there to talk about? I still live with my parents, but that isn't very interesting. You missed high school. Rumor had it that Clayton and I huffed gasoline fumes and then he got me pregnant. Everybody thought I had gotten an abortion, so nobody would talk to me. Then Clayton moved back to Santa Cruz with his parents. He said he would write, but he never did."

Kay laughed and then drifted off to the hum of the highway for an hour.

"I sent him a letter, James. It was about a storyteller in a village of mutes, who was banished after she wrote 'silence hurts' with a stick in the dirt. Years later, she returned with toy animals fashioned of iron and wood.

"He still never wrote back."

Kay laughed again.

"God, I love your car. I feel like I could just drive all the way to L.A. without stopping."

9. A Long Flight Home

Bernrd Red looked out the window on his return flight to New Orleans. The pregnant woman's husband. What was his name? It had unusual letters. An x or a q or a z. Xavier. Quinn. Zeke. Zach. That's it. His name was Zachary.

His mind flashed to the face of Zachary's pregnant wife and the beating he gave her, which triggered that infernal song, Crosby, Stills, Nash & Young's "Carry On," which hadn't wormed through his mind in years, since before his brother had visited him.

But now it was back. He thought about Dr. Beverly Farworthy and his time in the asylum. He thought about Jimmy's visit. The word "recidivism" popped into his head. He thought about his brother's getting drunk, how he had encouraged it in his own sick way. He thought about Jimmy's going to L.A. and about getting the news from his mother that Jimmy had jumped off the roof of a youth hostel in

Hollywood. He thought about Mr. Sunday at the funeral and his assessment of the ring. How he had blamed the ring for Jimmy's death.

Bernrd Red twisted the ring with as much friction and velocity as he could muster. He wanted to feel the burn.

10. Brotherless

Bernrd Red woke up brotherless in New Orleans. He opened a beer and drank it down. Then he drank two more and thought he had better eat something.

He rummaged through a kitchen drawer, looking for a spatula, and came across a cigarette lighter. Crosby, Stills, Nash & Young and the tendrils wormed through his mind. He needed them to cease immediately.

He recalled how twisting his ring had caused a pleasing burn, which had the added benefit of quieting his mind. He removed the ring and heated it with the flame of the lighter. Then he applied it like a brand to his wrist. The pain put an end to the music and made the tendrils wither.

He took off his pajamas and repeated the procedure on his chest and ribs like a doctor with a stethoscope. Then he methodically branded his way down to his feet. A tendril seemed to shrivel and die with each forming welt.

The song returned, but now it didn't seem to bother him. He recalled his childhood, when he had held a favorable opinion of CSNY.

"A favorable opinion," he said.

A feeling of eagerness overtook him. He put on his pajamas and slid his feet into a pair of slippers.

He stepped outside and started to walk down the dry black street. He noticed the weather, pleasant but windy. The wind blew copper leaves along the street. Then he noticed something else, which caused his enthusiasm to diminish. There seemed to be a pebble in his slipper, but when he removed and inspected it: nothing. He returned it to his foot. The irritant remained.

The ring, he thought.

He removed it from his finger and put it in his pocket, the brilliant ruby mixed in with so much loose change.

He continued along the street until he saw a teenage girl with a shaved head outside Café Macabre, leaning against a pole and smoking a cigarette. He looked into her eyes, which blossomed like sunflowers.

The tendrils inside his skull began to sprout like the stubble on the girl's head. All at once he saw Zachary and his pregnant wife, felt his pajamas snag the welts all over his body, and suffered the invisible pebble in his slipper.

He began to rant at the girl, some nonsense about wouldn't it be nice if she had some hair that could blow in the direction of the wind, and about his waking nervous as a bull thinking slow as cheese and the pebble in his slipper irritating him and making him moan. He felt like some kind of religious lunatic speaking in tongues.

The ring, he thought.

He reached into his pocket, grabbed a handful of pennies, and tossed them—along with his ring—into the street.

The girl scooped up the ring and the pennies and disappeared into the café.

The ring belongs to her now, he thought. It's the least I can do.

11. Five Years Later

Five years later the girl no longer had a shaved head, but she did still have the ring, which an appraiser valued at twenty-five thousand dollars.

She didn't want to keep it, and in fact sold it the day after her boyfriend proposed in order to finance the wedding, which was held on the white sands near Las Cruces, New Mexico.

"Do you, Jason Cooper, take this woman to be your wife, to have and to hold from this day forward, for better or for worse, for richer, for poorer, in sickness and in health, to love and to cherish, from this day forward, until death do you part?"

"I do," said Jason Cooper.

"Do you, Sarah Rayford, take this man to be your husband, to have and to hold from this day forward, for better or for worse, for richer, for poorer, in sickness and in health, to love and to cherish, from this day forward, until death do you part?"

"I do," she said.

PART II

12. Less Comfortable Than Cambodia

Kay Sutter made the trip from the Branhoovers' driveway in Pittsburgh to the youth hostel in Hollywood in four days. Driving six hundred miles a day was exhausting to be sure, but somehow it was less taxing on her than the flight to Cambodia after her parents had sold their church to Goldwatch.

Kay knew what it was like to be broke, at least until James had repurchased their church and, unknown to her for a time, kicked in even more money to finance her parents' current house.

But the locket had cost two-thirds of her personal savings, and gas and lodging were more expensive than she had anticipated.

"Maybe I should have taken your brother's ring and sold it, James," she said. "But he wasn't really going to give it to me, was he?

"Don't answer that," she said, managing to laugh. "I'll ask your mom if she can help, at least until I get a job."

Kay Sutter checked in at the youth hostel, dragged her bags to her room on the ground floor and crashed in her new bed, which was less comfortable than her bed in Cambodia.

In the morning she called Mrs. Branhoover, who informed her that her Volvo was secure in the Branhoovers' driveway, that she was going to FedEx James' notebook if not today then tomorrow, and that there was no way Kay was going to waste time seeking employment in L.A.

Mrs. Branhoover arranged for one hundred thousand dollars to be wired to a new bank account opened in the name of Kay Sutter.

13. An Open Door

James' notebook arrived in the youth hostel mailroom late the following morning. Kay retrieved it and was intending to return to her room to formulate a strategy for ascertaining the truth about James, when she passed by a room with an open door and glimpsed a chandelier hanging tenuously from the yellowed and peeling ceiling. And that was not all. Sitting unconcerned beneath the teetering chandelier were two young women of approximately Kay's age wearing Gothic clothing and makeup.

"Gracie, do you have any fives?" asked the girl on Kay's left.

"Go fish," said Gracie.

"Damn you," said the girl, who finally noticed Kay at the door.

"My name's Nirvana," she said. "We've been hoping to find a third. Wanna play?"

"Yeah, we've been expecting you," said Gracie.

Kay entered the room, took a seat at the card table, and looked over the new girls in their strange milieu.

"Your eyes are mesmerizing," said Nirvana to Kay.

"I wouldn't go that far," said Gracie.

"Gracie and Nirvana?" asked Kay. "Are those your real names?"

The girls looked at each other, and then Gracie scooped up the cards and began to shuffle them.

"And what's your real name?" she asked.

"Kay Sutter."

"Oh, look," said Nirvana. "Kay has a locket like mine."

"Though not as cheesy as yours," said Gracie.

Nirvana giggled. "There is nothing cheesy about Jonathan Scott-Taylor."

Gracie hissed.

"Who's that?" asked Kay.

"He played Damien Thorn in the Omen II," said Nirvana, who opened her locket to show the photo to Kay.

"Oh, how Goth," said Gracie.

Kay recalled the quiet man's "Damien Freakshow." It gave her the shivers.

"Do you have a photo in your locket, Kay?" asked Nirvana.

Kay opened her locket and showed the photo of James to both girls. Nirvana shrieked. Gracie became quiet and looked at the floor.

"You knew him," said Kay, solemnly.

"He's the boy who jumped off the roof a month or two ago," said Gracie.

"Yeah. I'd known him since kindergarten," said Kay.

"There's a lovely memorial up there, where he leapt," said Nirvana. "Do you want to see it?"

"Yes," said Kay.

14. In the Mind of the Boy

The three girls wound their way up the stairs of the five-story youth hostel, each attempting to place herself in the mind of the boy in Kay's locket who had ascended these same stairs on the last day of his life.

Kay Sutter was the last to step out onto the roof. The shrine was much larger than she expected. Flowers, candles, poems, and crucifixes lined the entire eastern edge of the roof.

"Oh, James, do you see it?" asked Kay.

Gracie and Nirvana looked at each other but didn't say anything.

"Oh, hey, look who's become one with the lilies," said Nirvana.

"Diego, what's up?" said Gracie.

Diego sat up, scattering the flowers and poems that were lying on top of him.

"Hey, Gracie. Hey, Nirvana," said Diego, startled out of his nap and pretending he wasn't really asleep, as if sleeping were something to be embarrassed about.

"Diego is the keeper of the shrine," said Nirvana to Kay.

"It's beautiful," said Kay.

"Show him your locket," said Nirvana.

Kay unclasped the locket and handed it whole to Diego, which made Gracie anxious and which Nirvana found endearing.

When Diego saw the photo of James, his spirit seemed to leave the roof and float off into the ether. Kay looked up after him, and when her eyes returned to level ground, she knew this was one of the street boys from James' notebook.

"You're in here," said Kay, handing the notebook to Diego.

"Oh, man, I've seen this. I mean, I never opened it, but I remember seeing it in his room. What's your name?"

"Oh, where are your manners, Gracie," said Nirvana, giggling. "Diego, Kay. Kay, Diego."

"I knew there was a girl," said Diego, believing that he finally comprehended what was going on and taking a step back.

Kay winced and looked down.

"Shit, Diego!" said Gracie. "Kay was his friend. She came all this way and moved into this dump because of him. She even talks to him. She's the only one he'll listen to."

Diego paused and attempted to assimilate what Gracie had said, all of which was incredibly bizarre and yet somehow rang true. "Well, maybe she feels guilty," he said, returning the locket and the notebook to Kay and heading toward the stairs.

"What's eating him?" asked Nirvana.

Gracie glared at her.

"It's okay," said Kay. "He's upset. I like how he stuck up for his friend."

Kay also liked how Diego didn't succumb to her innate charm. She liked how he challenged her witchiness.

15. A Living Representative

Kay returned to her room and took a much-needed nap. When she came to, she half-heartedly fanned through the notebook. Now that she had met Diego, a living representative of its pages, the words had lost their potency. She wanted to talk to Diego and hear everything he had to say about James. She also wanted to learn more about Diego himself.

"I like your friend Diego," said Kay to James. "You really left a lasting impression on him. And what about Gracie and Nirvana? I don't feel so different around them. Did you know them? I'm not sure I like them, exactly, but they make me feel less alone."

Kay looked around her room at the bare walls and languid furnishings. She wondered what her new friends were up to. She walked down the hall to Gracie and Nirvana's room. The door was still open. She looked inside. The card table and chandelier were gone, and there was no trace of

567

the girls. Kay jogged up the stairs to the roof in a mild panic, hoping to find Diego among the lilies of the shrine.

He wasn't there. What the hell is this place? she thought. She trampled roses, kicked over a candle, came to the edge of the roof, and looked down, understanding how a mind, friendless and confused, could want to divorce itself from the world.

16. Breakfast

Kay was up early the following morning, packing and unpacking, missing Mrs. Branhoover and her parents yet glad to be away from them, pining for Pennsylvania, hating Hollywood, and daydreaming about other places and other cities, when she heard a loud voice in the hall outside her door.

"Kay? Kay? We know you're in there. We can smell your brain." And then laughter. It was Nirvana.

Kay smiled inside her room and opened the door. All three of them—Gracie, Nirvana, and Diego—stood in the hallway.

"Oh, thank God," said Kay. "I thought all of you were gone."

"Gone?" asked Gracie, perplexed and concerned.

"I went by your room. I thought you had moved out."

"Well, we did move," said Nirvana, pointing to the end of the hall.

"It has fresh paint," said Gracie. "We couldn't pass it up."

"Hey, Diego," said Kay, with deliberate brightness in her voice.

"Hi, Kay," replied Diego, sheepishly. "Sorry about yesterday. I don't even know you yet, so I shouldn't have judged you."

"Right. Wait till you know her, and then judge her with impunity," said Gracie.

All four of them laughed.

"Hey, let's go to the beach for breakfast," said Nirvana.

"Oh, I don't know," said Gracie. "Do you really want to spend the day on the bus?"

"I've got a car," said Kay.

"Then let's get out of here," said Diego.

The four of them walked down the hall, out of the building, and into the parking lot.

"What the fuck," said Diego as they came upon the Mercedes.

"Oh . . . No . . . I . . . His mom insisted I take it for the long trip," said Kay, immediately comprehending her blunder.

"That's *his* car!?" exclaimed Nirvana.

"His mom insisted?" asked Gracie, skeptically. "I don't know. This is too weird."

"Can you wait here a minute? I need to show you something," said Kay.

Gracie shrugged.

Kay went to her room, retrieved the notebook, and returned to the car, relieved and somewhat surprised that all three of them were still there.

"Yeah, we know about the notebook," said Diego.

"But you don't know what's inside," said Kay, who was through humoring him. "James was convinced that he had gotten a man killed, but I don't believe it. His mom wants to know too, and she is helping me out. And that's all there is to it."

"We want to help, too," said Nirvana.

"You two didn't even know him," grumbled Diego. "Nobody did, really. Jimmy was always distracted."

"Well, that's a good start," said Kay.

"Can we discuss this in our room? I'm starving," said Gracie. "There's no way I'm going to make it to the beach. I think we've got bagels and beer."

Gracie and Nirvana's new room was the same as their old room, the card table under the chandelier and sundry trinkets on the walls: miniature stars, moons, and gargoyles, and an ironic crucifix. The only difference was the fresh paint. The toxic fumes reminded Kay of the high-octane sessions.

"We used to inhale gasoline fumes on my porch," she said.

"Then you must be feeling nostalgic," replied Gracie.

"Maybe that's why he jumped," said Diego. "Jimmy was always wasted. He just wasn't thinking straight."

Kay momentarily considered mentioning that James had rarely inhaled the fumes on her porch, but held back. "Maybe so," she said, taking a healthy swig of the beer Nirvana had opened for her and then reaching for the notebook with her other hand.

"You're in here," she continued, "but James mentions two other boys. Do they still live here?"

"People come and go around here," he said. "Not just Jimmy. Anyway, no, I have no idea where they are."

"Okay," she said. "At least I know James didn't make them up."

"Which means he *did* get a man killed," said Nirvana, with moonlight in her eyes.

"You're such a psycho," said Gracie.

"You're so snide," replied Nirvana.

"There was a homeless man down an alley off Hollywood Boulevard who really freaked him out," said Diego.

"Is he the one?" asked Nirvana.

"I don't think so," said Diego. "Jimmy really stuck up for him. He might still be there. I don't know."

"Is it far away?" asked Kay.

"Nah, walking distance," said Diego.

The four of them finished their bagels and beers and set off on foot toward Zachary R.'s stretch of pavement between medium buildings.

17. The Man in the Alley

As Diego led Kay, Gracie, and Nirvana down Highland and left on Hollywood Boulevard, he recalled his last encounter with the man in the alley. Though none of them acknowledged it at the time, the three street boys, Diego included, went to the alley that night to take out their grief on the homeless man who had made James crumble to the ground and who had discovered James' body on the night of his leap.

The three of them split up not more than a week later. The first street boy, Chase, got picked up by his parents. Diego was surprised by the enthusiasm with which Chase, their supposed leader, slid onto the backseat of his parents' car. The second street boy, Elliot, who had thought number one was his best friend, mumbled something about Portland and then disappeared. Which left Diego, the smiling one, keeper of the shrine, on his way to the alley again, but in the company of women.

To everyone's disappointment, but especially Kay's, the man was not in the alley.

"Are you sure this is the right one?" asked Kay.

Diego nodded.

"It's not a total loss," said Nirvana. "He wanted you to have these." She handed Kay the urn which once held Annabel R.'s ashes and now contained the sunflowers Sarah R. had replaced them with.

Kay held the urn and gazed at the wilted flowers.

"No. You're right. Her eyes *are* mesmerizing," said Gracie.

"I'm keeping these," said Kay.

Nirvana giggled.

"That's kinda gross," said Gracie. "Diego will buy you flowers. Won't you, Diego?"

Diego didn't respond. He was rummaging through a pile of items next to a dumpster.

"I recognize this stuff," he said. He moved aside a hat rack with a sailor's hat on it, a stack of magazines, and a neatly arranged row of empty beer bottles, some with the caps on, until he came across a clipboard with a sealed business reply envelope clamped to it. Diego instinctively handed it over to Kay.

Kay set down the urn and opened the envelope.

Inside were four pages of words and artwork scribbled on the back of used pleading paper. Kay admired the schizophrenic contrast between the staid Times New Roman type on the front versus the wild scrawl on the back.

The one-word title written at the top of the back of the first page was "SUICIDE," but it hardly seemed like a suicide note to Kay. It contained pictures, mostly. Pictures with captions. A drawing of a redheaded Goth Girl had the word "Protect" written beneath it. A drawing of a brunette Goth Girl was captioned "Torment." Several spirals of varying sizes were drawn on all four pages, each one captioned "The Cracked Snail." And then, inconceivably, on page three, a ruby ring and a nametag with the name "Bernrd Red," and on page four, three menacing-looking boys and one gentle-looking boy, a blond, who seemed to resemble both James and Kay.

Kay began to hyperventilate. "What is this? . . . Who are you? Why are you fucking with me?" she screamed, pounding on Diego's chest.

Diego attempted in vain to keep Kay at arm's length while imploring Gracie and Nirvana's assistance with his eyes.

"Kay! Kay! You don't mean Diego, you mean the homeless man. You mean who's the homeless man," said Gracie.

"I mean all of you," replied Kay. "How could all of you be in here? How could James and I be the same person? How could you have known about James' brother and his ring?"

"No, Kay, you mean the homeless man," Gracie repeated, not knowing what else to say.

Nirvana, attempting to quell the chaos inside of her, extended her arms for a hug.

Kay began to calm down when she registered the genuine confusion in Nirvana's eyes. Then she handed the note to Gracie. "Look, here you are," said Kay, pointing to the redheaded Goth. "And there's Nirvana and Diego," pointing at the brunette Goth and one of the three menacing-looking boys. "And there's James, but he looks like me, too. No, he mostly looks like me."

"It kinda does look like me," said Nirvana, the moonlight returning to her eyes.

"It really does," said Diego, examining the portrait of the brunette Goth.

Gracie flipped through the pages several times before agreeing that all the portraits were eerily accurate. Then she asked Kay about the "Bernrd Red" nametag and the ring.

"That's James' older brother," said Kay, quietly.

"No," said Nirvana, extending her arms again, but this time to show everyone her goose bumps.

"That's unbelievable," said Diego. "I mean, it's not much of a stretch that he could have seen all of us at some point. But the nametag is just freaky."

"Maybe he was some sort of tormented prophet," said Gracie.

"And there's more," said Kay. "James also put his suicide note in a business reply envelope. These drawings aren't a suicide note, but the word 'SUICIDE' is written at the top of page one, as if this homeless man knew. Hey . . . wait. What do you mean *was* a prophet?"

"Well, that *is* an urn," replied Gracie, pointing at Kay's new possession.

"Goose bumps," said Nirvana, grinning.

18. Leaps of Logic

Kay Sutter had left the alley with her three new friends, cradling the urn with the wilted sunflowers in her right arm and clutching in her left hand the business reply envelope with Zachary R.'s "suicide" note inside.

Now it was evening and she lay supine on her bed, thinking.

"Gracie makes these leaps, James. Leaps of logic," she said. "She's convinced that the urn in the alley means the homeless man is dead. And Nirvana and Diego just went along with it.

"She said I'm the only one you'll talk to. I mean, how could she possibly know that?

"And Nirvana is just this sweet psychopath. She's vulnerable and laughs so easily, but then she has a locket with a photo of the Antichrist inside."

Kay chuckled quietly, then closed her eyes and fell silent for several minutes.

"And Diego seems so normal," she blurted out of her dormancy. "Not at all how you described him. I think his grief over you made him grow up.

"I should call your mom in the morning to give her the lowdown."

At this Kay laughed, surprised by her choice of words.

"And why haven't my parents called? I mean, I'm sure your mom told them what I'm doing here. Maybe they're waiting for me to call them. I don't know. It's exhausting.

"James," she said. "How the fuck did that homeless man know about your brother? And how could he have possibly drawn me?"

Kay rolled onto her side so she could gaze at the urn and the note, which she had propped up against it. She fell asleep feeling vital to the world.

19. In One Word

Kay woke early the next morning with a sense of purpose she hadn't felt since the early days of the high-octane sessions strategizing against Patchouli Goldwatch. She quickly dressed and walked down the hall to Gracie and Nirvana's room.

Nirvana swung open the door. "Oh, hi, Kay," she said, her eyes beaming. "Gracie's not here. Can you come back this afternoon?"

"That's okay," said Kay. "Maybe we could hang out."

Nirvana's response to this was to smile and shut the door.

Kay was devastated. Her mind scanned all the people she had ever known, and none were as cruel as Nirvana. She considered an ascent to the roof to see if Diego was up there, but then she worried that he wouldn't be and that she would look over the edge again.

Oh, James, I get it. I understand completely. They want to steal the light from our eyes, she thought.

She returned to her room and shut the blinds. The sight of the urn and the note made her stomach churn. She opened the note and stared at the portrait of the brunette Goth. "Torment."

He summed her up in one word, she thought. And he wants to restore the light. His drawing wants to restore the light.

Kay Sutter took a deep breath and opened the blinds.

* * * * *

That afternoon Kay returned to Gracie and Nirvana's room. Gracie was there, as promised, but now Nirvana was missing.

"We're not Siamese twins," said Gracie.

Nirvana was right. Gracie was snide, but her snideness had a hint of comfort in it that Kay was coming to appreciate.

"Your roomie didn't want anything to do with me this morning," said Kay. "She basically slammed the door in my face."

Gracie shrugged. "Don't take this the wrong way. I mean, we're as blown away by yesterday as you are. Well, almost. But we've got other stuff to do, you know? I've got to work. So does Nirvana. Or . . . well . . . who knows what Nirvana does."

Kay managed to laugh.

"Wanna play some cards?" asked Gracie.

"I'd love to," replied Kay.

20. Wet Blanket

A week went by and Kay had made zero progress in her investigation beyond what she had found in the alley. The sunflowers in the urn were done. Kay attempted to preserve their dignity by hanging them upside down from a piece of twine she found in James' shrine on the roof. Nirvana suggested that Kay paint them black. Gracie said that would be too obvious.

Kay surmised that Gracie had spoken to Nirvana about the door-shutting incident, because Nirvana seemed to be making a determined effort to rein in her psychotic side. Kay still felt a sense of unease in their company, a sense of mystery, but there was also a suggestion of old-friendness that she hadn't experienced since her early friendship with James. This worried her, as did Diego, whom none of them had seen since the day in the alley.

Kay found it inconceivable that he could just leave after reading the homeless man's note.

"It's probably good news," Gracie had said. "He probably went home to his parents. Maybe the note inspired him to get a life."

Kay failed to see how getting a life could be more important than investigating the homeless man's note, which she considered to be nothing less than prophecy or magic or witchcraft.

To this Gracie had responded, "Do you know how Diego paid his rent? He was a prostitute. And he's not even gay, not that that makes much difference."

Gracie had a way of smothering flames with the wet blanket of the truth, which Kay found endearing in spite of herself. And she couldn't help but like Nirvana, despite her proclivities, or perhaps because of them.

Their similar sartorial tastes notwithstanding, the two young women couldn't have been more different. Kay admitted her fondness for them, but she couldn't reconcile their allowing the inertia of day-to-day living to grind her investigation to a halt.

When she confronted them on this subject, she said, "All these amazing things have happened, all these connections and coincidences, but it doesn't seem to change anything." Kay, of course, was speaking about her encounter with the quiet man at the funeral/wedding in addition to Zachary R.'s note. "I want it to mean something. I want to feel vital. I want something to happen."

Kay's speech ignited the moonbeams in Nirvana's eyes, but, predictably, Gracie asked, "What do you think is supposed to happen? Do you *really* want something to happen?"

"Killjoy," said Nirvana.

"Imp," replied Gracie.

21. Filial Duty

The next day Kay finally performed what felt like her filial duty to Mrs. Branhoover and called her. She knew the call was overdue, but part of her had to admit that she simply needed to hear a voice other than Gracie's or Nirvana's.

Kay debriefed Mrs. Branhoover on Gracie, Nirvana, and Diego, went into great detail regarding the homeless man's drawings (making sure not to mention the word "suicide," but, against her better judgment, describing to Mrs. Branhoover the sketch of the nametag with her eldest son's name on it), and gave an accounting of her expenses, which were negligible. Then she asked whether her parents had inquired about her.

Mrs. Branhoover found the debriefing to be incredibly unsettling, but forced herself to suppress the turmoil in her mind in order to tell Kay how delighted she was to hear from her. Her delight was genuine. She felt that she was finally succeeding as a surrogate parent with Kay, whereas she had failed as a real parent with Bernard and James. She thanked Kay on behalf of herself and James for providing such a thorough and fascinating progress report, then she explained that she had, in fact—surprising even herself—called the Sundays to let them know where their daughter was headed. She explained to Kay how Mr. Sunday believed his daughter was on a sort of pilgrimage. " 'Mission' was the word he used," she said. She explained that her parents believed it imperative that Kay not be disturbed during this important time in her life.

Kay was relieved to hear that her parents supported her in this endeavor, mainly because it meant they had gotten over her eulogy.

"I think your eulogy was beautiful," said Mrs. Branhoover. "Now, don't be a stranger," she said and hung up.

22. The Smallest Boy

Mr. Sunday's vote of confidence in Kay's mission revived her, fortified her against the dismaying, yet somehow understandable, detachment of Gracie and Nirvana, and Diego's baffling disappearance, which Kay considered an abandonment.

"James," she said, looking at his notebook, "I'm sorry I doubted you. I doubted you when you were here, and I still doubted you after you were gone, but I don't anymore. Everything you wrote in here is true. You said the man you got killed was downtown, and I believe you."

Kay shifted her gaze away from the notebook and toward the row of upside-down sunflowers, which, in their shriveled state, were starting to resemble bats. She laughed a little, wondering how long it would be before she started dressing Goth. Then she grabbed the keys to the Mercedes and set off toward downtown Los Angeles in furtherance of her mission.

* * * * *

It didn't take long for Kay to put together
that the homeless downtown were in a more
advanced stage of deterioration compared to the
homeless in Hollywood. Their features were
wilder, more pronounced. Their eyes deader. And
they weren't shy about approaching the
Mercedes, thumping their hands on the
windshield, kicking the tires and doors, looking
for any way to get inside, to tear it all apart,
including the pretty blonde.

In environs like these, the question of Kay's
witchiness seemed childish. Kay Sutter had no
superhuman powers. She was simply a scared
young woman in a borrowed car questioning her
judgment for putting herself in harm's way. She
considered stopping at the Union Rescue Mission
to inquire about robberies/murders around the
time James was there, but decided that she didn't
want to exit the car. She drove aimlessly down a
few more streets until a light turned red. As she

sat, idling, she watched a group of teens move diagonally across the intersection. What now? she thought. Then she saw the smallest of the group, a boy who was dressed differently, dart out from the cluster and then get yanked back in. "They're punching him!" she yelled. She scanned the intersection for the police or any other indication that somebody was going to intervene. Nothing, except cars honking to get by.

She switched on the hazard lights, leapt out of the Mercedes, and ran directly at the pack of teens. "Leave him alone!" she screamed to nobody in particular. For several seconds no one in the cluster registered Kay's presence. Finally, one of the larger boys glimpsed her, said "What the fuck, bitch?" and then swatted her to the pavement. Kay stood up just as red turned to green and the honking turned to her and her idling automobile. She hopped back into the Mercedes and drove back to Hollywood, bruised, scraped, flustered, and helpless to do anything on behalf of the smallest boy.

23. No Achilles' Heel

Kay Sutter kept it together until she made it back to her room. Though Gracie didn't seem like the type to say "I told you so," Kay was nevertheless pleased that she didn't encounter her in the hall, and for once their door was closed. "Do you *really* want something to happen?" played in her mind in Gracie's voice.

Kay walked briskly past their room, keeping her emotions in check until she had shut her own door. Finally hidden from the world, Kay half-heartedly washed up and administered first aid to her scrapes and bruises. Then she lay on her bed and allowed herself to cry herself to sleep.

When she woke, she looked at the clock. 4:13 a.m. In her mind she compared the day spent in the alley being amazed at the interconnectedness of the world and feeling vital to the whole process with the day downtown being thrown to the pavement like a sack of garbage.

She thought about the smallest boy, hoping that somehow he had made it home in better shape than she had. Then she began to formulate a prototype of invincibility. She started with the quiet man's assessment of her, that she could innately control people's thoughts and actions. Clearly, this wasn't enough and, in light of the past day's events, seemed almost entirely useless. If she did have some power in this regard, what good was it if she hadn't a clue as to how it worked and had no control over it. She shuddered at the image of the cluster moving diagonally across the intersection. Oblique movement. That would need controlling.

Who knows? Maybe her witchy mind control kept her from getting killed out there, but invincibility would require much more than this.

She looked at her cuts and bruises. Invincibility would require mastery of the physical universe. There could be no Achilles' heel, for example. If she were to be dipped into the River Styx by Thetis, she would have to shake free of her grip to make sure that every millimeter of her body came into contact with the magic waters.

There was too much. There was no way she could cover every contingency.

She would have to be impervious to all the elements: earth, wind, fire, and water. She couldn't be buried alive. She could dig her way out of any amount of dirt. She could shrink, if necessary, down to the molecular level. She could, of course, become invisible. She could stand in the bottom of a pit with hordes hurling stones at her and not be hurt. It would not be possible to burn her. She could be tied to a stake and lit on fire and suffer nothing. She could be thrown into Vesuvius and swim her way through the molten lava to safety. She could fly . . . into outer space if necessary. Breathing wouldn't be mandatory to her survival. She couldn't be drowned. She couldn't be consumed by sharks, suffocated by pythons, disemboweled by hyenas, and so on and so forth unto invincibility.

She looked at the clock. 6 a.m. She rolled onto her left side, her prime sleeping side. The dead weight of the bed tugged slightly at her flesh, agitating her wounds. She winced and then returned to sleep.

24. Fifty Feet Underwater

Kay Sutter moved through the lilies of Diego's shrine to the edge of the youth hostel roof. She sat down and dangled her legs over. She saw a homeless man coming up the avenue and wondered if he was the man from the alley who had combined her and James in a single sketch.

She pushed herself off the edge to meet him, only to find herself fifty feet underwater. The water was clear and warm, and breathing in it was as easy as breathing air.

She swam to the surface and turned three hundred and sixty degrees. It was nighttime. The sky full of stars. The moon a perfect circle. Dragonflies and cedars along the shore.

James and his father boarded a raft at the end of a wooden dock and rowed out to meet her.

25. Realms and Times

When Kay woke from her dream, she didn't move, not even a twitch, because she knew from prior dreams that movement in the conscious realm ended it, and she didn't want this dream to end.

But end it did. She lay there feeling as peaceful as she could ever remember. James was with his father and they were rowing out to meet her. This would have to be part of her invincibility, too. The ability to move between realms and times. Her mind flashed to the image of the homeless man coming up the avenue. She had pushed herself off the roof in order to meet him. This gave her the shivers, but not the creeping-death variety. These were the shivers that came in the aftermath of having done something brave.

Then her mind flashed to Gracie and Nirvana. She missed them. Her investigation regarding James seemed complete now. She put his notebook and the homeless man's drawings into her suitcase and snapped it shut.

PART III

26. First Gray Saturday

Kay Sutter spent the rest of the day of her underwater dream in her room, thinking about James and her childhood. She allowed herself to cry again. She had to admit that it helped, even if wrinkles were beginning to form around her eyes. Crying eased the burden of her fledgling grief and, beyond this, caused it to ripen. Kay felt that her progressing grief was the same as her progressing maturity, and permitting herself to weep was part of the evolution.

Another part of it was putting behind her the notion that she was some kind of witch possessed of abilities beyond others'.

"Are you a witch?"

"Through the ages."

This was mysterious to be sure, as were the homeless man's drawings and her dream. But there was no mystery in getting slammed to the pavement and injured. She focused on the reality of her aching bones until she fell asleep yet again.

603

In the morning Kay was awoken by the sound of four fists banging on her door.

"Kay! Kay! It's First Gray Saturday. Let's go," said Nirvana.

Kay swung open the door. "I've missed you two," she said.

"Oh my God, what happened to you?" asked Gracie.

"I got into a fight," said Kay.

Nirvana giggled maniacally.

"Freak," said Gracie. "Are you all right, Kay?"

"I'm fine. What's First Gray Saturday?"

"It's the first Saturday of May Gray, when we go thrifting," said Gracie.

"You know . . . Black Friday, Gray Saturday, ha-ha," said Nirvana.

Kay turned and looked out the window. Sure enough, the sky was gray. Her mind flashed to

Pittsburgh, where gray sky was hardly an occasion.

"It's been blue skies since I got here," she said.

"Right. First Gray Saturday," said Gracie. "You catch on quick."

Kay laughed. Another comforting Gracie gibe.

"Can we take my car, or are you two badass Goth chicks still freaked out by it?"

"So let's go already," said Nirvana.

* * * * *

Gracie and Nirvana introduced Kay to La Brea and Melrose Avenues, their secondhand stores with high prices and cheap incense. Kay had imagined herself in Goth attire like her two friends, but wound up spending five hundred dollars on what Gracie called organic hippie duds.

"I like them," said Nirvana. "They really suit Kay's personality."

"Um. Not," snorted Gracie.

The three of them sat in a coffee shop comparing and competing and generally enjoying one another's company until Kay pulled a nonhippie-esque spiked bracelet out of her bag.

"I don't remember buying this," she said.

"Oh, that's mine," said Nirvana, plucking it out of Kay's hand.

"That's odd. I definitely would have noticed the cashier putting that in my bag," said Kay.

"I put it in there," said Nirvana. "I ran out of room in my bag."

"Do I have to say it?" said Gracie.

Nirvana stomped her feet and frowned.

"Our good friend Nirvana is a kleptomaniac."

"And you put the bracelet in my bag?!" said Kay, loud enough that people in the café stopped whatever they were doing to look at her.

"Yelling. That's not very peacenik of you," said Gracie.

"Yeah, what's your problem?" asked Nirvana.

"I could've gotten arrested," said Kay, her mind flashing to the edge of the youth hostel roof. "And besides, stealing is wrong." Now she felt childish for having stated the obvious.

"It doesn't seem like a big deal when I'm the thief," said Nirvana.

Gracie chuckled. "Nirvana, say you're sorry and that you won't put stolen goods in Kay's bag ever again."

"Fine," said Nirvana. "I'm sorry and I won't do that again. I promise."

"Well, okay," said Kay, finally regaining her composure.

"So, who knew you were a flower child?" said Gracie.

"I did," said Nirvana. "Flowers in the shrine. Flowers in the urn. Flowers hanging upside down in her room."

"It's true. I probably got it from my parents," said Kay.

"Nirvana was raised by wolves," said Gracie.

"Gracie once dated a boy for a month before she noticed he was missing his right hand," said Nirvana.

Kay paused to consider the kind of person for whom this would be possible. Her eyes welled up. "That's so beautiful," she said.

"He was a lefty," said Gracie.

27. Kay Sunday

Nirvana's shoplifting notwithstanding, Kay considered First Gray Saturday to be a success. Back in her room she tried on all her new clothes. Reds, oranges, and purples predominated, except for a single black veil, which she attributed to Nirvana's thievery. She thought about her parents' spacey purple church. Kay Sunday: Flower Child, Witch, she thought.

She lay on her bed in a new dress, draped the veil over her eyes, and fell asleep. She had several dreams that night. In one of them, the homeless man from the alley drew her portrait. When he handed it over to her, she looked at him and said, "I'm going to help you someday."

28. Accustomed to Solitude

As was the case in the days after their discoveries in the alley, a week passed by after First Gray Saturday without the girls saying more than hello to one another in the hall. Kay was growing accustomed to the noncommittal nature of Los Angeles. She was growing accustomed to solitude.

In her new organic hippie duds, she went to Venice Beach and saw the Pacific Ocean for the first time, not counting looking out the window of the 747 over Southeast Asia. She ate in nice restaurants. She rented a bicycle in Santa Monica and rode it to Malibu and back, including a trip up the hill to see the Getty Villa, which impressed her enough to visit the main Getty Center, the

Museum of Modern Art, and the L.A. County Museum of Art.

At LACMA Kay lingered at a painting by Pacino di Buonaguida, circa 1340, called "The Last Communion of Saint Mary Magdalene." The placard read, "Two angels deliver Saint Mary Magdalene to priest Saint Maximinus, who administers her last communion. Clothed in her own golden hair, Mary Magdalene hovers miraculously above the ground. Church in Aix-en-Provence."

"You have her hair," said an elderly museum guard. Kay looked at him directly and nodded.

"Through the ages," she said.

* * * * *

Back in her room, Kay wondered whether she should return to Pittsburgh or whether L.A. was her home now. She thought about what kinds of jobs she could get and how much a proper one-bedroom apartment went for. Then, finally, a knock on her door. She could tell by the sound that it was Gracie and not Nirvana. She opened the door gently.

"Gracie, hi," she said.

"Hi, Kay. You know, I always forget how pretty your eyes are when I haven't seen you in a while."

Kay knew something was up when Gracie was being sincere. "Thank you," she said. "Do you want to come in?"

"Can I? It's Nirvana."

"Oh, no. What did she do now?" said Kay, attempting to add levity to her voice.

"You know how I said I have no idea what Nirvana does?"

"You mean jobwise?"

"Exactly. Well, I was helping her out for a long time, but, you know, I just can't do it forever. Anyway, I finally cut her off last week, and now I haven't seen her in three days."

"Well, then let's go find her," said Kay.

Kay and Gracie stepped out of Kay's room and stalked the halls of the youth hostel, slowing at each door to listen for Nirvana's presence. On their second pass through the building, on the third floor, Gracie heard a female voice behind a closed door.

"Are you sure it's hers?" asked Kay.

"Kay Sutter?" came the voice from behind the door.

"Nirvana?" said Kay.

The door opened, but the first face Kay and Gracie saw wasn't Nirvana's.

"Michael, are you getting Nirvana high again?" asked Gracie.

"And hi to you, too," said Michael, genuinely hurt by Gracie's curtness.

Kay wondered whether Gracie and Nirvana knew everybody in the building.

"What do you care, anyway?" said Nirvana, stepping out from behind Michael and into the hall.

"Okay, that's it. I've had it," said Gracie, grabbing Nirvana by the bicep.

"You kicked me out," said Nirvana. "Let go of me!"

"I didn't kick you out. I cut you off," said Gracie, releasing her grip on Nirvana's arm.

"What's the difference?" said Nirvana. "You know I don't have any money."

"Holy shit. Michael, what are you doing to her?" said Gracie.

"Don't even go there," said Michael, calmly but firmly. "I'm letting her crash here until she finds work, and that's it."

Gracie stepped back. "I'm sorry. I was just so worried about her," she said.

"I understand," said Michael.

"He's been really sweet," said Nirvana. "He showed me creepy-crawling, and next week we're going to Disneyland."

"You mean like Manson?" asked Gracie.

"Well, yeah, except for the murders," said Nirvana, giggling. "Prowling in the hills at night is exciting."

Kay had heard enough. "I can give you some money, but I think you should move back in with Gracie."

"That sounds like a plan," said Michael, who paused and then added, "And just so we're clear, the creepy-crawling was her idea, not mine."

"Duh," said Gracie, allowing herself to smile.

29. Her Legal Name

The next morning Kay took Nirvana to the bank and transferred money from her account to a new account opened in Nirvana's name, which, of course, wasn't really "Nirvana," but she asked and Kay agreed to look away when she wrote her legal name on the bank documents.

Kay couldn't help but compare this transaction with James' buying back her parents' church. She felt pangs of grief.

"What now?" asked Nirvana, stunned and confused by the freedom conferred upon her by financial independence.

"I thought we could go job hunting," said Kay.

"But we can do whatever we want," said Nirvana, pouting. "Let's go to Disneyland."

"The money I gave you isn't going to last as long as you think," said Kay. "But if we get jobs, at least our savings won't decrease, and we can quit if the jobs suck. I believe it's called 'fuck-you money,' " she concluded, laughing.

To Kay's surprise, Nirvana didn't laugh along.

"The job *will* suck," she said, flatly. "*All* jobs suck."

"Gracie has a job," said Kay.

"Why do you think she's always so snide and bitter?" asked Nirvana. "Look, you said this money came no strings attached."

"It does," said Kay, exhaustion setting in.

"Can we go tomorrow?" asked Nirvana. "I've had a hard couple of days."

"All right," said Kay, calculating in her mind how long it would take for Nirvana to be broke again and creepy-crawling with Michael.

30. Windfall

Nirvana wasted no time in putting her windfall to use. She paid a visit to Michael and procured a dime bag, an eight ball, and some Valium. Then she took the Red Line downtown to Union Station, where she boarded a train to Anaheim. In Anaheim, her final destination, she hailed a cab, which took her directly to the Disneyland Hotel.

In her room she lay on the king-size bed, rolled a joint, smoked it, rolled another joint, took one long drag, and then fell into deep thought regarding her strategy for the park the next day.

She questioned her judgment in purchasing the eight ball and buried it deep in her bag. Then she figured she'd smoke the rest of the pot first thing in the morning and then, once inside the park, take one Valium after each ride until she reached an agreeable stopping point to be determined at a time and ride of her choosing. Who says I don't have a job, she thought, and then giggled intermittently for the next thirty minutes until she fell asleep.

Nirvana rose at sunrise and faithfully executed her plan. She smoked the rest of the weed, entered the park, downed a pint of ice cream at the Carnation Café on Main Street, took a Valium, went to Tomorrowland, rode Space Mountain, took a Valium, rode Star Tours, took a Valium, went to Fantasyland, rode Alice in Wonderland, took a Valium, road Mr. Toad's Wild Ride, took a Valium, went to New Orleans Square, rode Pirates of the Caribbean, took a Valium, rode the Haunted Mansion, took a Valium, went to Critter Country, ordered a burger, fries, and a Coke at the Hungry Bear Restaurant, sat at a picnic table overlooking the Rivers of America, fumbled in an attempt to get another pill onto her tongue, vaguely heard an elderly park janitor say, "Looks like you got yourself an E ticket," and then her face hit the wooden table, out cold.

31. Two Days Later

Two days later, Kay and Gracie sat in folding chairs at the foot of Nirvana's bed at the Thalians Mental Health Center of Cedars-Sinai. Nirvana's trip to Disneyland was ruled a suicide attempt by the authorities, so she was under evaluation for possible committal to an institution.

"Will you please tell them there's nothing wrong with me," she said.

"You almost died," said Gracie. "Why does everyone in our building want to die?" She started to cry, but then, through sheer force of will, reversed the process, as if the tears climbed back up her face and into her eyes.

"It was an accident, I swear," said Nirvana. "I just . . . miscalculated. I should have eaten something before the Haunted Mansion. That's when I started to go. Oh, Kay, I thought of you in the Haunted Mansion at the end of the ride when the ghost hitches a ride in your car. It reminded me of James riding along with you in his car."

"Goose bumps," said Gracie, attempting to prove she was herself again.

Kay laughed, but she was distracted. She was mentally comparing how she gave Nirvana money and it almost got her killed with how James gave the homeless man money and it did get him killed. She wondered whether this whole trip was some sort of test. Maybe her dad was right. Maybe this was a mission. Maybe Nirvana's not dying was a second chance for both Kay and James. Maybe that's why the portrait in the "suicide" note resembled both her and James. Maybe James *had* hitched a ride. Maybe their mission was to make sure Nirvana lived. Maybe they were supposed to nurse her back to health. Nurses. Charles and Betsy Larson were nurses. Maybe she and James were supposed to become nurses and go on missions. Maybe back to Southeast Asia. Maybe back to Cambodia . . .

"Um, Earth to Kay," said Gracie.

"Oh, don't stop her," said Nirvana. "I love when her eyes get all wide and start spinning."

Kay laughed again, but now she was present. She reached into her bag and pulled out a deck of cards.

"Wanna play?" she asked.

Nirvana sat up and smoothed the bedsheets.

Kay dealt three hands.

"We've been expecting you," said Gracie.

Acknowledgments

Special thanks to my editors, Jen Richardson, Laura A. Lionello, and Greg Dalgleish, for their expert guidance in the evolution and completion of this book.